Falling For You

ROOHI BHARGAVA

BLUEROSE PUBLISHERS
India | U.K.

Copyright © Roohi Bhargava 2025

All rights reserved by author. No part of this publication may be reproduced, stored in a retrieval system or transmitted in any form or by any means, electronic, mechanical, photocopying, recording or otherwise, without the prior permission of the author. Although every precaution has been taken to verify the accuracy of the information contained herein, the publisher assumes no responsibility for any errors or omissions. No liability is assumed for damages that may result from the use of information contained within.

BlueRose Publishers takes no responsibility for any damages, losses, or liabilities that may arise from the use or misuse of the information, products, or services provided in this publication.

For permissions requests or inquiries regarding this publication, please contact:

BLUEROSE PUBLISHERS
www.BlueRoseONE.com
info@bluerosepublishers.com
+91 8882 898 898
+4407342408967

ISBN: 978-93-6452-794-1

Cover Design: Sadhna Kumari
Typesetting: Pooja Sharma

First Edition: January 2025

Prologue

"Life is unpredictable."

You never know what turn your life will take. You have to just go with the flow. You need to work hard, sacrifice, and love life the way it comes to you.

"Love is beautiful."

Love happens. It happens when you least expect it. The way a person looks at the surroundings or people around them, leads to love. Two people might have differences, but the differences seem beautiful, and this is how love happens.

Both life and love go hand in hand. When two people come together and have mutual feelings, it creates an indescribable feeling. Love is a feeling that cannot be explained, but you can experience it. It's about understanding all the love shared between two individuals.

Love is a beautiful emotion, just like the beauty of those who are in love, in a lovely relationship, or in a close friendship. When a relationship is built on trust and friendship, it becomes the strongest and most beautiful thing in the world and everyone wants to own it. Not everyone has the patience to nurture their relationships. However, when there is trust, love, affection, and positivity in every aspect, the relationship can last longer than expected. You'd be glad to be home with someone who loves and celebrates you. Moreover, the two souls share love and are pillars of strength for each other.

This is one such story of friendship, love, trust, pain, and companionship. All the elements are necessary in life in order to have a successful relationship. The story revolves around two souls who are childhood friends and end up falling in love with each other. It is all about falling for someone who's been your light in the dark, who's the light of your soul, and who's your healer and has healed you in an alluring way. This is the story of **Ruhana** and **Vineet**, who pave their way towards love, holding all the elements intact in their journey.

*****

Ruhana Mehra is a fun-loving, full-of-life, and happy girl. Her world revolves around her parents and a young boy who means home to her. He is **Vineet Malhotra**, her childhood friend. These two souls have been together since former's birth. Vineet is two years older than Ruhana and has already vowed to protect her through all the thick and thin that comes their way in their lives. They've always trusted their friendship and believed in each other for a long time.

Life has taken a toll on both of them in different ways. However, they have their own ways to deal with their real-life situations and hardships. Obviously, life is never smooth; it's us who make it smooth by concentrating on the right side and making things look better on the outside. You may have a smile on your face, but you might be crying inside.

Nobody knows, and nobody cares either. You have to help yourself, compose, and move on—this is what life is all about.

Vineet and Ruhana are being their own selves; they have devised their own ways to heal themselves. She finds her happiness in small things, while he prefers to stay silent and do his work. He's an introvert, while she's an extrovert, trying to keep herself and her best friend happy. She's the only one who prefers staying home with Vineet and her parents rather than going shopping or to the movies with her friends. The past incidents have made Vineet a silent person, which he was not in his childhood.

Ruhana finds solace in Vineet's presence. When he smiles, she feels herself smiling and can do anything to cheer him up. This is a very different kind of feeling that she feels, but she's unable to name it. She's always happy to have him around, and she's trying her best to bring her best friend back on track so that she can share her heart with him. She has a lot to say to him and a lot to hear from him.

It's their story of discovering their friendship and love.

Contents

1. Unveiling the Unknown 1
2. The Heart of Discourse 6
3. Outburst Echoes 14
4. The Rejected Apology 22
5. Contemplating the Feelings 28
6. Banters & Arguments 34
7. Embracing the Truth 45
8. Trailing through the Past 54
9. Finding Happiness 63
10. Day of the Trip 71
11. Beginning of the Trip 77
12. Landing in Mumbai 84
13. Witnessing the Oceanic Beauty 89
14. Oceanic Talks 96
15. A Joyous Ride of Life 104
16. The Trifle 113
17. Her Anger, His Grief 123
18. Whispers from the Past 130
19. A Day Out - Solace in Chaos 138
20. The Reconciliation 150
21. The New Beginning 157

22. Surprising Her: Meeting her Rockstar 164
23. The Journey Back Home 171
24. News about the Fest 180
25. Profound Conversation 189
26. Healing needs Time 196
27. Life Goes On 203
28. Love of a Family 209
29. Healing Each Other 216
30. Planning for College Festival 222
31. The Musings and the Fest 229
32. The Heated Argument 236
33. Contemplating Thoughts 244
34. The Confession 250
35. A New Beginning 258
36. Epilogue 267
37. About the Author 270

Chapter 1:

Unveiling the Unknown

Living in the city of dreams is beautiful. But there's a lot of struggle in realizing those dreams. But you do not stop dreaming, do you?

"No," is the answer. You should never stop dreaming.

Always chase your dreams. Everyone should chase a better future and a happy life for the happiness of their loved ones, shouldn't they? And chase love? That is the most important and beautiful thing to do.

Vineet and Ruhana have a lot of dreams in their eyes. She keeps telling her parents about her dreams, while Vineet is the silent soul among them. He keeps his feelings, aspirations, and dreams to himself. He doesn't like to share them with anyone. Though he is very open with Ruhana's mom and shares his feelings with her, Ruhana is always trying to help him, but sometimes she gets irked. Why wouldn't she? He's not supporting her; he's not responding to her attempts and tricks.

*****

A boy and a girl are standing on the terrace of the house, watching the sunset. The boy is six years old, while the girl is four years old. It is part of their daily routine. They would stand on the terrace of her house and watch the sunset. The orange-reddish-hued sky, the slightly cool breeze, and the birds flying in the sky make it all the more beautiful when you look at the sky with your naked eyes.

The sunset is surely an elegant and beautiful sight. Not only adults but kids love it too, especially the bright colors.

"This is so beautiful!" the boy says, exclaiming at the moment.

"Yes! I love the orange color over there," the girl says, pointing towards the orange hue in the sky.

He smiles at her softly. They're little kids, and she is the innocent soul who says everything that comes to her mind. They are best friends, and they make sure that they spend ample time together. All they need is each other, and the duo stands by each other. She usually saves him from his mom's scolding while he takes her out for strolls, and they go for ice cream.

The bond that they share is blissful, beautiful, and emotional. The day the girl was born, the young boy promised himself that he'd take care of her in every possible way. He does that every single day. They hang out together, play together, and study together, always by each other's sides. Life's not hard for these two as long as they're together.

"I like it too. I love to watch the sunset," he says, a slight smile adorning his features.

"It is fun with you, always. Now, let's play before Aunty comes to take you home. She won't let us play then," the girl says innocently, her gaze fixed on his face.

He laughs, and they break into a run. He's chasing her now, all around the terrace. The whole house is filled with giggles. Finally, they stop as he holds her by the wrist. They are panting heavily, and at the same time, they hear his mother calling him, and it's time for them to part.

They touch their foreheads together; it's their signature step when they meet and part. They've created their own ways and actions to tell each other that they are always rooting for one another. The boy looks at the girl, instructing her to finish her homework. He also tells her that they will have ice cream the next day since it is Sunday. Their moms have decided timelines for certain things. The girl jumps on her toes, and the boy smiles. They run down the stairs, where their mothers are sitting and talking. The ladies are discussing about their kids since they share a close bond of friendship and are inseparable. Soon, they say goodbye to each other. A fun day has come to an end for the two best buddies.

*****

Many years have passed. Fifteen long years. They are grown up, but their routine hasn't changed. They are again standing on the terrace, watching the setting sun. The sun is orange-hued, and the sight is as beautiful as it was in their childhood. The sight is beautiful as ever but they have changed a lot over time. Today, they are standing together, hand in hand, watching the sight.

Vineet is staring at the setting sun. His lips are pursed in a single line, and it seems like he is hiding something. The girl shifts her gaze between the beautiful sight of the sunset and the young man standing beside her. He has grown into a fine young man. He's handsome, and the growth of a little beard makes him look elegant. He's her best friend, but he hardly talks to her or anyone else. She wishes to initiate a conversation with him, but he seems uninterested. Ruhana sighs deeply; she wants him to speak, to share the pain or agony that he's been hiding in his heart. She decides to initiate a conversation with her best friend.

"It's beautiful, right?" she asks him while looking at his handsome face.

"It is! Though life is not that beautiful," he says in his deep, crisp voice, though he doesn't look at her.

Ruhana looks at Vineet. He's tall and broad-chested, and his crisp voice makes her heart skip a beat. She tugs on his hand and looks at him. He looks pained and sorrowful. He's not conversing with her like he used to in childhood. His eyes are fixed on the setting sun, while her gaze is set on him.

She calls his name to get his attention, and he looks at her, setting his gaze on her. He squeezes her hand lightly. She gazes into his eyes; his black orbs seem like an ocean hiding many secrets beneath. She feels that he wants to share something, but there's some obstacle preventing him from saying anything to her. However, he's unable to find appropriate words to describe his feelings. She puts forward her first question, for which he is unable to find an answer.

"Why can't you be the same friend of mine whom I know?" she asks, her tone soft yet firm.

"Because you won't find him anywhere," he replies bluntly, his tone louder.

"Why not? Why do you want to lose yourself? Your life hasn't ended yet, Vineet," she exclaims, concerned about him.

"Ruhana, please! Don't take me back into the past," he says, his tone blunt and cold.

"The past was painful; I agree. But we have some beautiful memories, don't we? Can't we move on, imbibing the memories in our hearts?" She asks, her tone questioning and her eyes are filled with hope.

He sighs deeply. He has gone through a painful, rough past that no child deserves. He has grown up to be a silent person who keeps everything in his heart. He doesn't share his pain and agony with anyone, not even Ruhana. She tries to convince him yet again, and he bluntly asks for more time.

"I need time," He repeats the same line he has been using for many years, especially since they crossed their teen years.

"Take your time. But give me my best friend back, please, Vineet," she requests, her tone laced with concern for him.

He looks at her briefly and leaves the terrace without answering her, while Ruhana sighs, letting out the tears she has been hiding for a long time. Frankly, she is tired of having him silent around her. She wants him to share his heart and the pain he has been holding. Yes, she might not understand the intensity of his pain, but she'd surely help him ease it.

They are best friends, or even more than that, as she sees it. Ever since childhood, they have been inseparable, but Vineet has grown indifferent. She is fun-loving and chirpy, while Vineet is silent. Ruhana's parents are also Vineet's guardians. Everything has changed, and Ruhana knows she has to work hard to bring Vineet back to his usual self.

Ruhana is determined to do so; she wants Vineet back to the person he once was. She wants him to be the same soulful person who knows how to love and care.

Chapter 2:

The Heart of Discourse

Vineet asks for more time, and Ruhana sighs deeply. She grants his wish and he walks down the stairs. He's teary-eyed by now. He believes that she's demanding much more than he can afford to give her. He's been asking for time constantly and it's been years now, and Ruhana is irked about it. Sometimes, she feels that Vineet doesn't want to heal himself. Okay, it's hard to heal; she agrees. But it's not impossible. He needs to try.

And he doesn't want to try at the moment. She's afraid of the outcomes of his rigidness.

She doesn't want to give up on him. She knows that one day, her hard work will pay off. He will become the guy she wants him to be. And she will wait.

Even if it means waiting until eternity, respecting someone's time means caring for them. Healing is hard. It is hard to cope with the loss of love, family, and joy that someone has gone through so far.

It's hard to come back to life, but one can't live holding grudges from the past. You have to tackle all the obstacles that come your way and live your life on your terms. That's the real meaning of living a beautiful life.

Always live in the moment. Things will happen—some will bring joy, and some will bring sorrow. We can't hold on to the happenings and stay still. Life is not easy at all; we have to make it easy. We have to always move forward in our lives.

Vineet sighs deeply and leaves the house. He needs some alone time. Usually, no one disturbs him at home as well, yet he goes to the park to spend some time in silence. He has no complaints from Ruhana, yet he needs time.

*****

Ruhana watches him leave the house and sighs deeply. She feels that her attempts have again failed. Are fifteen years not enough for him? Yes, she knows that his loss is big and he needs more time to heal, but every time she talks to him, he is always ready with one or the other excuse and it hurts her. She is worried about Vineet, and she wants him to come back to life. She is lost in her own thoughts when her mother pats her shoulder. She looks at her mom, who smiles sweetly at her daughter.

"Give him some time, honey," she says yet again.

"How much more time, Mumma? It has been fifteen years already, since that incident. Why can't he come out of it?" Ruhana asks; she's tired of waiting for him.

"Everyone takes their own time to heal, baby," her mother, Rekha Mehra, says, trying to convince her.

Ruhana nods negatively. Though she knows that everyone has their own ways to heal themselves, she can't take Vineet's rudeness anymore. She knows that the incidents that happened in his past have made him silent. but he has to try to overcome them. Only her attempts won't work. He has to make efforts to come out of the cage that he has built around himself. He has to learn to overcome them and lead a happy life. He has to realize that he is not the only one who is suffering in this world.

He has to try, and eventually things will fall into place. Ruhana believes so.

Ruhana's parents consider him their son. They admire the bond between him and their daughter. Rekha takes care of all his needs. Moreover, he calls them Maa and Dad, just like Ruhana.

Okay! She understands that Vineet has lost his mother, and whatever her mom does, she cannot take the place of Vineet's mother in his heart. She knows that Vineet respects her mother in the same way he did for his mother, but exceptions prevail. At the moment, she just wants her best friend back. She just wants him by her side, laughing, giggling, and happy.

Ah! He looks so cute when he smiles, and it makes her smile automatically.

So precious is the relationship between them. Her mom's words break her trance, and she looks at the lady.

"He will heal. You have to keep trying, Ruhana. Your father and I are always with you, honey. He will heal himself one day. He will love you and care for you in the same way that you are doing," her mother says, her tone soft and convincing.

"Are you sure, Momma?" Ruhana asks, her tone laced with unsurity.

She wants to believe her mother, but a part of her heart is unsure because Vineet keeps asking her for time. She can't make herself believe it.

"Yes, honey. We need to believe in him. I know that fifteen years is a long time. But he will heal. I believe him, and you also trust him, right? Just keep doing your part, honey. This is your duty at the moment," Her mother says, her tone soft, encouraging.

Ruhana nods positively. She knows her mother is right. She will do everything she can, to heal him. She just wants Vineet to be happy and sound, just like they were in childhood. She can go anywhere and do anything to please Vineet, but she cannot forget him or let him ruin his future.

Their friendship needs to survive, and she will make sure that he revives his old self. She hugs her mother and kisses her cheek, telling her that she needs to see Vineet. Her mother smiles affectionately and watches her leave the house.

*****

Ruhana reaches Walker's Park and looks around to get a glimpse of him. She finds him sitting on the bench near the fountain. He is watching the sunset. The orange-hued sky is looking beautiful. The birds are returning to their nests, and the cool breeze is making the trees sway to their tune. His eyes are fixated on the sky, while she is just gazing at him. For her, seeing him sit in peace is a happy moment. It's part of his routine that he comes and sits here for hours, watching the sunset. She sits beside him, gazing at the setting sun.

"You can't see such a beautiful scenario without me, Vineet," She says, her eyes are fixated on the beauty of nature around them.

"What are you doing here?" he asks, a little startled to find her by his side.

Ruhana glares at him. She knows he cares for her, but she also can't see him alone but he thinks otherwise. He feels that the girl is not living her life the way she should, all because of him. She's always behind and beside him, so she should concentrate on herself and not on him. His reverie is broken when Ruhana keeps her head on his shoulder and her eyes are fixated on his face.

"I can ask you the same. If I should be home, then you should be home too. Mum and Dad don't say anything to you; it doesn't mean that you'll do anything that you like," she says, her tone laced with concern for him.

"I wanted to be alone," He speaks briefly, his tone carrying resignation.

"You're always alone, Vineet. You stay alone at home. You never share your problems with me. You don't tell anyone; it's fine that I know where to find you. It is Mumma who believes you otherwise; you can't escape," she complains.

He smiles lightly. He knows that he can't escape her. It's her parents who believe him. She truly cares for him. This is the reason she is here beside him. She chides him, teases him, and scolds him, but she cares for him as well. She's the only light in his life, and with her by his side, he feels that life is a little better.

Ruhana calls him again, but he doesn't reply at the moment. Oh! She's irked. He never tells her what is bothering him. He never thinks that his silence is hurting her, and she gets upset with herself. He is just thinking about his pain and not about others' pain. He never tries to understand her point or her view that she wants him to be fine. She sighs deeply; she doesn't want to argue with him on this topic. She just wants him to understand her the way she understands him.

Is it too much to ask for? She breaks the silence prevailing between them.

"Vineet! Don't keep your feelings to yourself. Share it. I know what you went through, and I want to help you. You know it, right? I want my best friend back," She says it meaningfully.

"It's not easy, Ruhana," he says, it's something he says every now and then.

He's been giving the same reason for a long time now. On the other hand, Ruhana feels that it's humans who make things easy. Only those people emerge as winners who are able to tackle everything smoothly. Well, it's difficult for everyone, though.

"Nothing comes easy in life, Vineet. It's we who make even the simple things complicated. It's you who are making yourself complicated," She says, her tone soft yet firm, reassuring him of her words.

Vineet stays silent; he doesn't have any answers to Ruhana's questions. She further says,

"Do you think it is easy for me to do what I do? I am not doing it for myself. I am doing it for you. I want you to live your life the way it should be. Aunty is only looking at you. She'll be happy when you're happy," Ruhana explains, her tone filled with concern.

Vineet nods in affirmation but doesn't reply at the moment. He knows she is right, but he is hesitant. He doesn't want to get hurt anymore; therefore, he stays away from people. He's happy with Ruhana, but it's only Ruhana who talks, and Vineet listens silently. Things have changed between them as compared to their childhood. His reverie breaks as

Ruhana pulls his hand away to take him home. He lets her take control of himself. They reach home and find her parents having coffee. Rekha looks at Vineet. She knows they might have arguments, so she asks Vineet.

"All well?" she asks.

"Yeah! except that our little girl is angry," Vineet comments teasingly, taking his seat near her father, Sanjeev Mehra.

"All because of you, big boy," Ruhana retorts, glaring at him.

"He's responsible, though," her mother comments, praising Vineet.

"Yeah! He's responsible, and that's why he leaves the house without telling anyone and you don't scold him," Ruhana complains to her mother.

"Maa knows everything, and she doesn't roam behind me," Vineet says it teasingly.

"So, I roam behind you? I disturb you; that is what you want to say," Ruhana glares at him, though she's only faking her anger.

"Obviously, Ma doesn't do that. You do it," He says it teasingly and hides his face on her mom's shoulder.

Ruhana looks at him as he laughs, accompanied by her father. She knows he's teasing her, yet she can show some attitude. She can show some anger and get his attention. She makes a face.

"Haww! That's so bad. Okay!! Now I'm not going to talk to you. and I'll not come behind you. and you will miss it the most. Huh!" She shouts at him and moves to her room.

Vineet smiles at her. She looks annoyed at the moment. He feels that they've only been teasing each other until now, but things have changed. She's angry, and she runs to her room when he's around. Ah, things are difficult. Sanjeev persuades Vineet to go and convince Ruhana, which is going to be hard.

Chapter 3:

Outburst Echoes

Ruhana is in her room; she's angry at Vineet. Not really, though. She knows Vineet teases her in front of her parents. They have fun; she mocks anger at him and is never serious about the mock plays they do. At least he has a smile on his face when he teases her. That's enough for her. When he's happy, her heart flutters with joy. *That's all she wants!*

Though today she is feeling an adrenaline rush through her nerves, he just said that she roams behind him and coaxes him to do certain things. Is it really like this? Does he really feel this way for her? Or is it a prank? Well, she knows that Vineet won't ever mean the words he said. She's trying to calm herself, but she's unable to do so.

It might be a joke for him, but it has hurt her. She has never thought of coaxing him; she has always given him time and accepted his silence wholeheartedly. Is it wrong on her part? Is it wrong to be considerate towards her best friend? Yes, she stays with him because she feels that if she keeps him company, he will share his heart with her, but she's proven wrong. He has just declared something that she hasn't done so far. Having him by her side makes her happy and boosts her confidence as well.

She comes out of her trance when his voice falls in her ears. She doesn't respond to him, for, she doesn't want to melt at the sight of him. She picks up her novel from the side table and begins to read it. He again calls her by her nickname, she ignores him yet again. He's the one who serves her silence every day and then teases her with something he didn't do for her.

"Ruu.."

The nickname that he's used is just reserved for him. Her nickname in his deep, crisp, and perfect voice sounds like music to her ears. She is amused at how affectionately he calls her name. They're best friends, and this is a certain kind of love, she supposes. Her mother tells her that every relationship holds a different kind of love and has a different kind of meaning. *Love isn't something that two lovers share; it prevails in every relationship.* He again calls her name—her full name now.

"Ruhana!! Listen to me," He calls her again, his tone soft yet filled with emotion.

"I don't want to talk to you," She says this, folding her arms across her chest and turning away from her face.

"I was kidding," He says, his eyes never leaving her face.

"But I'm not kidding. Go! Leave my room," She says, her tone stern at the moment.

Vineet is astonished, for, she has always been soft towards him. It's going to be hard for him to convince this pretty girl, as she's adamant enough. He can bear everything, but not her anger. He looks at her once again, trying to convince her.

"Ruu, please. You know, I cannot bear your silence," He says it innocently, and he means every word.

"And what do you give me every day? Your silence?! Am I here to understand your silence? Or should I say that I am the only one who is understanding among us? Can't you handle a little silence from my side?" She shouts, losing her cool.

Vineet is shocked. A little teasing has ignited her anger. He tries holding her hand, but she jerks him away. She is right; he can't deny it, but he didn't mean to upset her.

"Stay away, Vineet! Until you promise me that you will grow past your silence. don't talk to me," She says, pushing him away.

" Ruu! Listen! We can talk," He says he is trying to calm her.

"I also come to talk. And what did you say? I roam behind you. I don't do that for my own good, Vineet. I do it for you so that you don't feel lonely. I don't want you to feel left out. But no, you have to stay alone. Then fine, stay with yourself. I won't come behind you. I won't coax you anymore," She shouts at him and turns to the other side.

Her eyes are teary by now. She wasn't angry, but when he mentioned silence, she lost her cool. She always tries to make him happy. She knows he has been through a rough childhood, but they can make a better future together, can't they?

Vineet and Ruhana have grown up together. Though Vineet grew up to be silent, his care for Ruhana has never changed. He always takes care of her and makes sure that she is fine. She also does the same. The only difference is that she makes an effort while he stays silent.

Ruhana wants him to laugh, talk to her, take her out on strolls, and have ice cream like they did in their childhood. It's not that she can't go alone. But she loves to share these moments with him. She can't blame him, but it's his life. He can come out of the bad phase and start afresh. Ruhana and her parents love him. He's not alone in the world. Vineet reaches to hold her hand again, mustering the courage to speak. He knows that she is angry, but he wants to convince her for now. He looks at her innocently while she glares at him.

"These gestures won't work today. I've always been too easy on you. I always melt because I cannot see you sad. I always forgive you for all the scoldings. But it's not happening today. When you can't take in my silence, why do you serve the same every day? I also cannot accept your silence, but I do. I give you time to heal up because mom says that time will heal everything, but now! Now I feel like you don't want to heal yourself. So, I give up! Do whatever you want to. You're free," She shouts at him, venting all her anger, and leaves the room.

He stands still, processing her words, Teardrops escape his eyes. He has hurt her, and he has to make up for it. But how? He has to figure it out, but for now, it's best to know her whereabouts. He knows it, maybe!

*****

Ruhana leaves the house in a jiffy. He knows she's very angry with him. It's not that she doesn't understand him or his feelings; it's just the variation in understanding between the two. The things that matter to her don't matter to him anyway. She wants him to laugh and enjoy life as they used to do in their childhood. *Is it wrong? No!* Vineet needs to grow out of his cage and start his life afresh. He knows it, but he's been denying it for a long time.

Ruhana walks towards the park situated on the society's premises. It's her safe place near the pool in the park. Whenever she's sad, angry, or upset, she comes here and sits for a while. The surrounding environment and natural beauty help her calm down. Today, she's angry at Vineet. Just a mere word—silence—caused her anger to fire up. The only reason is that she experiences his silence daily. He never tells her about his feelings or if there's something he wants her to know. She's fed up with his behaviour.

She settles on a bench near the pool and fixes her gaze on the flowing water. Her mother's words echo in her ears. She says that *water keeps flowing; you'll never find the same drop of water again. Every drop is new,* and Ruhana agrees with it. Similarly, life is a maze, and you have to keep moving on.

Life won't cause pain every time. Your age won't return once it passes by. You'll grow up, from a kid to an adolescent to a middle-aged person, and then grow old. You have to live through all ages with the same zest. You have to be playful and curious in your life, just like a little child is. Life is hard, but you have to overcome the obstacles and lead a life of your choice. It's your life; it's better to live it under your own conditions.

*****

Ruhana sighs as her trail of thoughts pauses with a sound. She looks up, only to find a few children playing in the pool. One of the kids who knows her asks her to join them in the pool. She denies it politely. A small smile makes its way to her lips. Vineet should learn how to live life from these little children. She always wants him to be happy, but he chooses silence. Today, she has decided to be silent. She won't talk to him. If he can serve silence to her, then she can do the same. After all, she's getting hurt at the end of the day, all because of his rudeness and silence. She spots an ice cream stall and moves towards it. She purchases a chocolate cone and pays the money to the vendor. A familiar voice falls into her ears.

"You'll catch a cold, Princess," Vineet says, his tone soft.

He knows her better, and here he is, convincing her. She ignores him and begins to have her ice cream. He follows her until they reach the pool area. She sits on the bench and continues to have her ice cream while scrolling through her phone. Vineet sits beside her.

"Sorry, Ruhana," he apologizes.

Ruhana glances at Vineet, and he smiles cutely while she turns her face away from him. She has decided to make him realize how it feels when your loved ones hurt you. She turns to the other side again. She can hear his loud sigh.

"Ruhana! I am sorry!" He apologizes again.

"Don't say sorry, Vineet. You never meant it," Ruhana retorts, glaring at Vineet.

"I mean it, Princess. You know me. I promise it won't happen again," He says it softly.

There's pain reflecting on his face. He knows what she means to him, and she has always been by his side. When she was born, he promised to protect her. She takes care of his happiness, his likes and dislikes, and even makes him smile. It seems like his smile is her treasure. But today, the pretty girl is angry. It won't be easy to convince her. Vineet changes sides and sits in front of her. She turns her face away, stating her displeasure with him.

"Ruhana, sorry! Please understand. If you won't understand me, then who will do that?" he asks while looking into her eyes.

"Have you ever tried to understand me, Vineet? Whenever I ask you about your problems or if anything is bugging you, you always scold me. You don't tell me anything. You always serve silence to me. Then what should I do? When you don't feel that I am able to understand you, then why should I understand you?" Ruhana says, venting her anger at him.

"I fight with everyone—I fight for you, Vineet. I leave the parties with my friends just to be with you. I choose you over myself. I do everything that pleases you. And what do I receive in return? Your silence! Why Vineet? Am I bound to understand you? If you cannot understand me, then why do you expect it from me?" She looks at him angrily while he is shocked with her choice of words.

Vineet knows that Ruhana is right, and so he hangs his head low. She's right enough; she does everything as per him. He doesn't like to go out to parties, so she cancels her parties. She chooses to be with him rather than her best friend. Vineet means a lot to her, more than her friends. She's frustrated with his behaviour when he's not ready to change. Her voice broke his trance.

"Even I miss Aunty. She always took care of me in my mother's absence. She used to make my favorite cuisines better. She was the one to hold me in her arms before my own mom, Vineet. I know I can't fill her presence, and neither can Mumma. But can't you get out of it? It's been fifteen years, Vineet. Please," She chides him angrily.

Vineet sighs deeply. She's right, his mother had been concerned about Ruhana while her mother has always showered love on him. It was Ruhana's dad who used to take him on outings. Her mother used to cook his favorite sweets, while his mother used to cook Ruhana's favorite dishes. Since his mom's demise, Ruhana's mom has taken care of him. Even at night, it used to be him who used to snuggle close to her. He knows he should move on, but he's unable to. He doesn't know how to respond to her.

"Speak something, Vineet. You know I am right, don't you?" She asks, her tone filled with rage.

"It's not easy," he whispers, downing his gaze.

"Look at me. Why is it not easy? Vineet, you're hurting your mom like this. She didn't raise a weak boy. My best friend isn't weak. Your smile makes my day, Vineet. And what do you do? You hurt me," She says, her tone laced with concern for him, while her eyes are still fixated on him.

"Think about your doings, Vineet. Mom, Dad, and I want you to be happy. Dad trusts you. Don't you think you should move on in life? We are there. I am there to hold your hand," She says she is cupping his face with her hands.

Vineet doesn't reply. She looks at him another time, but he lowers his gaze. He knows that Ruhana is right, and he should help her get what she wants from him. She turns angry again at his silence.

"Fine! If you don't want to answer, then don't talk to me. Stay with your silence, forever," She says.

Ruhana gazes at Vineet and leaves the place. Vineet is still standing still at his place, reminiscing about her words. She's right, and he's lost in deep thoughts, all about how to convince her and how to be the person she wants him to be.

Chapter 4:

The Rejected Apology

Ruhana leaves the park after the trifle with Vineet. She's tired of his silence and rudeness. She wants him to be his real self. As always, he doesn't have any answers to her questions. He doesn't know what to say; all her accusations and reasons are correct. He's at fault, for he's unable to let go of what happened to him at a tender age. It's hard, though, but it's not impossible.

If a person is determined to do something, he or she can attain it.

Then, why is he not willing to try? This question keeps bugging Ruhana. She doesn't have an answer, and Vineet doesn't want to talk about it. Ruhana reaches home and moves straight to her room. Vineet follows her inside the house shortly. Rekha looks at them and knows that the two friends had a tiff. Even Rekha longs to see the same person in Vineet as he was in childhood. Okay, Vineet has turned mature, but he has caged himself, and the lady wants him to be carefree and enjoy his life.

Voids can't be fulfilled, but new memories can be made with the people who are still around you and who love you the most.

Rekha sighs deeply. She has seen life more than her children, and she knows that life is how you make it. It's you who nurture and carve your life with your own hands. She needs to convince Vineet and make him realize reality. Rekha keeps her hand on his shoulder.

"What happened, Vineet?" she asks softly, reading his sad face.

"She's very angry," he says softly, guilt building in his heart.

"Give her some time. You know, she can't stay silent and away from you for a long time," she says, her tone exuding a warmth.

"But I'm the reason for her anger. I don't want to be the reason for her anger, Ma," he says disappointedly.

Rekha makes Vineet sit on the couch. She's his mother as well, and she knows what is going on in his heart and mind. Like Ruhana, Rekha also wants him to share his feelings, but she knows he will take time, so she has given him the liberty. She hasn't given birth to him, but she loves him like her own son. She cups his face softly and kisses his head.

"Relax Vineet. I know what bothers both of you. Ruhana is right at her place. You're her only friend, Vineet. You guys have been best friends since you were little kids. She dislikes going to social gatherings. She says she is happy with you. And if you serve her silence, then she'll be hurt. It's better that both of you sit and talk about it. She's not demanding too much from you," She says it meaningfully.

Vineet looks at her innocently. The lady smiles and keeps her hand on his head, pressing it softly. She knows what Vineet is going through, but it has been fifteen long years since that bad incident. He has to cope with his past and live in the present. She cups his face.

"What do you think? Am I just your mom's namesake? No, you're dear to me, Vineet. You're my child. Your mom gave your responsibility to me. And it's not because you've been living with us; it's because whenever your mom used to scold you, you used to come to me. For you, I was your saviour. You used to convince your dad [Ruhana's dad] to take you on long drives. Do you think I can see you sad? No, son! No mother can see her children sad. I care for you and Ruhana equally. I know what bothers my children. Try opening up your heart, son. Ruhana only needs her childhood best friend. Can't you be the same boy as you used to be in your childhood? " She explains her concern.

Vineet sighs deeply. He knows his mother is right. He fears being the same person again. He feels that if he trusts others, he will be hurt again, and he doesn't want that. He fears opening up, even if it is to Ruhana. But he also knows that life doesn't go the way a person wants, but he refuses to grow up. He looks at his mother. His eyes are teary, and he apologizes, for not being the person they want him to be. His guardian lady understands this, and she looks at him.

" Maa! I am sorry," he says softly, and Rekha smiles softly.

"Don't be sorry, Vineet. But I'd like to say something. Not every phase is the same, and neither are the people around you. I tell Ruhana that everyone deserves a certain amount of time to heal. Take your time, but don't lose your real self. I don't want my children to change," She says, her tone soft yet meaningful. She kisses his forehead while he closes his eyes to feel her motherly warmth.

She asks him to freshen up and come down with Ruhana, as she will be preparing dinner. Vineet nods and moves to his room. On his way, he peeps into Ruhana's room. He finds Ruhana sitting on the bed, clutching her teddy bear. Her eyes are teary. She's angry at him, and she's crying as well.

Why? Seeing her cry pinches his heart. He's guilty because he's the reason for her tears. He wants to convince her, but he knows that it's hard as well. He sighs deeply and knocks on the door. She looks up and frowns as their eyes meet.

"Vineet, please, if you have come here to apologize, don't do it. Because you won't mean it," She says, her tone firm.

"Ruhana, try to understand. I said sorry. I promise I won't do it again," He says, his tone low and filled with genuineness.

She snaps at him angrily. She is well aware of his habit of sugarcoating his words, and then he pulls away from all his promises. She couldn't believe him in the first place. Secondly, she doesn't want to get hurt again.

Hurt by him!

He will promise, but then do the same thing again. He has done it numerous times, and she doesn't want him to repeat it again and again. He looks pained at her reply. He walks towards her while she turns away from him. He manages to hold her hands, and the warmth of his hands makes her turn her face at him, but she glares at him. Vineet is tense because she isn't talking to him.

The girl who follows him everywhere, the one who makes sure he's fine, the girl who always finds time and moments to be with him, is angry with him. He is suddenly missing everything that Ruhana does for him. He is used to it now, and he can't deny it. Even if he serves her silence, she never stops doing things for him. She never backs off her duties, and all she tries is to make him feel happy and better. Now, he wants her to run behind him to coax him to do things her way, but she is serving him silence.

He deserves it. Yes!

He deserves her silence.

She jerks his hands, and he comes out of his trance. She is really angry; she doesn't want to melt for him so easily. She wants him to understand that she can be silent as well. She pushes him lightly.

"Vineet, please. If you can get angry, then I can do the same. Your sad faces won't work today. Just leave me alone. That's your way! Right?" She snaps at him, her tone harsh.

A lump forms in Vineet's throat. She has never been so angry at him. She can't be, but right now, she is mad at him, and it's for all the obvious and right reasons. It's hard to convince her. She shows him the door.

"Leave my room, Vineet. You should be happy that I won't coax you anymore," she says angrily.

"But I want you to do it. I miss it all," he says emotionally.

"Oh, please, Vineet! Stop talking. I don't want to do anything. When you understand how silence feels and tastes, then you will understand my pain. Now leave my room. I have to change," She says this and pushes him out of her room.

Vineet is astonished. Ruhana isn't of this kind. She always wants him to be by her side. She feels better when they study together in her room. There are times when she goes to him or calls him in order to seek his help. But today, she is angry. Vineet feels guilty. He understands her pain now that she's not behind him. He moves to his room and moves into the washroom. He splashes water on his face and looks at his wet face in the mirror. He moves out and changes into casual. All the while, he is thinking about what to do to convince Ruhana.

He scans his room. Everything is in its place. It must be Maa who does it all for him. And not to forget, Ruhana as well. His eyes land on his guitar, and he knows what to do to convince Ruhana. He silently wishes that she will forget her anger and forgive him.

Chapter 5:

Contemplating the Feelings

Ruhana is upset because Vineet doesn't understand her perspectives. He should not expect something from her if he can't give it to her. She is fidgeting with her thoughts when there is a knock on the door. She looks up to find Vineet at the entrance, and she ignores him willingly. He sighs deeply, watching her facial expressions.

"Ruhana!"

"Roo, please, listen to me,"

He calls her name lovingly, but she ignores him. He feels bad about her behavior but knows he's at fault. He was rude to her, and now that she's doing the same, he's hurt. She always jumps to respond whenever he calls, staying close whether he needs her or not. She knows his wants, needs, likes, and dislikes. Now, she's hurt, and he knows; he's the reason. Her silence pinches his heart, but he refuses to understand that his actions and silence might have caused her pain. He wants her to forgive him, despite knowing she's mad. His heart knows he deserves it, but he doesn't want to lose her. He wants to apologize to her right now.

"Ruhana, please listen to me," he says, his tone soft and laced with guilt.

"Do you listen to me? NO! Then why should I do it?"

"Do not expect me to do something that you don't do, Vineet. Please know that I can also do those things that you do with me constantly," Ruhana screams, her gaze sharp and intense, fixated on him.

He sighs deeply. He knows her anger is genuine, but he needs to pacify her. He needs her, after all. She is his source of sunshine. He looks at her and finds her looking into her book. He glances at the guitar in his hand and begins to play her favorite song on it. Ruhana looks at him for a moment but looks away in the next instant. He sits beside her and begins to play the song, trying to cheer her up and seeking apology. However, this time, she isn't easy to please. She only glares at him and hops off the bed towards the window. He follows her and keeps his hands on her shoulder.

"Ruhana, I am sorry," He apologizes again, his tone honest.

"Your sorry won't take away my pain, Vineet. It won't bring your old self back. You'll convince me, and then you will behave in the same way tomorrow," She snaps at him, her tone laced with annoyance.

"I will try to be the way you want, Ruhana. Lend me some time, please." He says, his tone firm yet convincing.

She glances at him, and she can see the tears building up in his eyes. Though she feels that he's telling the truth, she's doubtful that he will stick to his words. This time, she doesn't want to melt for him.

"I've given you ample time, Vineet. I've tried to convince you many times. It's been fifteen years since that bad incident, but you don't want to understand my perspective. So, it's a waste of my time, isn't it?" She snaps at him and he lowers his gaze.

"You're taking so much time that you're hurting me and Aunty as well. Do you know she's up there looking at you?

If she sees you like this, she'll be sad as well," Ruhana says, putting her thoughts in words.

"It's better to move on, Vineet. I know your grief is big, but it's life. It doesn't stop for anyone. Aunty's death was destined, Vineet. By being silent and rude, you're hurting her and me as well. Why can't you be happy with what you have? Are you not happy with us? Tell me! I will stop doing things for you—those things that I do to make you feel better," She says that, and Vineet knows she's being modest and honest.

"Even I miss her, Vineet. She didn't give birth to me, but she took care of me. So, I love her the same way you do. But why am I suffering amidst this? I don't deserve to lose you," She says it angrily, and her eyes are watery.

Vineet takes a deep breath. He knows she's right. But he has refrained himself from becoming the old soul that he was. Or maybe he doesn't want to do the same.

"Now say something? How long do I need to wait, Vineet? What do you want? I am an idiot who's always running behind you, but you never pay heed to me. Do you?" She asks, her tone cutting through the silence in the room.

She has had enough of his tantrums. He should know how she feels when he ignores her or doesn't listen to her. She wants him to understand the pain she feels when he serves her with his silence. His pain is not hidden from her, but he can't move on in his life. She only wants him to open up and share his feelings with her, and she believes that it is not too much to ask for. She looks at him again.

"I know you, your past, everything about you, Vineet. I could leave you easily. But I didn't, I stood by your side, and I am still by your side. I want you to be the amazing person that you are. Why do you hide under the masks of silence?" She asks, her tone laced with concern for him.

"I am trying," he says, though he knows that he's not trying.

"Really! I don't think so, Vineet. If you were trying, it would have been visible. Just tell me, what do you want? I didn't want to talk to you. I already freed you, and yet you're here. So, tell me, what's the problem?" She says it angrily, annoyed with his behavior.

"Ruhana, I know I have hurt you. But I am trying," He says, his eyes teary at the moment.

"If you'll leave me alone, then I won't be able to do anything," He says it, and it is the truth from his end.

Ruhana is the only force that makes him come out of his shell. Otherwise, he is always silent and lets things happen as they come to him. It's only Ruhana who coaxes him, and he knows that she is doing it for him, so out of courtesy, he has to agree with her. Ruhana knows that some of the things he does are just formalities. Yet she looks at him, and he assures her that he's telling the truth. He holds her hands in his.

"I'll need you. I know it's hard for me to express my feelings, but I know you're also trying hard for me. I will surely try harder," he says, holding Ruhana's hands.

"I understand Vineet. Only if you look back at me. Please know that hiding things or being silent won't solve your problems. You will need someone, and I am always there," Ruhana says, trying to compose herself, while he doesn't have any answers to her questions.

"Will it make any difference, Vineet? You've promised me several times, but you always break the promise," She says this rather than complaining to him about his deeds.

"I will try my best not to repeat it," he says softly.

Ruhana looks at him. A part of her heart wants to believe him, and the other part thinks the other way around. She doesn't know what to do. She looks at Vineet, who is gazing at her intently. She takes a deep breath, as she can't see him sad or upset, and she can wait until he truly smiles.

"Fine! You are forgiven. But Vineet, remember that you promised me to be happy and sound," she says, her hopeful glance falls on him.

He smiles positively and pulls her into a hug, reassuring her that he will not give her any reason to complain. They part ways when Ruhana's phone rings, and she gets excited with the news that is bestowed upon her.

"Really!! Is it true?"

"That's great? We'll go, and we will enjoy ourselves. It's going to be fun,"

"Mom and Dad will allow; I will talk to them, and I will convince Vineet as well,"

Ruhana replies to her friend while glancing at Vineet, and she disconnects the call. He raises his eyebrows at her; it's his habit to question her without speaking a word. Ruhana clings to him and tells him that the college is organizing a trip to Mumbai. She is quite happy with the news, but he denies it with a straight face.

"No!" he denies straightly; he doesn't want to go, obviously.

"Please Vineet!! It's a beautiful place. Let's go," She clings to his shoulder.

"Then you ask Ma and Dad, please. I don't want to go," He denies shrugging his shoulders.

"Huh! See, you are again breaking the promise you just made, Vineet," She pouts at the moment.

"I have other responsibilities," He says this, turning the other way, and Ruhana gets hyper.

"Yeah! You're the only one who has responsibilities in this world. You know what to do for other people, but you don't know what you should do for your loved ones, and I hope I come in your loved ones," She snaps at him sarcastically.

"When you can't keep your promises, why do you make them, Vineet? You always forget your promises to me. Whatever I demand, all you can say is no. See, I am proved wrong again," She shouts at him.

All her good mood is spoiled in a second. Yeah, he could say yes for her sake. When she can do anything for him, why can't he do one little thing for her? She turns away, and Vineet sighs deeply.

He knows that she's right. It happens every time Ruhana demands something from Vineet. She walks out of the room to talk to her parents. She doesn't want to talk to him anymore. He knows that it'd be a very tiresome task to convince her another time.

Chapter 6:

Banters & Arguments

Ruhana walks out of her room to talk to her parents. Vineet follows her and her mother looks at Vineet and smiles. She knows that her children patched up, but Ruhana is upset for another reason now. Even the lady thinks that Vineet is being harsh. She gazes at Vineet.

"Why is she angry, son?" she asks softly, only to be answered by her daughter.

"Mom, don't ask him. I will tell you. Our college is taking us to Mumbai for an educational tour. It's for the whole college and it's a great chance for Vineet as well. But he doesn't want to go. As usual, he doesn't want to agree to what I say. However, he promised me that he would try to change his ways. Yet again, he denies me. If someone else asks, he will agree. But because I asked him, he will not do it," Ruhana replies, her tone laced with anger.

She is upset that he's again breaking the promise he made to her. Meanwhile, Vineet's phone rings. He moves aside to attend the call. He hums in reply and then agrees to report to the college early the next day. He turns around only to face Ruhana and her mother.

"What happened, Son? Why so serious?" Rekha asks him, noticing his facial expressions.

"We can go. Go, do your packing. We have to get the registrations done in the morning," he says lowly while looking at Ruhana, and she is shocked.

"Are you okay? You straightaway denied me. Why do you agree to go now?" Ruhana asks doubtfully.

"I have some duties to do. I will have to go," he says, feeling her gaze fixed on him.

"Oh! So this is not for me. You could have agreed when I said that, but you agreed when you were given some duties. It's unfair, Vineet," She says it, her tone cold.

Ruhana walks into her room. Vineet doesn't say anything, but he knows he has to hear it from her. He has already broken the promise he made to her a couple of minutes ago. He's the prefect in college, and he knows that he will be needed on the trip. Though she is not pleased, she calls Priyanka and Akshara to inform them that she and Vineet will join the Mumbai trip.

*****

An hour later, after the family finishes their dinner, Vineet tells them that he's heading on to the terrace, at which his Maa nods affirmatively. Ruhana helps her mom finish the chores. She then prepares coffee for Vineet and herself and moves onto the terrace. She can't break the routine that they have been following for many years. She hands him his cup of coffee and sits beside him on the swing. She looks at him and finds the lines of deep thoughts etched on his face. She initiates the conversation and asks him about the trip, and he assures her that he will not change his plan now. She hums in agreement, and Vineet knows that the girl is still upset.

"Ruhana, I am sorry! I know, I denied, but you know..." He says so, but Ruhana cuts him off.

"Yeah, you just promised me that you'd try to be happy. What's wrong with you? You agreed to go on the trip because management asked you. Why couldn't you say yes for me, Vineet? *Agar mere kehne par tum maan jaate, toh kya hota?*" She asks him, but her tone is still cold.

"No wrong, it's just that......" Vineet says but falls silent, feeling her gaze on himself.

"You never try to understand me, Vineet. Ever never. And I always melt for you. I am angry. Stay alone," Saying so, she moves to her room, angered at him.

Vineet is sad, and he's unable to express his feelings.

*****

Ruhana moves into her room and sits on the bed. She's angry and tears begin to trickle down her eyes. She takes out her diary from the side table and begins to pen down her feelings.

"Today, I failed again. I failed to make him understand that everything is not the way he thinks. I have known him since childhood. He was not as stubborn as he acts these days. He's 24— the most mature person I know. Still, he acts immaturely. I don't know when I will have to convince him. When will he change his ways? He promises me but again breaks it. Just like right now.

Why? Why is he like that? Okay, I can't change his past, but I can help him create a better future. I need to bring my best friend back. He needs to learn to trust again. He needs to believe in love and trust. I wish to be successful. That's all for today! Good night!"

Ruhana caresses what she has just written in her diary and keeps it in the drawer. Her gaze falls on the photo frame on the side table. It is her and Vineet's childhood picture. He is standing a step up and has his hands on her shoulders. She smiles as she remembers something from the past.

"Ruhana, please stand still. If you'll keep jumping and moving, don't blame me for the bad picture," Little Vineet scares her.

"Vineet, I dare you to do something with my picture. .Click on a nice picture. Otherwise, I will kill you," she replies angrily, and he giggles at her.

That's when her father comes there and asks him to stand with her so that he can click a picture. He runs and stands behind her. He holds her ponytail to irritate her, as she doesn't like anyone touching her hair except her mom. She gets irritated, and her dad clicks a few pictures.

This is the best of all the clicks, and she smiles at the sweet memory.

*****

She's lost in her thoughts that revolve around Vineet. These days, he doesn't even smile; forget about laughing freely. She comes out of her trance to hear his voice. She finds him standing near the door.

"Ruhana, Be early tomorrow! Finally, what you want is happening!" He says it softly and lowly.

She looks up at him but chooses to ignore him. His sight is causing her displeasure, which she doesn't like personally. She sighs deeply; he's not realizing that he broke his promise, and she's upset. Though they are going on a trip, his eyes show no emotion yet again. He is a quiet person these days, totally opposite of what he was in their childhood. She pats her hand on the space near her, gesturing for him to sit down. He did so. She wants to convince him again. He looks at her, and she doesn't look okay.

"Are you okay, Ruu?" He asks.

"Yes! I will have to be fine. Because you're not doing what you're supposed to," She snaps at him.

"Ruu…please!" He says it but falters momentarily.

He knows that she will come up with something, and she's right; only he can't find a way out of his cage. She's tired of all his silly reasons, and she decides to be the person that she is. She chuckles, telling him that she's excited to go on the trip. He's still caging himself, and she needs to free him.

Life happens, and you need to always move forward.

She knows he will never share his feelings. She still wants him to open up and share all the pain, sorrow, and fears hidden in his heart. But it seems like she needs to wait a little longer. Vineet looks at her. She looks happy, and she continues to talk about her plans. He tugs the loop of her hair behind her ears.

She's beautiful!

He always feels that way. She has always been the pretty soul who gives him light and paves his way. Ruhana casts a look at her and hugs him; maybe she wants to request something for another time. He hugs her back, locking his arms around her petite waist.

She asks him to come out of his cage again. Vineet sighs deeply and glances at Ruhana. Her eyes are closed, and she has placed her head on his shoulder. The moment seems to stop. He trails back into the past, when she entered his life.

*****

Ruhana has been a bubbly girl since her childhood. She has never worried for anyone or anything. She's been the apple of her parents' eyes. Also, she's Vineet's best friend. They seem perfect for each other. Vineet, being short-tempered, always calms down if Ruhana is around. And she always believes him; right and wrong don't matter to her.

This friendship began when Ruhana was born. Vineet was 2 years older than her, and he had cared for her since she was a little baby. He was happier when his mother told him that he would soon get a new friend to play with. He started making plans for what to keep for his friend and what to share. Their mothers often laughed at him when he used to pick up his toys and keep them for his new friend. He grew protective and caring for Ruhana over the years. She,too, loves being around him. She would play pranks just to irritate or tease him. He never got irritated with her pranks; actually, he loved them. Whenever she sat down like a good girl, he knew something was wrong.

Even he, like every good boy, used to approach her and ask her about the problem. She would look at him and hug him the next moment, blurting out everything. He smeared her back to make her calm. Eventually, she'd calm down and smile. He seemed happy to make her feel relaxed!

But, as they say, time never remains the same. Many things happened in their lives.

No! Actually, in Vineet's life. His life is ripped apart, and he's left alone.

The reason is his father's harshness and rudeness towards him and his mother. Sometimes, he would come home drunk and argue with his mother. Adding to this, an accident happened that shook his life completely. How does it affect this little boy, who's merely 9 years old? His parents' divorce and then his mom's death shattered him. Even when his father came to take him, he shouted at him, saying that he couldn't love him the way his mother did; actually, he never loved them. He was happy to stay with Ruhana and her family.

He started living with Ruhana and her parents, though he was lost. He would get irritated when she teased him, and sometimes he would shout at Ruhana, making her sad. She knew he was sad, so she always tried to cheer him up.

*****

His trance is broken when Ruhana nudges him. He finds her staring at him. He parted the hug, glanced at her, and asked her to rest, as they had to leave early for college. They have to go for registration and other formalities. She nods her head like a little girl while he smiles lightly. He places a soft kiss on her forehead and leaves the room.

She watches him go. She wants to see him laughing and happy, like in their childhood. He needs to trust people and start loving again. She promises herself to make this ten-day tour life-changing for him. She caresses his picture, hugs it close to her heart, and dozes off into her dream world.

*****

The next morning, Ruhana is the first one to wake up and get ready. She's an excited being. She has made a promise to herself, and decided to stick to it. She picks up her bag, rushes to her parents' room, and asks her father for registration money, which he obliges. Well, she's taken her saved money also, yet her father is going to give her money for registration. Ruhana hugs him out of excitement. She's happy; she will get extra time with Vineet, and she'll try to bring him back. She rushes out of her father's room as her mother calls them for breakfast.

Vineet is the silent being, listening to Ruhana's father intently. Her eyes are fixated on him. She just wants to see his charming smile and his usual self. Vineet is hiding his feelings behind his duties. The small family of four finishes breakfast, and her dad offers to drop them off at college, and they agree. Soonish, they leave for college. Ruhana takes her seat in the back of the car, and Vineet sits in the passenger seat.

"This is going to be fun," she chuckles and jumps to her place.

"Yeah! But you don't have to act kiddish, honey," Her father says it teasingly.

"Oh, Dad! Please! Vineet is enough to be the serious one. I don't want to be like him," Ruhana makes a face.

"He's a kind gentleman. Dare you trouble my son?" Her father glares at her through the rear mirror.

"Oh yeah! A kind yet stubborn boy," Ruhana makes a face, causing the men to giggle.

"Just like you, Ruu! You're one stubborn and adamant girl," Vineet breaks the silence.

"Only because of you, Vineet. You never listen to me. And Dad, you never scold him. But he does all the pranks. He troubles me; I don't trouble anyone," She says this, complaining to her father.

Her father laughs. He knows what she's talking about, and he agrees with every word of it. He gazes at both Ruhana and Vineet.

"Give him time, honey. You know well how to handle this young boy," her father says softly.

"Oh yes! He'll be under my care on the trip," Ruhana smirks.

Vineet smiles. He knows what she's up to. He wants to be the way she wants him to be, but his past stops him. He doesn't know it, but there is some barrier that is stopping him. She slaps the back of his head.

"Put a small smile on your face. Being goofy and silent won't help you, Mister," she whispers in his ears.

He smiles lightly, and her smile widens seeing that small curve on his lips. Meanwhile, they reach the college. Their father asks them to take care of him and leaves. They enter the college, and Ruhana spots her friend, Priyanka, at a distance. She gives Vineet a quick hug and tells him that once she is free, she will meet him only at the gate. He agrees, and they walk in different directions.

*****

Ruhana meets Priyanka, and they begin to walk towards their class. Priyanka glances at her friend and asks her about Vineet. She knows that her friend is very concerned about Vineet.

"Is Vineet coming for the trip?" she asks.

"He has to come. Even though he didn't want to. But his duties are pulling him," Ruhana says softly:

"Oh! So he denied it at first?" Priyanka asks, her curiosity piqued.

"Yeah! He has to deny my words always," Ruhana shrugs her shoulders.

"And you're always after him," Priyanka looks at her friend.

Ruhana shrugs her shoulders. She looks dejected, but it's true. She loves to be around Vineet. She loves to be in his warmth. When he's around her, she feels safe and secure. She's happy to be with him. Now, she's glad that Vineet will be with her on the trip.

"He will be there, and I'll be glad for it, Pri!" Ruhana says, a smile lighting her face.

"Mad in love, you are!" Priyanka says, slapping Ruhana's shoulder lightly.

Ruhana giggles. She doesn't know if it's love, but *Vineet certainly holds a special place in her heart and in her life. His silence, his smile, his words, his voice—everything about him matters to her. She can't help but smile while thinking about him.* Her trance is broken by Priyanka, who is sitting by her side on the desk.

"Stop daydreaming, baby. Go and tell him your feelings," Priyanka nudges her another time.

"Yeah! And he'll push me out of his life. He's still far away from me. I can't risk it, darling," Ruhana says softly:

"Oh! But you should, before someone else enters his life," Priyanka says.

"Noo!! It won't happen!" Ruhana says, and she's startled at her words.

"Then tell him what you feel about him," Priyanka says, chiding her best friend.

"Oh! Shut up, Pri! Nothing of this sort will happen. He won't let anyone come close to him. I know him," She says it confidently.

"Quite confident! Then I wish you luck, babe!" Priyanka says it with a smile.

Ruhana smiles and holds Priyanka's hand. She knows that her friend will always be by her side, and she's thankful for that.

"I need it, truly. I have made a promise to myself. I will bring Vineet back on track. He has to come out of the cage of silence and sadness. He promised me to come out, yet I doubt him," Ruhana says she's thinking about him.

Priyanka tends to agree, and soon the class begins. A long day lies ahead.

*****

Vineet moves to the headmaster's chamber and learns about his role as the administrator of the trip. He is the head boy, and he has the duty to maintain the students and keep an eye on the students who are going on the trip. He can't neglect his duties at the college. Talking with the head, he approaches his class and meets his best friend Rohan on the way.

"Going on the trip?" Rohan asks, his curiosity piqued.

"Yeah! "I got the duties for the second year," Vineet says.

"Ruhana would be happy, no!" Rohan comments.

"Yeah! But she's angry," Vineet lets out a deep sigh.

"You know what she needs," Rohan says.

Their eyes meet, and Vineet understands the meaning behind his words. Vineet tends to think about her, and at the same time, someone comes up to him and says something that leaves him raging, and he begins to leave the place, but someone stops him on the track, and he's surprised to hear them.

Chapter 7:

Embracing the Truth

Ruhana is quite excited about the trip to her dream city, Mumbai. Vineet is also accompanying her and she is glad to spend some time with him. She always wishes for his happiness, and she wants to take away all his pain. She wants him to smile as if there's no end to their lives. Though she knows, it is hard. However, life is hard and harsh; it's a reality.

Nothing exists like a fairy tale in real life.

Yet Ruhana wishes that Vineet would open up and live his life to the fullest. It's hard to bring out the real person when they have locked themselves in a cage. Ruhana silently prays for her success during this trip. After all, Vineet matters the most to her.

Her trail of thoughts is broken when Priyanka nudges her. She finds their teacher gone, and it's a free lecture. They move out and move towards the library when Ruhana spots Vineet with someone—a girl whom Ruhana doesn't like.

*****

As Rohan and Vineet are talking, someone stops Vineet by calling his name. She is Rhea and she belongs to the wealthy family of the college trustee and tends to get whatever she wants. She's always trying to get the attention of guys, and right now, she's focused on Vineet. Ruhana rages to see Rhea near Vineet. She finds Rhea talking to Vineet, actually asking him out for a coffee date. She slaps his arm, as she does with other guys.

"Come on, Vineet! Can't we go on for coffee?" She asks, her tone flirtatious.

"I don't want to go, Rhea. Please go ahead," Vineet replies, his tone calm and composed.

"Oh! Vineet! Can't you keep a girl's word? I mean, guys run behind me, and I am here, asking you out. I am requesting. But you're denying it—how rude!" Rhea shouts, unable to accept the denial.

"Oh please! I know who is behind whom! Now leave my way," Vineet says it firmly and he gives her a push, shocking her.

"No! Until and unless you say yes, I am not going," Rhea shouts at him, trying to hold his hand again.

"Can't you understand that I have denied you? I am not interested in you and your stupid activities," Vineet shouts, this time shocking Rhea.

"How can you be so rude to a girl? I am requesting it! How could you deny a girl?" Rhea tries to hold his hand for another time, but Vineet jerks her hand.

"Vineet, please don't do this. Why are you creating a scene here?" Rhea says, sounding emotional.

"You're creating a scene here, Ms. Rhea. Don't you understand the meaning of the word "NO"?" Ruhana shouts at Rhea, intervening between the two.

"Oh, please, dare you teach me? Who are you?" Rhea shouts at Ruhana; she can't take anyone shouting at her.

"You don't deserve to know me, Miss Rhea!! But look at your deeds first. You're a girl, and that's why he didn't hit you. Else, you'd have been in the hospital," Ruhana says it hatefully, clutching Rhea's face with her hand and leaving her with a jerk.

"Who are you to barge in between us? Stay away!" Rhea shouts at her, showing her index finger to Ruhana.

Ruhana holds Rhea's finger and twists it. She hates Rhea, and she can't take it if she comes near Vineet. And at the moment, she is bothering Vineet, and she can't take it. She shoots an angry glare at Rhea.

"Don't you get it when he denied it at first? Why don't you buy some brains instead of makeup and short dresses? You need it badly. Your mind is so like your mini dresses. Mind your own business. Next time, if I see you bothering him, I'll surely punch your nose," Ruhana says this and leaves Rhea's hand with a jerk.

Rhea is about to fall, but her friend supports her, and they leave from there. Rhea passes angry glares at Ruhana, but the latter isn't concerned. Ruhana shrugs her shoulders, and Vineet glances at her only to find her staring at him.

"What is this, Ruu? You didn't need to do that," Vineet says, trying to dismiss her action, but he knows that girl, Rhea needed the same.

"She needed to know her place. And of course, if someone will bother you, it ought to be done, Mr. Vineet," Ruhana glances at him.

"That's wrong, Ruhana. It doesn't suit you," He tries to convince her.

"And it doesn't suit you to stay calm when people like Rhea cling to you; you entertain them, and when I do the same, you shout at me, asking me to be quiet. It doesn't suit you either, Vineet. And you needed to get rid of her," Ruhana says, her tone calm yet firm.

That's true; he tried to let go of Rhea, but she didn't go away. Instead, she began holding his hand, and he didn't like her touch. Actually, he doesn't like anybody touching him—especially any of his friends. This is only allowed for Ruhana and her mom. Ruhana holds his hand and rubs his palms to calm him. She knows him; he is surely calm-headed, but he needs to deny people; he has to learn to raise his voice, just like he shows anger to her every now and then.

"Vineet! Stay away from Rhea. Anger usually sits on your nose. Why could you not confront Rhea with your rage? She deserved it. It's not good to be soft every time. I mean, you deny me even if I ask a simple question while Rhea was trying to hold your hand. If I had been there, you'd have jerked me, but with Rhea, you didn't. Think of your deeds," Ruhana says it meaningfully.

Of course, she didn't like this gesture from Vineet. They're childhood friends and if Vineet can't let her hold his hand, why is every other person doing it? She can't understand the reason for his rudeness towards her or his care and concern for others. Vineet glances at her, and she smiles lightly. She knows he understands his point, but he's reluctant to accept it. She tugs at his hand.

"I know you are getting my words. You need to accept it. You let go of people easily, but you're not letting go of your past. I knew it was bad. But it is long gone, Vineet. Until when are you going to stay in that cage? There are people like Rhea who are ready to take advantage of your simplicity, and then it's me! I want you to be who you are. I think you understand the difference," Ruhana says this while looking at him.

Meanwhile, her phone rings, and it's Priyanka, who's waiting for her in the library. She looks at Vineet and finds him lost in his own thoughts. She shook him and told him that she would meet him at home, as she and her friends were planning to go to the nearby market to do some shopping. He agrees, and they leave for their respective classes.

*****

The day passes in a blur. Vineet reaches home and tells his Ma that Ruhana will be coming late. The lady nods affirmatively; her daughter has already told her about it. She gives him coffee and she finds him thoughtful.

"What happened, son?" she asks.

"I don't know, Ma! There are many things that I want to do; there are some things that Ruhana wants from me, but I am unable to do them," he replies, looking at his mother figure.

"Think with a calm head. Your mom will always be proud of you, and she will be happy when she sees her son happy! And you want her to be happy, right?" she says.

Vineet nods his head affirmatively and keeps his head in her lap. She smears his head softly for a while and then asks him to change. He nods and moves to his room. He decides to take a shower so that he can calm down. He steps into the shower and closes his eyes. Ruhana's words echo in his mind. He takes a deep sigh, and then he opens his eyes. It seems like he has an answer to her questions. He finishes his shower, and after getting dressed, he moves out of the room. Ruhana is already home, but she's showering.

Later that night, after dinner, Vineet is on the terrace. He's thoughtful after the college incident. He realizes that Ruhana is right. She only wants his happiness, nothing else. She finds time for him; she is always around him, and he serves her silence.

He also realizes that her anger is apt; he lets Rhea come close to him while he always pushes away Ruhana. He's been polite with Rhea, but when Ruhana questions him or asks him something repeatedly, he shouts at her and scolds her every single time. That's the difference. The girl who wants to see him smiling is scolded and served with silence, while the others are handled calmly.

After spending some time with her parents, Ruhana reaches the terrace. She finds him holding the guitar, and her lips curve into a smile. She is glad to find him holding his guitar, and it's a sight she wants to see every single day. She hugs him and takes her seat on the swing. He acknowledges her with a smile. He begins to play her favorite songs, and she savours the music with closed eyes. Vineet stares at her for a while; there is a calmness on her face. He suddenly stops playing the guitar and kneels before her, holding her hands. She opens her eyes, feeling his touch, and she looks at him.

"What happened? Why did you stop playing music? All okay? " She asks, placing her palm on his cheek.

"I am fine, Ruu! It's just that I realized the reality. And I should thank you for it," Vineet says, his eyes fixated on her face.

"Vineet! Can you please speak in simple words?" Ruhana looks at him; she's puzzled at the sudden confession.

"I am sorry!" he says, downing his gaze.

"Sorry! But why? You're never mistaken, Vineet. Then, why are you seeking an apology?" Ruhana looks at him; she is bewildered by his act.

He has never apologized to her. Well, she doesn't mind it either. He tightens his grip on her hands. He knows many questions are bubbling in her mind, and he wants to clarify them. She makes him sit on the swing and look at him.

"Is something bugging you? Look, Vineet, whatever I said in college was right. I am sorry if it hurts you, but you do it every day. You shush me whenever I ask you anything; you shout at me; you ask me not to pry into your matters; but if others do the same things, you either calmly talk to them or you just deny, just like you did today. I do it for you only. I can't imagine my life without you, buddy," She says this as water wells up in her eyes.

Vineet glances at her, and he knows that she's being honest with her words. He has grown up to be a silent guy, and she's the only chirping bird in the house. All she wants is to have him by her side, and she makes sure that it happens every day.

Her trance is broken as Vineet holds her hands in his and looks into her eyes. She can see some uncertainty in his eyes. He takes a deep breath.

"I know; you do it all to make me happy. But, you know, I try, but I am unable to do it. I don't know why," He takes a deep breath.

"Try doing it for yourself, Vineet. Or for me! If you still consider me your friend," Ruhana says.

"You're the only friend I have. All others become selfish," he whispers, but he's being honest with his opinion.

"That's why I ask you to smile; I ask you to bond with others. Silence is good for the people you hate or the ones who underestimate you; not for me, I suppose," Ruhana says this while looking into his eyes.

"I am not able to forget what I have gone through," He says dejectedly.

He stands near the railing, keeping his hands on it. Ruhana looks at him and moves to stand beside her buddy. She keeps her hand on his and looks at the moon.

"*Chand ko bhi toh grahan lagta hain*, Vineet. Its brightness lessens every day, but it comes out every day. The moon knows that he will diminish, yet he comes out and gives us a cool, serene light. It shines with all its might. In the same way, you need to get out of it. One incident can't affect you this much," Ruhana says while Vineet glances at her understandingly.

"I know it was bad; even I miss Mom. (Vineet's mother). But it doesn't mean that you put a shell around yourself. At least I don't deserve this. We used to have so much fun back then. Why not now, Vineet?" Ruhana asks as she reaches out to hold his hands.

"It's not so easy!" Vineet says it again, his gaze fixated on the moon yet again.

"Life is not easy, Vineet. Do you remember when my grandpa passed away? He told me that he'd become a star in the sky. I don't know if it's true, but she's surely seeing you from the heavens above. Why can't you smile for Mom's sake, if not for mine?" Ruhana says.

Vineet takes a deep sigh. He knows she is right. He should move on, for the sake of his loved ones, for Ruhana, and for her parents. He sighs deeply. She's looking at him keenly, waiting for a response. He holds her hands and gazes at her beautiful face.

"You're right, Ruhana. Maa said the same thing to me today: I am sorry for hurting you," He says it, and Ruhana smiles.

"Vineet, take your time, but open up. Don't live in your shell. I am not asking you to forget her; she's your mom. You can't forget her, but you can move on. She's in my memories too, but we can't live our lives this way. You're getting me, right?" Ruhana looks at him.

" I know, and I promise, I'll try my best this time," Vineet says, gazing at her.

Her lips curve into a smile, and she hugs him while he embraces her in his arms. She thanks him for understanding her viewpoint, while he's lost in his past. He says something that leaves Ruhana shocked; it's hard for her to believe.

Chapter 8:

Trailing through the Past

Vineet envelops Ruhana in a warm embrace. As they hold each other, he takes a stroll down memory lane and shares a secret with Ruhana, leaving the young girl in disbelief. She looks at him with her eyes wide open, trying hard to understand what he just said and find out more about it. This is the first time he has talked to her about his feelings; otherwise, he never says anything about his mom or family. She looks at him and finds tears forming in his eyes. She softly touches his cheeks.

"It would have been better if Mom had divorced him," Vineet whispers in her ears, still in her embrace.

"What is this? What are you saying?" She asks softly, taken aback slightly.

"You're getting it right, Ruhana. My mom was supposed to leave him. I heard Maa (Ruhana's mom) talking to my mom about it. But I really liked my dad. He always got me toys, and I didn't know the truth until that night," He says this and looks away towards the railing.

Ruhana gently places her hands over his, which is resting on the railing. She remains quiet, encouraging him to express himself. He squeezes her hand firmly and starts to narrate an incident from their past.

Flashback Begins

Little Vineet was playing with Ruhana in her room. Both kids were colouring in the colouring book. Their moms were talking while sitting in the living room. Little Ruhana finished the drawing and rushes to both the ladies.

"Mumma! I am first. I finished the drawing before V!" She chuckled, showing her drawing to both ladies.

"Take the full name, baby!" her mom said.

"Noo! He's V for me. Right, Vineet?" She turned to Vineet as he stood by her side.

He nodded in agreement, and she giggles. They both displayed their drawings and then Ruhana's mother suggested they watch television in the bedroom. The children laughed and rushed into the room.

As the ladies engage in conversation, Vineet stepped out to pick up his ball. Suddenly, he became alert to some noises. His mother was in tears, and Ruhana's mother was comforting her.

"Why are you here? Why don't you take Vineet and leave him?" Ruhana's mother asked, her tone concerned.

"No! I can't. Vineet loves him; he always waits for him. What will I tell him? I don't want Vineet to hate his father," His mother, Shivani, cried.

"But Shivani, you can't stay with him and ruin your and Vineet's lives. You have to take a step. For Vineet, for your own good," Rekha, Ruhana's mother, said this while looking at Shivani.

"But how? Vineet doesn't know his real face. I know he loves me as well, but he is very attached to his dad. I can't do it, Rekha!" Shivani said, crying bitterly.

"But you have to, Shivani. He can do anything with you and Vineet. Vineet is a kid; he doesn't know reality, but for his

betterment, you have to take this step, Shivani. Otherwise, I'll have to take the step. Vineet is no different from Ruhana for me; I have the right," Rekha said, her tone laced with concern for her best friend. .

Shivani didn't answer; she just cried while Rekha embraced her in her arms. Seven-year-old Vineet is taken aback. He understood his mom is talking about his dad, but he's confused about why another woman is saying she should go away from his dad. What could his dad have done that's so bad? Most importantly, why is his mom crying?

"V-Vinu! Where are you? Let's finish the game," Five-year-old Ruhana stood by his side.

"I am coming," he said, and this broke the trance of the ladies.

Shivani wiped her tears, and Vineet rushed by her side. He wanted to know the reason for her tears and he wanted to make sure that she is fine and safe. He held her hand.

"Mumma! Why are you crying?" He asked; he has already noticed her tears.

"Nothing, my son! Come on, finish your game, and then we will go home. I have to purchase some items from the market," Shivani said, patting Vineet's cheek.

"Aunty! Can I come with you?" Ruhana asked innocently and then looks at her mom.

"V promised me ice cream," She said it innocently, and it made the two ladies laugh.

"Dad will take you and your V! Let him come home," Rekha said this smilingly.

"Noo! Ruhana wants to go with V and Aunty!" the little girl said, her tone soft.

"Okay okay! Let's go!" Shivani said and assured Rekha that she will drop Ruhana home safely.

Rekha agreed, and Ruhana chuckled. She wore her sandals and left with Vineet and his mother. Shivani gave ice cream treats to Ruhana and Vineet, and they return home.

*****

Later that night, Shivani made Vineet sleep. But she's lost somewhere. Vineet held her hand, and the lady looked at him.

"Ma!" he called her; it's the word that melts Shivani.

"Ma! Why are you crying? And why was Rekha Ma asking you to leave?" He asked innocently.

"It's nothing! She wants to take you somewhere along with Ruhana," Shivani made up a story.

"No! I am not going without you and Dad," he said innocently.

"Okay relax! I am not sending you anywhere! Now, please sleep. It's too late!" Shivani asked her son.

Vineet looked at his mom, feeling unhappy, but he hid his feelings and hugs her for comfort. Later that night, he woke up and tried to get some water, but his tumbler was empty. When he went to fill it, he heard scary sounds from his parents' room. Curious, he peeked inside and saw something really scary: his dad, whom he always admired, is hurting his mom badly. She can't defend herself, maybe because she asked for a divorce, which made his dad really angry.

Scared by his dad's loud anger, Vineet rushed back to his room, trembling. He hid under his blanket, crying, until he fell asleep. He's so scared of his dad that he avoided talking to him for a long time.

Flashback Ends

"Before I could ask Mom to leave him, Mom left me alone. She bore his torture for me; I can't forgive myself, Ruu!" He says it, his eyes teary.

"It wasn't your mistake, Vineet. It was fate. But you have to grow past it, for me and for Mom and Dad. Please Vineet. Mumma has every right over you; you say so, right? You should break out of your cage," Ruhana says as she cups his face in between her hands.

"But he hurt you too!" Vineet says, his tone laced with guilt.

"It's still in my memories, V! And I don't want those bad memories," Ruhana says her eyes are equally teary.

Vineet embraces her in his arms, hiding his face in the crook of her neck while she smears his back, trying to console him. They embrace each other, still floating in the past. She wants him to come out of the pain that he's bearing. For the first time, he has shared something with her and she's happy. At least he's trying to keep his promise. Yes, she knows everything about his parents, but having him share his pain and thoughts is a new feeling for her. It feels like her efforts are being acknowledged. She's happy that he has finally decided to speak but sad for the reason that he took a lot of time doing it.

Right now, he is not ready to leave her. He tightens his embrace around her waist. She's glad in her heart, for he's been this close to her for the first time. She separates herself from the hug and rubs his tears away. She can't see him crying; his tears cause pain in her heart. She says nothing; she wants him to cry his heart out. He needs it badly.

She takes him to his room and makes him lie on the bed. He needs to rest and put all his disturbing thoughts to rest. As she begins to leave, he holds her hand and asks her to stay by his side. Ruhana is surprised, but she knows that he is weak at the moment; he has told her a secret—that moment of the past. And she needs to heal him. She sits beside him, and he rants a little more about his dad and then compares him with her father, who has always been gentle with him. Soon, Vineet falls asleep. She covers him with the duvet, switches off the bedside lamp, and then moves to her room.

*****

She closes the door to her room and cleans her desk first. Picking a book from her bedside table, Ruhana settles into bed, leaning on the wall behind her. She relaxes herself before opening the book to read it. But soon, Vineet takes his place in her mind. He's told her about that painful memory of his childhood, which triggered her memory of when his dad behaved wrongly with her. She walks down memory lane.

Flashback Begins

It was a fine day; Ruhana's parents left her at Vineet's place as they had some urgent work, and Ruhana denied going with them. Shivani, Vineet's mom, assured her friend that she would take good care of Ruhana. Rekha smiled and left with her husband. Vineet took Ruhana to his room, and the two kids started playing. Meanwhile, his mother brought pudding for both of them. Ruhana chuckled when she saw it and thanked her for the yummy treats. Shivani asked the kids to have the pudding and play in the room itself. The two kids played along; they made a castle with the building blocks, and Ruhana chuckled.

"This is ours; promise me, you won't give this to anyone." Ruhana looked at Vineet cutely.

"No! Let's keep it here," Vineet said and placed the castle on his study table.

Ruhana smiled and watched him as he stuck two stickers on the castle, which happened to be the first initials of their names. Ruhana chuckled and hugged Vineet out of excitement. He laughed, and then they began to chase each other as he teased her. Ruhana ran out of his room, and Vineet ran behind her, but before he could stop her, the little girl bumped into someone—his father.

Vineet shivered as he saw him. Since that incident when he saw him beating his mom, he had been distant from his dad. Vineet held Ruhana's hand, but it was too late. His father shouted at them, especially Ruhana. The little girl shivered at his loud voice. She hadn't met him so far because usually, Vineet came to her house, or when she came to his place, his father was usually out for work.

The man scolded both kids until Shivani came onto the scene. She asked Vineet to take Ruhana to his room and lock the door. The boy obeyed his mother, and the two kids rushed to his room. Ruhana sat on the bed holding her hand, just as his father had held her hand tightly, and the finger imprints were visible. Vineet held her wrist carefully as if it would heal the pain, but the girl kept her head on his shoulder as they sat silently. She neither asked about his dad nor did she question him, for the loud voices from outside the room were answering their questions.

Flashback Ends

Ruhana comes out of the trance; finds her hugging herself. She runs into Vineet's room and finds him sleeping soundly.

She sighs; her eyes are teary. She wipes the tears away and looks at him intently.

"It wasn't your fault, Vineet. It's your dad's fault. You can find love twice, and you can't force love on anyone. And I don't want you to regret it. You refer to my parents as Maa and Dad; please move forward in your life for their sake," Ruhana says, her tone soft, knowing that he's fast asleep, yet, she wants to speak out her heart.

She finds the same castle they built in childhood sitting intact on his study table. She holds the castle in her hand and looks at his sleeping form.

"If this can stay as it is, irrespective of everything that happened in the past or still happens, why can't we? Why can't we walk past the bad memories?" Ruhana looks at Vineet's sleeping form and finds him awake.

He looks at her intently, then at the castle in her hand. She places the castle on the side table, and he glances at her another time. She is truly the light of his life. She has said the right thing. He should surely move on in his life. Ruhana smiles at him. She knows that he has heard her. She smears his head.

"I am not forcing you, Vineet; I just want you to be happy. Shivi Aunty will stay in our hearts forever. She is right there in the sky, looking at us. You know how much she loves us," Ruhana says, her tone laced with affection.

"You're right, Ruu! I promise I will keep my word. Ma says it right: It takes time, but things heal. That's the reason thinking about him doesn't hurt me anymore," Vineet says.

"He's not worth it, Vineet," Ruhana says, her tone blunt.

Vineet nods his head affirmatively and pulls Ruhana into a hug. She begins to pat his back to calm him. The young lad falls asleep again. She makes him lie properly on the bed and covers him with the duvet. She sets the temperature of the AC and then pecks his forehead, wishing him good night, and she leaves the room.

While leaving his room, she glances at his calm face; maybe the new morning will bring her old friend back. Silently praying for the same, she walks to her room and calls it a night.

Chapter 9:

Finding Happiness

The next day, Ruhana wakes up before her alarm rings. She sits on the bed and ties her hair up in a bun. A soft wind makes the curtains move gently. She gets off the bed and opens the curtains to enjoy the fresh morning air. The cool breeze feels soothing and it makes her smile. She stops for a while, thinking about a sad memory she and Vineet share. It's something they both wish they could forget. Ruhana hopes that today will be better. While looking at the sunrise, someone touches her shoulder, making her jump. It's her mom, and she hugs her warmly, saying good morning.

"All good?" her mom asks her as she folds the duvet while Ruhana makes her bed.

"I woke up early. That's the effect of reading books," She giggles as she ends her statement.

"But you weren't here until 12," her mother says.

"Vineet and I were on the terrace," Ruhana informs her mother.

"How's his mood?" her mom asks, as she is aware of his foul mood since he spent the evening in her embrace.

"I hope he will be fine today. Otherwise, you check on him. Maybe he's sleeping yet," Ruhana shrugs her shoulders.

"He is an early riser," Her mother retorts, and she moves to check on Vineet.

Ruhana smiles and gets ready for the day, feeling happy and excited. She's really glad that Vineet opened up to her, showing his trust. She's also looking forward to their trip to Mumbai. What makes her happiest is that Vineet will be coming along. She hopes this trip might help fix their friendship. With these thoughts on her mind, she prepares herself for the day and exits her room, grabbing her bag on the way out. She's all set for another day at college.

Ruhana makes her way towards the dining table; she spots her father and Vineet already seated there. Her father is savoring his tea, while Vineet is enjoying his black coffee. She takes her coffee cup and settles down beside her father. She glances at Vineet and inquires about his mood. He assures her that he's doing well and flashes a smile at her. His small smile reassures her that he's truly feeling better.

Considering the emotional breakdown he has experienced the previous night, seeing him in improved spirits brings Ruhana happiness. They have breakfast, and Ruhana's father offers to drop them off at college, and they agree. He takes his bag and leaves with Vineet and Ruhana.

*****

Ruhana's father drives them to college and then departs for his office. Upon arriving at the campus, Ruhana notices her friends - Priyanka, Akshara, and Prisha - standing near the garden. She greets them with a wave and then turns to Vineet. She tells him that she'll catch up with him at the main gate after her classes. He nods in agreement, and they both head to their separate classrooms. Ruhana approaches her group of friends, and as she does, Akshara exchanges a knowing look with her, fully aware of everything that transpired between her and Vineet.

"Everything okay?" Akshara inquires, her tone concerned.

"Yes, much better now," Ruhana responds with a smile.

"It looks like you had a heart-to-heart with your best friend," Priyanka remarks, arching her eyebrows.

"I did, and I'm glad he opened up. He's even joining us on the trip. It's going to be a blast," Ruhana says, her hands clasped together.

"Yeah, then you'll be spending less time with us," Akshara teases, earning a smile from Ruhana.

"Don't worry; he'll be there, and that's all I need," Ruhana reassures them with a gentle smile.

Her friends know how much she cares about this guy. He's not just a friend; he's really special to her. She is really happy, but then the school bell rings and they all hurry to their classes.

The day goes by quickly, and finally, the last class ends. Ruhana and her friends leave the classroom and find a big crowd in the hallway around a new notice. They push through the crowd to read it, and they get really excited about what they see.

Priyanka and Akshara exchange awestruck glances as Ruhana excitedly jumps on her toes. Akshara gazes at her, curiosity brimming, and can't resist asking about the source of her joy. Ruhana's smile stretches from ear to ear; her happiness is simply uncontrollable. She hugs Akshara out of excitement.

"It's a kind of lottery for me. It's an educational tour; Vineet is coming along for the tour, even if it is due to office duties, and we'll attend the RD's concert. *Itni saari khushiyan!* Oh my god!" Ruhana chuckles, her tone laced with excitement.

"Who's this, RD?" Priyanka rolls her eyes at her best buddy.

"He's the famous singer, Raj D'sena. He's installing his band, and he has sung some beautiful songs. I just love him. Vineet plays his songs on guitar for me," Ruhana says, and her excitement is clearly visible on her face.

"Such a crazy girl!" Akshara taps her head, smiling.

"Yess! I am! And I am so happy!" She chuckles as they move out of the college building.

Ruhana hops out of the college building and she can't hide her excitement. She is happy to learn that their tour will also let them attend a rock band concert. She jumps on her toes, as the rock band belongs to her favorite pop band singer.

R.D! Okay! She doesn't mind if he's not so popular, but she loves the singer and his songs. She believes that one day he will be a rock star.

Ruhana runs out of the college building and finds Vineet at their usual meeting place. Her eyes softened at his sight. This boy is always on time.

Vineet doesn't really care about what others think, but he always cares about her. That's something she really likes about him. They might argue or not talk sometimes, but they always look out for each other. She always knows where he is, and he looks out for her too. Usually, they go home together at the end of the day, unless one of them has something else to do.

Ruhana tells him that they will get the chance to attend R.D.'s concert. Priyanka and Akshara tease her about the same.

"She's going to meet the love of her life, am I right, Ruu?" Priyanka eyes her bestie, who blushes momentarily.

"Who? What is she talking about?" Vineet asks, breaking the hug. He is clueless at the moment.

"She's talking about Raj. **Raj D'sena**." Akshara chuckles, her smile never fading.

"Who's he, now?" Vineet whispers and glances at Ruhana confusingly.

"He's a musician and singer. We will meet him in Mumbai. There's a concert, and college will be taking us there," Ruhana chuckles, her eyes brimming with admiration for the said man.

"You and your fantasies!" Vineet smiles lightly, ruffling her hair, and moves forward.

"My fantasies are about you,"

Ruhana whispers softly and Vineet turns to her, asking if she said something, but she denies it. He then tells the group that they will be leaving on Saturday and returning after 7 days. Also, he tells them to get themselves registered for the trip. The people agree, and after that, Vineet and Ruhana walk home.

*****

Ruhana and Vineet arrive home and retreat to their respective rooms for a quick refresh. Ruhana's mother, aware of their evening routine, prepares coffee for them. Ruhana shares details of their Mumbai itinerary and the upcoming live concert with her mother, who chuckles at her enthusiasm but acknowledges the thrill of meeting someone one admires. Vineet playfully teases her about it.

"I might just leave you alone with him, you know! Enjoy your time," Vineet teases, initially provoking a playful protest from Ruhana.

"Sure, I'm fine with that. But you'll be so bored without me," she retorts, playfully clicking her tongue at him.

"You'd really leave us?" He asks with an exaggerated expression of surprise.

"Haha! Yes! It could be nice to take a stroll with Mr. RD. It'll be fun!" Ruhana says, wrapping her arms around herself.

"But why would you do that?" Vineet asks, his tone turning serious.

"Because you never take me out for walks anymore. You don't talk and walk like you used to. You've changed a lot," Ruhana replies, her words carrying a deeper meaning.

Vineet stares at her for a few minutes and bows his head. The girl is actually right. It has been ages since they went out to have ice cream. Also, he's a little possessive; he felt a little unrest in his heart when she talked about RD. Okay, he knows that is not possible, but having Ruhana talk about him has made his heart beat faster. He doesn't know what it is, but he feels uneasy.

These days, it's Ruhana who plans things for just the two of them, and whenever he denies it, she pulls herself back. He sighs deeply. Her parents never stopped them from going out together. They respect their relationship, and her dad never stops him; rather, he asks him to take care of Ruhana in his absence. His trance breaks as Ruhana keeps her hand on his shoulder.

"Running from everything is not a solution. You know it better than me. You're more mature than me, Vineet. And we already talked about it yesterday," Ruhana says softly, looking into his eyes.

"We will be happy when we move on. Life is hard, but we have to go on," Ruhana speaks again when she finds him silent.

"I said, I'll try my best, Ruu," He says this, breaking his silence.

"We will start it today. We will go for ice cream after dinner. You'll be paying like always," Ruhana chuckles, her happiness evident on her face.

"Oh yes! Who else will?" Vineet says, a small smile lighting his face.

Ruhana grins widely, for there is a smile on his face, and it means the world to her. She knows she has to get things done with him, and for that, she needs to make decisions. She hugs Vineet tightly, and the duo begins to make lists of the things they'll need for their trip. Ruhana's mom helps them with the list and also promises to help them pack.

Meanwhile, Ruhana's dad returns home, and the family of four has dinner together. Her father teams up with Vineet only to tease her, but in the end, the truth is that the two of them love her the most.

Later in the night, after helping her mother finish up the work, Ruhana asks her mom to go out for a stroll and have ice cream with Vineet. The lady allows her, Vineet, and Ruhana to rush out of the house.

*****

Ruhana is happy as she holds Vineet's hand, thanking him. He is amused and looks at her with surprise. He's always been this innocent. Ruhana slaps his cheeks lightly and thanks him for coming out on a stroll. Vineet smiles lightly as they reach the stall, and he purchases two ice creams—chocolate chip for her and vanilla for himself. Ruhana grins widely at him as she snatches the ice cream from his hand. She thanks him, and he's surprised.

"Why do you keep thanking me?" He asks though he knows the reason.

"Don't act unknown. You know why I am thanking you?" Ruhana says this while savoring her ice cream.

He doesn't respond at the moment. She holds his hand with her other one.

"You know you mean the whole world to me. You're not just my best friend; you're more than that. I can't drop you. I want to hang out with you. You've made me happy today, so thanks for that," Ruhana says it genuinely.

"I had to do so. I know what you want from me! And I promise, I'll try to be the one you want from me," He says it, and she knows he's being honest.

"Really?" Ruhana looks at him keenly, and he nods affirmatively.

Ruhana jumps on her toes and hugs him out of happiness. This gentleman has promised her something, and she knows he will abide by his words.

"I am really glad about it, Vineet. Thank you. This trip will be memorable. Our Mumbai Trip!" Ruhana says, and Vineet smiles softly.

The girl is back to her usual self. They reach home holding hands and rush onto the terrace to spend some quiet time.

It's necessary, after all.

Chapter 10:

Day of the Trip

Several days have elapsed, and Vineet has begun the journey of rediscovering his former self. However, breaking out of one's comfort zone is challenging. He is determined not to let Ruhana down, as her excitement and inner happiness mean the world to him. Soon enough, Saturday arrives, marking the start of their ten-day trip to Mumbai.

Saturday morning stands out from the rest, filled with a unique energy. Ruhana is brimming with excitement about their upcoming trip to Mumbai, which happens to be her dream city. She has always heard of Mumbai as a bustling metropolis where she might have a chance encounter with her favorite celebrities. What makes it even more special is the prospect of attending Raj D'sena's concert, affectionately known as RD. While he may not be an internationally famous singer, he possesses undeniable talent in his craft. Moreover, her college has organized this concert, and she is determined not to miss this golden opportunity.

Ruhana feels really excited and can't stay still. She's bouncing around the room, showing how much she's looking forward to something. Her mother is busy packing food for their journey and offering words of caution to take care of herself and Vineet, naturally. Ruhana embraces her mother warmly.

"Relax Mom! We will be fine. After all, we are much older, and Vineet is there; why are you so tense?" She asks her mom.

"I am not tense. I just want you two to be fine. Okay?" Her mom replies while looking at her.

Ruhana smiles at her mom, grateful for her concern. She gives her a gentle kiss on the cheek. Ruhana knows moms always worry, but she wants to show her they can handle things. Even though Rekha believes in her kids, she still gets worried sometimes because that's just what moms do.

"Relax Mom! You needn't worry until Vineet is with me. And I know you trust him more than me," She finishes her statement.

Her mother smiles at her and decides to tease her. She knows she doesn't need to worry until Ruhana and Vineet are together, but she's a mom, after all.

"Of course, I believe in my son more than you. At least he is quite responsible," She says it teasingly.

At the same time, Vineet arrives there, holding his bag. He greets his mother and then looks at Ruhana. By his looks, he seems to be back in duty mode. He is concentrating on the duties that are given to him. He glances back at her; he knows that she's ready, yet he tells her to brace herself.

"Ruhana, Be quick! We're getting late. The buses will leave by 8:30," He says this as he picks up a glass of water.

She offers a warm smile to her closest friend, understanding that he's likely in a hurry due to pending tasks. Giving him a light hug, she reassures him that her father will ensure they arrive at college on time. Her dad has a deep affection for both of them, treating Vineet like his own child, and had already promised to drop them off at college before their buses depart.

Meanwhile, he notices her mother is busy packing some snacks. She's well aware that her children have specific preferences when it comes to healthy food, so she's thoughtfully preparing their favorite snacks with an abundance of love. Rekha affectionately pats Vineet's cheek.

"Calm down, Son! I know you have some official duties given to you by your professors, but it will be all fine. You'll not be late! I will get you some coffee. Your dad will be home soon," She says it, and he smiles and nods affirmatively.

Vineet knows he can't deny his Ma. This lady has been his mother since his own mother left him alone. He might get angry with Ruhana; he might scold her or ask her to hurry up, but to her parents, he's one obedient boy. He never speaks a word to them. His trance is broken as Ruhana pulls him away, makes him sit on the couch, and looks at him. Not getting any words out of her mouth for quite some time has amazed him. She is just looking at him, and he decides to tease her.

"What? Why are you looking at me like this? Is there something on my face?" he asks, trying to be unknown.

She says nothing, clicks out her tongue at him and slaps his arm, at which he whines in pain; actually, he mocks a whine. She makes a face; she knows he's doing a little drama to tease her.

"Please keep aside this grouchy look, Vineet. We're going on a trip. At least, show that you're happy. Aren't you excited?" She asks, looking at him

He smiles at her. He knows that she is super excited to visit Mumbai and so forth; she cannot contain her excitement to herself. She wants him to do the same. She feels that he's again going into his silent mode, and she wants to bring out his real self in the 10 days of this trip.

"Are you going to let anyone show their excitement?? Let anyone speak?" he asks her, clicking his tongue out at her.

She glares at him. She knows he is trying to divert her, but she won't let him succeed.

"But, at least, don't behave so seriously as if you're going to give an exam!! Switch off this all-time serious mode! We are going to a concert, not someone's funeral," She says it in a warning tone, which makes him smile, and she slaps his arm.

Meanwhile, her mother comes with coffee for both of them and instructs them to take care of themselves. As a mother, she is worried for both Vineet and Ruhana; after all, Vineet is the only mark of her friends' existence.

"Oh, mom, how many times are you going to tell us the same thing? I told you no; we will take care. And if not me, Vineet is mature enough to take care of both of us!" Ruhana whines; maybe she is done listening to her mother's instructions.

Just then her father comes inside, and after giving both Ruhana and Vineet a kiss on their foreheads, he moves to take a quick shower before going to drop them off.

*****

After having a quick breakfast with their parents, Vineet and Ruhana leave for college after taking blessings from their parents. Their college is at a distance of 15 minutes of ride from home. Ruhana seems quite excited, while Vineet is a silent listener. Her father smiles at her excitement.

"Ruhana, I know, dear, you're excited, but atleast, keep it up to you. Look at Vineet; he's so quiet. Learn something from this gentleman," He says this while looking at her babbling image in the rear view mirror while Ruhana whines.

"Dad!! He is always quiet, you know. Ask him to keep his serious mode off; otherwise, I am going to smack him," She replies to her father, smacking the back of his head in an irritating tone.

Vineet is astounded at her action and rubs his head while she pouts at him. Her father and Vineet smile at her antics. Her father stops the car as they reach the college and looks at her.

"Grow up, Ruhana! You're no longer a kid," He says this as he kisses his daughter's head.

He may say it, but deep down in his heart, he wants his daughter to keep chuckling all the time. He can't see her sad or teary-eyed, and he wishes the same for Vineet. They're his kids, after all. Ruhana smiles as she hops out of the car. She knows they wouldn't want her to grow up. They love the kid in her. Vineet takes out their bags while her father kisses her forehead again, hugs Vineet, smearing his head, and asks him to take care. He assures him, and soon after, he leaves for home while both Vineet and Ruhana rush inside the college, more like Ruhana dragging him inside with her.

Vineet instructs her to be with her friends. He knows that she can take care of herself, but he can't stop himself from checking at her. That's how they have been since childhood – checking on each other, and knowing what the other is up to. This is how life goes for them. Ruhana agrees and finds her friends at a distance. She walks towards them while

Vineet walks into the principal's office. Ruhana holds on to his luggage too. She gets busy chit-chatting with her friends while he looks after the students. Her friends start teasing her about how she blushes every time he kisses her on the forehead.

"Stop it, guys. He is just my best friend," She snaps, blushing a deep red as she looks at him talking with a professor.

"Oh, come on, Ruhana, you know you like him. Ignore all you want, but let me tell you that Rhea has her eagle eyes on him," Priyanka tells her, making her whip her head to Rhea, who was, by the way, looking at Vineet with hawk eyes.

Ruhana feels a rage building inside her. Meanwhile, the announcement for boarding the buses is made, which would lead them to the airport. Making everyone settle inside the buses, the professors and other office bearers board the bus, including Vineet. He boards the same bus as Ruhana did. He glances at her to assure her that she is okay. And so forth, trip to Mumbai begins.

Chapter 11:

Beginning of the Trip

Ruhana is quite excited about the Mumbai trip. Firstly, Vineet has promised her to be in his own skin as before while they are on the trip. Secondly, she will be attending the concert by her favorite singing sensation. What more could she ask for? She's content with what she has in her hand right now.

As per Vineet, he's trying to change himself. He is still introverted and doesn't share his feelings as much as she does. Well, it won't change the scene for Ruhana, for she understands his silence as well. Even if he doesn't say anything, she knows what he wants or how he feels.

Momentarily, Ruhana feels angry as she finds Rhea looking at Vineet. Oh! She can't bear that. This girl surely needs a lesson. She's again clinging to Vineet. She could feel a rage building inside her as she finds her clinging close to Vineet, Meanwhile, her eyes meet his and he assures that he is fine and she feels her rage simmering.

Ruhana smiles to herself before looking away from Vineet. Yeah, her friends are right. She really likes him, but the secret is that she holds something more for him. However, she's scared to lose his friendship. Seeing him smile, her lips curled into a smile as well. The way he takes care of her, his way of making her smile, and his way to hide his pain and smile at her are what she loves most about him. He would do anything to make sure that she was safe and sound. But this is nothing exceptional, as she does the same for Vineet. Her only goal is to make him happy, and that's what she's doing.

Suddenly, she realizes the way she raged when her friends told her about Rhea. She doesn't know why she felt so strange and angry when she found Rhea looking at Vineet. She wants to smack her so badly on the face that she is not able to look at him. Her trance is broken by Vineet's voice, who is sitting beside her now.

"What happened to you, Ruhana?" He asks out of concern, as he finds her lost at the moment.

She glances at him briefly. The concern on his face and the care in his eyes are what she melts for.

Oh! How cute he looks when he calls her name and asks about her!

His voice seems like a soft melody to her. He's looking at her, waiting for his answer. He won't be satisfied until and unless he gets a satisfying answer from her. He nudges her again, making her look at him.

"Where are you lost, Miss Ruhana?" He pats lightly on her cheeks, and she looks at him with a smile on her lips.

"Nothing wrong, Vineet! Are you okay?" She counter-questions him.

She is highly concerned for him. He can see all the love and care in her eyes. A while ago, he was running from one place to another as he had some official duties given to him by his professors. Now he remembers Ruhana. Her parents allowed her to go on the trip, and he's glad that they trust them. They're not little kids now. They're mature enough, though. Ruhana acts childish sometimes, but Vineet knows that it's for him and her parents only. To the outside world, she's mature and can make any decision she is willing to. Vineet has promised to always be by her side. She comes out of her trance when he lightly slaps her head, and she glares at him for spoiling her hair. He giggles at her reaction. It's their usual banter. He teases her and she whines, and on the other hand, when he's sad, she is the one to take care of him.

She nods affirmatively at him. He smiles, moves towards the driver's cabin, and settles down on the front seat. He sighs deeply, as the morning hour is hectic for him. He relaxes on the seat, knowing that everything is under his control. Ruhana's trance is broken when Priyanka nudges her. She begins to tease Ruhana while the latter makes a face.

"Ruhana, where are you lost? We know you like him, but at least don't stare at him like that," Priyanka says it teasingly, earning a glare from Ruhana.

"Hey!! I know what you're thinking. Now, don't stare at me open-mouthed. Have some chocolate cake," Priyanka says it teasingly and forwards a piece of cake towards Ruhana.

She is savoring the cake when Vineet announces that they will be reaching the airport in the next five minutes, so they should gather all their stuff and get ready to leave.

Ruhana takes hold of her bag when she realizes that Vineet has left his bag with her. She smiles but her thoughts overpower her senses. She realizes that she was so busy pondering over him that she didn't realize that he left his belongings with her. She takes hold of both bags, and soon they halt in front of the airport.

Before she can move, he signals for her to stay back. She didn't know why; she stood still at her place, letting others move out. Her friends ask her to move, but she persuades them to move out and wait for her outside. They agree and get out of the bus. The bus gets empty when both Ruhana and Vineet get off the bus after checking everything thoroughly. She is just gazing at him while he is doing his check. He nudges her again when he is done. She asks him to be happy and knows that he is trying his best to be the one she wants him to be. He assures her that everything is fine. He slid his hand around her shoulders, and they moved to the place where all the other students and professors were waiting. After a few more instructions from the professors, they walked inside for the security checks, and the flight was to take off in the next forty-five minutes.

******

Ruhana stands near her friends while waiting for their flight. She begins to smile while talking to them. Vineet finds himself staring at her. He's relieved to find that she's sound and safe among her friends. Their gazes meet again and she smiles.

Oh! Her smile!!

He loves it when she smiles at him, and it comforts him in many ways. He smiles to himself, thinking about her. Or, it would be more precise to say that he can't live without her. He needs her to be fine. She has been his guiding light, and how can he face the light of the world without this girl?

Having her around brings him a kind of peace, but he doesn't want to admit it. For the last fifteen years, Ruhana has been his sole reason for living in this whole wide world. It won't be wrong to say that whatever she did in the past or whatever she is doing in the present is for his well-being. She is a great friend. Vineet takes a deep breath while he rests his gaze on Ruhana, who's busy talking to her best friends.

She has put his broken pieces back together, and she is always there whenever he needs her. She leaves her friends just to be with him and her parents believe him more than they trust Ruhana.

Vineet has always proved himself perfect for Ruhana, be it by fighting for her, saving her from any dangers, or being a good friend to her. The only thing that he lacks is to be the same friend to her as they were in childhood.

This is the beauty of their relationship; they can converse even in silence. Moreover, Ruhana does it every now and then. She understands his silence and comforts him when he needs it. However, they share a glance again. At the same time, Rhea stands by Vineet's side and begins to talk to him. Ruhana watches as Rhea holds his hand and it rages Ruhana for another time.

Oh! Rhea! This girl is crap; she won't understand the polite way.

It seems like she has forgotten the incident that happened a few days ago at the college. Rhea is a flirty kind of girl and is egoistic as well. Many times, she breaks into a fight with Ruhana. Vineet glances at Ruhana and finds her glaring at him. Maybe she's seen Rhea approaching him. Fortunately, his phone rings, and he excuses himself. The call is from one of their professors, and after attending the call, Vineet turns to check on the students, and he finds them lost in conversations with each other.

Thirty minutes later, after all the security checks, they boarded the plane. Luckily, both Ruhana and Vineet get adjacent seats. The morning hours have been hectic today. Vineet takes his seat near Ruhana, relaxes on the seat, and closes his eyes. He smiles, only to hear whispers from other girls.

Yeah, about him. Of course, why won't they discuss him?

He's young, handsome, and a perfect gentleman.

All girls want a guy like him, but he's committed to only one person, and that's Ruhana. He never talks to anyone like that. Since he shares a close relationship with Ruhana, he feels as if the girls gossip because they are jealous of Ruhana. Sometimes, even Ruhana teases Vineet as girls drool over him, and she doesn't like it. He opened his eyes and found Ruhana glaring at him.

"What happened, Ruhana?" He whispers in her ears.

She turns her face towards the window in anger, while Vineet smiles at her antics. He knows that she has heard the girls' talks, and she must also have seen him smiling. He leans towards her and whispers in her ear.

"Okay, if you don't want to talk to me, I will talk to Rhea," he says intentionally to tease her, earning a tight slap on his arm, which only makes him giggle.

"Dare you talk to her? I will kill you!!" she says, gritting her teeth.

Vineet smiles at her words. He knows that Ruhana doesn't like Rhea. She can bear anything, but she can't tolerate Rhea around herself or Vineet. He smiles and decides to tease her further.

"Why? What's wrong? And why are you so angry?" He asks, his tone laced with naughtiness.

He loves the way she gets angry at Rhea's mention. Her clenched fists and her light slaps and punches on his arm show what she feels for him. Though he can't pull himself away from his past, he feels blessed to know that he still matters to someone. He looks at her, and she's calming herself. Maybe she has suddenly realized her reaction to what he just said. He taps on her shoulder, and she looks at him, smiling briefly.

"I am sorry, Vineet!" She stutters as she glances back at Vineet.

She is apologising. Did she think he is hurt? No, he has been enjoying her reactions. He smiles, takes her hand in his, and squeezes them lightly.

"It's okay, Ruu! I was just kidding! I didn't know; you'll feel bad," Vineet explains.

She smiles at him. Okay! She feels bad. She feels jealous to see Rhea around him. He means the world to her. He is not only her best friend but also more than that. Maybe she feels for him; maybe she loves him. but she is not sure. Ruhana smiles lightly at Vineet.

"Yeah Vineet. I know. But I mean what I said," She glares at him.

He smiles at her possessiveness. Meanwhile, the pilot announces that the flight is going to take off and that they should tuck in their seatbelts. As soon as the flight takes off, Ruhana keeps her head on his shoulder and falls asleep. Her lips curled into a small smile with his closeness while he kissed her head. This girl is really a bundle of joy, at least for Vineet. He takes a deep breath and rests his head on hers. The journey has just begun.

Chapter 12:

Landing in Mumbai

The flight to Mumbai turns out to be shorter than they expected. They didn't realize how long it took, but they woke up to the announcement made by the pilot. Ruhana whines sleepily and adjusts her head on his shoulder comfortably. Vineet smiles and pats her cheeks in order to wake her up. She slaps his hand lightly, asking him to let her sleep. He smiles at the fact that she's so sleepy that she is not realizing that they are about to land in Mumbai. He whispers the same in her ears, and she sits straight in her seat. She squeals with joy at just hearing the name of the city. She holds his hands excitedly.

"I am so excited, Vineet! This is almost like a dream come true." She speaks, her lips curving into a wide smile.

She looks at him happily, but he only smiles a little, mostly just for her. His eyes don't show any feelings or excitement. She sighs sadly, feeling let down. He stays there, humming a sad song quietly. It's not unexpected because he usually acts this way. He jokes and teases her, but his eyes always show he cares a lot. But right now, he doesn't feel as excited as she does about the journey.

She has resolved to rediscover his true self, but doubts linger within her. Can she truly achieve this? She questions whether it will be a straightforward task to rekindle his enthusiasm and if he can let go of his lingering sadness.

He really cares about her and worries when she's not feeling like herself. But while trying to help her feel better, he's become quiet, shy, and keeps to himself. This part of him bothers her because he stays quiet most of the time and only talks when he has to. Even though he's always there for her and listens carefully, he hides his own pain from her and everyone else. She sighs and holds his hands gently.

"Not again, dude! The least you can do for me is smile. Please, Vineet, don't act like this. You can be happy only if you want to. Just because something happened in the past, you cannot live with it for the rest of your life. Please, Vineet, give me my best friend back. Pretty please," she says innocently, actually requesting him.

He smiles and nods affirmatively at his best friend. This is the least he can do for Ruhana, who's always there for him. She hopes that she will be able to bring out his real self.

*****

Vineet requests the pilot make an announcement for the students and he obliges. He comes back to his place and asks her to tie her seat belt, at which she glares at him, but he smiles a little. She shakes her head, knowing that it would be hard to bring him back to life.

His past made him quiet. Ruhana wakes up from her thoughts when Vineet nudges her gently. They've landed at the airport and will get off the plane soon. When she tries to move, she feels him holding her hand firmly. She looks at him and sees that he's busy guiding the students while holding her hand. She smiles and stays where she is, liking how he's holding her hand so lovingly. She knows he cares a lot about her, which is why he's holding on tight. She appreciates it and doesn't want to let go. Soon, she ends up walking behind him towards the plane's exit. Normally, she'd let go and walk ahead, but today she wants to follow him and let him lead. Like a good kid, she just follows him.

They get off the plane, and Vineet goes with the professors to learn more. He finds out they're staying at TAJ VIVANTA, a special hotel for the students. Buses are ready outside to take them there. Vineet and others help the students get on the buses. He tells Ruhana to get on a specific bus for her group, and she nods to show she understands. Later, he gets on the same bus.

After a while, the group of students reached the hotel, humming tunes and occasionally sharing laughter. The sheer beauty of the hotel leaves them in awe. Ruhana is captivated by the surroundings, and her excitement prompts her to tightly clutch his hand. Vineet appears delighted to witness her laughter and happiness. The professors allot the rooms and everyone disperses to their respective rooms to freshen up and rest for a little while. Proper rest is required, after all. He says it all so plainly, and she is disheartened. She wants him to be happy and not roam around in his all-time serious mode.

Everyone freshens up and changes into clean attire. After lunch, the professors announce that their first destination will be the Gateway of India. Ruhana is way too excited, as she practically bounces on her toes; it's as if her dreams have come true. Concealing her enthusiasm is a challenge, a fact that Vineet is well aware of. He simply smiles at her and shakes his head. A glance in her direction reveals she's engrossed in a conversation with her friends, radiating happiness.

Over the years, he's realized that this is a tranquil sight, one he hadn't fully appreciated until now. It's Ruhana and her actions that have kept his faith in friendship alive. Whenever she's near, happiness envelops him. He snaps out of his reverie when his friend Rohan taps his shoulder. Vineet greets him with a smile, responding to Rohan's friendly nudge.

"What? Where are you lost, dude? I know you like her." He says it teasingly as he catches him staring at Ruhana.

"It's not like that," Vineet argues but Rohan cuts him again.

"Don't fool yourself, Vineet! You also know the truth! She is more than a friend." Rohan says.

Vineet looks at Rohan in disbelief. Yeah, he didn't want any relationships in his life. Friendship is beautiful for him, and he wants to be Ruhana's friend forever. Rohan shakes his head.

"Yeah, and you turn overprotective for her. She's not a baby, but you treat her like one. She's not a mere friend." Rohan emphasises his words, making him realize what Ruhana means to him.

Rohan knows there's something special between Vineet and Ruhana. He can see how much they care about each other without saying a word. He's sure it's love, but Vineet says it's not and changes the subject to the professors who are watching them. Silently, Rohan follows his friend. He knows Vineet inside and out and understands that he struggles to acknowledge his love for Ruhana. Growing up with her makes him feel like he needs to look out for her, but he goes even further, always making sure she's okay. He cares about her in a special way that sometimes confuses him. Rohan stops thinking about it and goes over to Vineet.

Having received their instructions from the professors, they are all set for their first excursion to the Gateway of India. The pre-booked buses are ready, and the organisers take charge of their respective groups.

And so a new adventure commences.

Chapter 13:

Witnessing the Oceanic Beauty

Following an hour-long journey, the students and professors arrive at the Gateway of India. The students, especially the girls, start giggling when they see the huge Arabian Sea. Everyone is amazed by the beautiful sea, no matter if they're boys or girls. The water moving back and forth on the shore makes a calming sound that captures everyone's attention. The girls enjoy the peaceful scene and have a fun time together. Meanwhile, the boys talk excitedly about the history of the monument as they head towards the shore too.

Ruhana finds Vineet talking to Rohan, and she sends a tug on his hand. He turns around to find Ruhana beaming at him. She sends an annoying look at the two boys. Vineet knows the reason for her annoyance; that is, they're just discussing some duties and they're not enjoying the view around them.

"What are you two talking about? There is a vast ocean around! Come, let's go and enjoy!" She asks them annoyingly.

"I asked him the same, Ruhana. But he wants to hear the boring history of this place. So arrogant he is." Rohan shrugs his shoulders and makes a face at Vineet.

"Hey!! He's not arrogant. Dare you call him like that?" Ruhana glares at her friends, while Rohan giggles at her words.

Rohan expected Ruhana to respond quickly, and he's not surprised. He knows Ruhana can hear conversations, but he also knows she won't stand for anyone saying bad things about Vineet. She gets upset with anyone, even Vineet himself, if they talk badly about him. A small smile appears on Rohan's face.

"I know. But your friend will only listen to you. I leave him to you." He winks at her and leaves the place, leaving Vineet and Ruhana alone.

Ruhana casts a glance in his direction, her expression forming a warm smile. In her eyes, Vineet is always kind and thoughtful. He's been there for her since she was born, understanding her feelings when even her parents couldn't. Without saying anything, she takes his hand and leads him to the shoreline. He understands her without needing to ask any questions and follows along.

Ruhana laughs happily as she watches the waves dance. She spots a boat in the distance and wants to go on an adventure. She looks at Vineet, who understands without words. She decides to ask the professors about boating, and Vineet agrees and talks to them. Ruhana gathers her friends, and luckily, the professors say yes. Some students stay on the shore, but others eagerly get on the boats. Vineet leads one boat and invites Ruhana and her friends to join. He starts paddling.

Vineet keeps watching Ruhana, who's laughing and playing in the water. Her hair is blowing in the breeze, and he loves seeing her happy. He gets lost in her world until she splashes water on his face, bringing him back. She's splashing water on everyone, and her laughter makes him smile. She sees his smile but wants him to be more present.

She wants him to enjoy the moment and she encourages him with her eyes and words.

agrees with what she says. He knows being sad won't make things better. He understands that Ruhana knows him really well; even his feelings he doesn't say out loud. She always tries to make him happy, but he's the one choosing to stay quiet.

Lost in their thoughts, they arrive at the shore, and Vineet helps Ruhana and her friends get off the boat. They hear the professors calling them. Ruhana holds his hand and looks into his eyes.

"Vineet, please, let your happiness shine through. Staying in your own world won't help." She keeps her point; her words are a gentle request for him to make a change.

Vineet meets Ruhana's gaze, but he remains silent. He then leads her towards the professors, leaving her with a sigh of disappointment as she follows him, her spirits subdued. Akshara and Priyanka offer her their support, taking her to an ice cream stall. It's been a good day, and while they enjoy their treats, the professors summon them, signalling the time to head back.

*****

Ruhana feels comforted being with her friends and enjoying ice cream at the beach. Everyone is happy, some going boating and others learning about the Gateway of India's history. Even though they've been here a while, time flew by. It's getting late, and the professors want everyone back at the buses to go back to the hotel and rest. Ruhana doesn't want to leave this beautiful place. She's still watching the waves calmly hitting the shore. The peaceful sound of the water helps calm her busy thoughts. She's so caught up in watching the water that she doesn't hear her friends calling her.

Meanwhile, Vineet is busy making sure all the students on his bus are accounted for. He realizes Ruhana isn't there and asks her friends, who point towards the shore. Seeing Ruhana lost in the scenery, he understands her love for the beach, but it's time to leave. Ruhana is standing by the ocean, totally focused on the view. He calls her name loudly, but she doesn't hear. With a sigh, he tells the other students to get on the bus and goes to talk to her. He remembers they're on a college tour and need to follow the teachers' instructions, not just come here for a vacation.

He goes over to her and sees her big smile. Her happy face makes him happy too. He lightly taps her shoulder to bring her back from her thoughts. His caring touch brings her back, and she looks at him again.

"It's time to go, Ruhana." He says this as he reaches out for her hand.

"Vineet, some more time, please. It's so calm and beautiful here. I don't feel like going from here." She says it innocently.

He wears a contented smile as he gazes at her. The beauty of this place is simply enchanting, and its scenic beauty is a visual delight, leaving a lingering desire in her heart to keep savoring it. The soothing flow of the water has a calming effect on him too, but just as all good things must conclude, this day too is drawing to an end. It's time for them to make their way back to the hotel, fully aware that another beautiful day awaits on the horizon.

Vineet tries to convince her, but Ruhana can't decide if she wants to leave the beautiful place. She pretends to be upset, making them both laugh. Even though they know they have to go, neither of them wants to say goodbye to this amazing spot. Ruhana asks Vineet to promise to bring her back here, and he agrees to make her happy. Ruhana is someone who goes after what she wants, like how she acts with her parents and Vineet. They start walking to the bus, and Ruhana finds her friend has saved a seat for her. She sits next to her friend while Vineet sits in the driver's seat. She watches him talking to the bus driver, and her friend Priyanka nudges her, starting to tease her.

"So, Ruhana, what did Vineet say to make you return without any interrogation?" Priyanka smirks as she finishes her question.

"What do you mean, Priyanka?" Ruhana rolls her eyes playfully at her friend, fully aware of her teasing tone.

Priyanka continues her playful teasing, "I mean, did he confess his love for you?" She teases, receiving a playful slap on her cheek.

"What's wrong with you?" Ruhana responds with a playful grin.

"I know you like him. Just don't say he's just a friend!"

Priyanka gives her a knowing look, and Ruhana, momentarily lost in her thoughts, doesn't respond at the moment. She knows that Vineet means more to her than just a friend. He holds a special place in her heart, which is why she chose his company over that of her friends. She longs for him to return to his cheerful self, as Vineet's happiness is her own, and his smile never fails to bring joy to her heart. Such sentiments go beyond the bounds of friendship, and Ruhana is keenly aware of it.

As Ruhana glances at Vineet, she finds him deeply immersed in thought. Their eyes meet, with Ruhana appearing slightly irritated, while Vineet smiles warmly. In the midst of their unspoken connection, they arrive at the hotel.

The students are instructed to meet in the hotel's restaurant by 8 p.m. Ruhana checks her watch, noting it's 7:15 p.m. She begins to head towards the garden when her friends call out to her.

"Where are you going? Take a rest and freshen up before dinner," Priyanka expresses her concern for her friend.

"No! This place is too beautiful. I'll stay here a while. I'll swing for a bit." She gestures towards a swing in the garden.

Priyanka and Akshara exchange knowing sighs, realizing it's not easy to convince her. Although Ruhana generally doesn't like being alone, there's something enchanting about this place, or perhaps she desires some time apart from her friends. After some negotiation, her friends depart, with Ruhana promising to join them in their room in twenty minutes.

Ruhana settles into the garden and gently sways on the swing, savoring the cool breeze. Suddenly, someone gives the swing a push, and she turns to find Vineet behind it. He beams at her and pushes the swing once more. She giggles as the brisk wind brushes against her face.

"What's on your mind?" he inquires while looking at her.

She shakes her head negatively, but he joins her on the swing and lifts her chin with a gentle touch.

"I know there's something bothering you. Please share," he urges.

She looks at him, surprised. He's really good at understanding what she's thinking and feeling, even when she doesn't say anything. He figures out solutions to her problems, even ones she hasn't talked about. He looks at her and raises his eyebrows, telling her it's okay to talk.

"You'll get mad if I tell you," She glances at him playfully.

"You'll be upset, so I'm not going to tell you," She further teases him, seeing him smile.

Vineet's laughter sounds so melodic to her, something she always loves. Seeing him happy like that means a lot to her. They look at each other, with him asking something with his eyes and her answering with a smile. Sometimes, not saying anything says a lot. She leans her head on his shoulder, something they do often, almost like their own heartbeat. Her cheek brushes against his shoulder, and she closes her eyes, enjoying the peaceful moment. When she's upset, they usually sit like this on a swing at home, and he plays guitar for her. It's a comforting feeling that they both understand, even if they never talk about it to each other.

While they were enjoying the calm moment together, Vineet's phone rang. He answers it, and then they head to the restaurant for dinner.

Chapter 14:

Oceanic Talks

Following a tiring day, students and professors make their way back to their individual rooms. Ruhana eagerly awaits their upcoming visit to the Elephanta caves, as recommended by the professors during the dinner. Ruhana, Akshara, and Priyanka are all staying in the same room together. They engage in conversation until midnight, gradually drifting off to sleep one by one. Tomorrow promises to be quite an eventful day.

*****

The next day, Ruhana wakes up with sunlight on her face. She's fresh like a flower as the morning breeze touches her face. She checks her phone and finds a message from Vineet asking her to meet him at the hotel lobby by 9 a.m. She likes that he's thoughtful and on time.

Ruhana feels excited to see Vineet and gets out of bed quickly for a shower. She wishes Vineet could feel happier, even though she knows he's sad. She hopes he can find happiness again.

Approximately twenty minutes later, Ruhana finishes dressing up for the day, wearing jeans and a black kurti. She walks out of the washroom to find her friends awake but busy with their respective phones. Ruhana informs them of the need to be in the hotel lobby by 9 a.m. The girls hop off the bed, preparing for their outfits and also taking the opportunity to tease Ruhana with Vineet's name.

Indeed, they understand Vineet's significance in Ruhana's life. He's not just her best friend; he holds a special place in her heart. Ruhana is aware of it, although she remains uncertain about Vineet's feelings. Ruhana's friends know about the special connection she has with Vineet. Even though they tease her when Vineet's name makes her smile, they can't help but playfully joke about it. Akshara and Priyanka especially like teasing her, and Ruhana enjoys their friendly teasing. Anything related to Vineet always makes her happy.

The three girls reach the restaurant right on time. The professors are telling the students that they will leave after breakfast. Everyone is quite excited. After breakfast, they move out of the hotel. They have buses booked to the Gateway of India, and from there, they will travel by boat to the Elephanta caves. Soon, the journey begins.

*****

Everyone appears excited at the moment. Some people are engaged in conversations, while others are immersed in card games or musical games. Amid this lively scene, Ruhana finds herself staring at Vineet. He's busy conversing with Ruhana. Ruhana snaps out of her trance when her friend Priyanka playfully scolds her and starts to tease her.

"Don't even try to deny it! I saw how you were gazing at Vineet without even blinking!" Priyanka says it with a mischievous tone.

Akshara chimes in, "Why not share your feelings with him?"

Ruhana, without making eye contact with her friends, responds, "No, I can't say anything! And no, I don't love him,"

"Don't kid yourself! You absolutely do love him," Akshara playfully teases her with a gentle tap on the back of her head.

Ruhana shakes her head and shoots an annoyed look at her friends. At the moment, she feels a sense of frustration. It's true that she has deep feelings for Vineet, but she doesn't know if he feels the same as her. Furthermore, she hopes he can come to understand the significance of love.

"Can we talk about something else?" she asks, eyeing both Akshara and Priyanka.

"Do you have time to think about anything else other than Vineet?" The two continue teasing her.

She lightly taps their hands playfully just as they announce they've reached the Gateway of India. Everyone gets excited and gets off the buses eagerly. The professors say it's a day tour to the island where the Elephanta Caves are. Everyone's really happy. Some boats are ready for the students, and they hurry towards the sea's edge. Ruhana stands there, watching the waves. They crash onto the shore like music to her. Her friends call her, but she's lost in the moment. Vineet snaps her out of it, putting his hand on her shoulder and smiling kindly at her.

"Are you going to stand here only? Don't want to see the island?" he questions her, boring his eyes in hers.

"No! But it's very calming right now. It's a natural chord producing serene music," Ruhana replies, looking at her.

Both of them gazed at the sea waves flowing up and down for a brief moment. He gently holds her hand and leads her onto one of the boats, steering towards the island. When she steals a quick look at him, she feels a calmness that makes her really happy. But what she really wants is to see him smile again. She really wishes to see that happy smile on his face, but all she sees is a serious look. He cares about her, but he's a bit reserved.

Sometimes, when she's around, he does manage to smile, but real laughter seems hard for him. He's trying to be the person he used to be, but something's still missing. She really wants to bring back his liveliness and revive who he used to be.

The way they were! In their childhood! Ruhana wants Vineet to be happy. Happy with her, maybe!

*****

Soon enough, they arrive at the island, famous for the Elephanta Caves. They didn't know much about it before. Ruhana happily jumps as they get there. Water surrounds the small island from all sides. Lots of green plants make the island look beautiful, and there are caves made of stone a little away from the shore. Everything is new and exciting for the young girl. She giggles, seeing how pretty the island is. Vineet smiles at her excitement. He knows she's thrilled to be in Mumbai. He takes her to where the other students are. A guide is there to show them around. Ruhana joins her friends as they explore the island. She listens carefully to the guide. Suddenly, her friend playfully taps her on the head, and she looks back at her friend.

Actually, she's listening to the guide and staring at Vineet. She is not the kind of person to listen to old stories, but today is another day. She wants to listen to the stories because Vineet is taking a keen interest in listening to them, and she wants to stay close to him. Her friend makes a face.

"No! That's super boring. Let's go somewhere else," Her friend Akshara insists.

"Noo, I want to listen!" She glances at her friend.

Her friends were not happy with her decision. She wanted to be with Vineet instead of checking out the place. They found out from the guide that the cave island had two parts: five caves for Lord Shiva in one area and smaller caves for Buddhists in another. Following the guide, Ruhana saw her friends going towards the Buddhist caves. She rushed to catch up and found them sitting on the stairs outside those caves. She joined them and sat down too.

"What is it? Why are we here?" She asks Priyanka.

"We are here so that you can talk to us," Priyanka chides her.

"That's what I am doing," she replies with a smile.

"No! You're not here. You're physically here, but mentally somewhere else," Akshara speaks teasingly and winks at her.

Ruhana sighs deeply. She's highly irked at the moment. She doesn't like her friends teasing her. It's not like they are saying it in the wrong way, but she doesn't like it. There's a reason that she can't express her feelings to Vineet. She loves him; that is true, but she doesn't know if he loves her in the same way. Sometimes, she feels that he doesn't believe in love anymore. She sighs deeply at her thoughts.

"Ohh...not again! Can we just move into the caves?" Ruhana replies irritatedly.

"Where are you running from, Ruhana? We know you like him! That is why you carefully listen to every word he speaks," Akshara says.

"I do. He's my best friend, and I have the responsibility to keep him happy, and this is exactly what I am doing," Ruhana says, shushing her friends.

Ruhana shakes her head. That's true. And she is not running from it; rather, she is trying to maintain a distance. She wants him to be happy in the first place. She wants him to realize the love that he holds and the love that he has earned.

She sighs, as she can't make her friends understand the same. They don't know what Ruhana and Vineet are going through. They can never understand why she listens to him or obeys him. They are far from the kind of relationship that she shares with Vineet.

"Okay fine! If that's the thing, then we will see it later, but for now, can we move? Professors must be searching for us, " She says this because she knows that Vineet will panic if he doesn't find her around himself.

Priyanka nudges her teasingly. She never misses a chance to tease Ruhana.

."No, No! Not professors; you must say Vineet is waiting for you. Right?" She looks at Ruhana, who doesn't reply to her.

"Your silence says everything. Even if you don't agree. Now, let's go!" Akshara says, holding her hand, and the three friends move out.

Ruhana doesn't reply to them. They can never understand her love and feelings for Vineet. Everyone was scattered in various directions, savoring the beauty of the island. Ruhana moves towards the shore and sits on the sand. She is playing with water and thinking about something. The words spoken by her friends are echoing in her head, and she can't jerk them off.

*****

Obviously, she is thinking about him. Vineet is always in her thoughts. He has been her only friend since her childhood. From fulfilling every wish of hers to saving her from her parents' scolding, he has been with her even now. So, is it more than friendship? What is it, actually?

She knows it is more than love. But she can't express her feelings for her best friend, Vineet.

Her trance is broken by some drops of water. She looks up to find Vineet sitting beside her. She looks at him, and before she could say anything, he says.

"What are you thinking?" he asks.

"Nothing!" She says this, looking into the water and moving her hands into it.

"Really! Then what has made you so silent?" he asks, looking at her.

She smiles, and he knows everything about her. Her gestures and her actions always tell him her state of mind. Is it more than what friends do? She looks at him, and their eyes meet. She smiles lightly.

"You made me silent! It's all your fault," she says naughtily.

He looks at her and sighs. He knows she's right. His silence has always affected her. Yet, he asks him, being unknown.

"What did I do?" he asks with surprise in his voice and fear visible on his face.

She starts laughing, looking at him. He is bewildered at her reaction. She controls herself and pulls on his cheeks.

"Look at your face, Vineet! You look so cute!" She says, her eyes filled with admiration for him.

He looks at her with his all-time serious look. She looks at him cutely.

"Okay, okay, I am sorry! Now keep away from this serious look. We're here to enjoy, right?" She looks at him.

He nods seriously. She sighs, looking at him. She knows he's back to his serious mode, and she will bring him back.

"Vineet, you remember, you promised me something. You'll be happy. At least for me," she says, holding his hand.

He didn't say anything, and suddenly he jerked his face as Ruhana sprinkled water on him, and their usual chase began again.

Will Vineet realize the reality? Will he come back to his real self and love Ruhana back the way she deserves?

Only time will tell.

Chapter 15:

A Joyous Ride of Life

The day concludes on a joyful note and it's time to head back to the hotel. They had a great time on the island, taking lots of photos and having fun. Everyone is happy. After a two-hour journey, they arrive at their hotel. The professors tell the student leaders to meet them in their room. All the students move to their respective rooms and be reminded to gather at the hotel restaurant for dinner at 9 p.m.

Following dinner, the group disperses in various directions. Ruhana is enjoying herself with her friends when she comes across Vineet sitting on the swing, the same spot she had occupied the previous day. A smile lights up her face, prompting her to excuse herself from her friends and approach him.

Vineet appears lost in thought, but Ruhana nudges the swing gently to bring him back to the present. He snaps out of his reverie and gazes at her. She sits close to him on the swing, smiling, and holds onto his arm. She loves being near him and really wants to see him smile.

"What's occupying your thoughts?" she inquires, playfully poking his arm.

"Planning tomorrow's day," he responds softly.

"Planning tomorrow's schedule already?" she asks, ending her question with a chuckle.

He nods in confirmation, but when she glances at the list, it's empty. It seems he's having trouble formulating a plan, so she gazes at him and playfully encourages him to share the details. She's eager to know his plans since he's the one in charge of planning the day. She glances at her.

"What's your plan? Why do you look lost with an empty schedule? Are you trying to make us fall asleep?" She jokes, pretending to be a bit annoyed.

"Nah, I'm just not sure how to plan out where we should go. We've only got five days," he explains.

"Take a breath and think about it. You'll figure it out," she says, trying to reassure him.

"Planning a trip isn't easy, Ruhana," he insists.

"You've handled tougher stuff before! I believe in you," she encourages him.

He glances at her and knows she's right. He usually has a solution for her when she's feeling down. She always looks to him for help in tough times. He gathers his thoughts and looks at her.

"Okay, so this time, you'll help me, right?" he asks, wearing a smile directed at her.

"How can I assist you?" She inquires with a touch of innocence.

He smiles. She understands the unspoken request, but she wants to hear it from him.

"Give me a list of places we can visit tomorrow. Let's figure out how to make the most of our day," he suggests.

She chuckles in response to his request. She knows he already has everything planned out and solutions ready, yet he's asking for her input.

"Well, we could start our day by visiting the renowned Ashtavinayak temple in the morning," she suggests, looking at him.

He nods in agreement, realizing he hadn't considered that option before. He jots it down on the list.

"That sounds great! In fact, we should have done it today," he remarks.

"No worries, Vineet. We can save it for tomorrow. So, we'll start with the temple," she says as he nods and takes note in his diary.

"We could also explore the wax museum, visit Marine Drive, or head to Juhu Beach. Don't forget the Rock Garden and the Bollywood Tour!" She replies with enthusiasm.

He smiles at her childlike excitement, especially about the Bollywood tour.

"Who's going to let us enter Bollywood?" he asks teasingly.

"But we can take a tour of Film City. Please say yes!" She requests, holding his hand.

He chuckles at her plea, and she gives him a playful glare when he smiles.

"It's not that simple, Princess," he remarks, and she pouts.

"Fine then. You plan the day all by yourself. I don't want to talk to you," she declares before moving to the side.

He laughs at her playful antics. She always acts like a child when she's around him, but he knows it's a special side she only shows him. She doesn't behave this way with anyone else. She's mature enough to handle him, his roughness, and his silence. If she can manage him, she can handle any challenge in her life.

"Okay, fine! Don't leave me alone out here. Help me plan the day. I'll see if we can get a glimpse of Film City," he says, although they both know it's all in good fun.

She looks closely at him, trying to figure out if he's being serious or just kidding around by studying his face. He playfully taps her on the head.

"Stop giving me that look; lend a hand!" he says, his tone innocent.

She makes a sad, childlike face, and then she glances at her best friend.

"Alright, but you must keep your promise. Will you do that?" She looks at him, a gentle reminder of his promise to be his true self.

He smiles and nods in agreement. Soon, they discuss the places they can visit, and in about half an hour, their itinerary is set. They're both delighted. Ruhana jumps for joy.

"Thanks for keeping Juhu Beach on the list for tomorrow," she giggles, eager to visit the temple.

He simply smiles, his usual reaction whenever she's around. In his words, she's his good luck charm. Even after his mother's passing, she's been the only one he would listen to and loved being with. Her anger, irritation, care, and frowns— he adores everything about her. Despite being two years older than her, he often feels like she's the older one. He cherishes her scolding, just as he appreciates the way she would stand up to him when he scolded her for her carelessness. She's made him realize that his feelings haven't completely vanished. He still cares, even if he struggles to show it. He knows she's perfect for him.

He snaps back to reality when Ruhana takes his hand and leads him back to the hotel, as they need to gain the professors' approval for their schedule. She jumps with joy when he informs her that their schedule is confirmed. She hugs him tightly and then hurries to her room while he stays still at his place, watching her go.

*****

The next morning comes quickly, and Ruhana is really excited. Vineet added her favorite place to the plan, and the professors said it's okay. She's super happy about getting to walk and talk with him, making memories. The professors said everyone needs to be in the hotel restaurant by 8 a.m.

Ruhana gets ready early. She's so happy to help Vineet lead the group. When her friends Akshara, Priyanka, and the others wake up and see she's ready, they playfully tease her.

"Ahem! Someone's absolutely brimming with excitement!" Akshara teases with a sly smile.

"Up and ready so early, Ruhana! What's got you so fired up?" Priyanka inquires, well aware of the reason behind Ruhana's enthusiasm.

"It's nothing, guys. Aren't you both thrilled about our Mumbai sightseeing tour?" Ruhana responds, her smile radiating from her two closest friends.

"Oh, is that the only reason, Ruhana, or is there something—or someone—else on your mind?" Akshara playfully raises an eyebrow.

Ruhana smiles softly, knowing her friends won't stop teasing her. They get why she's so excited - Vineet asked for her help with the day's plan, and that makes her really happy. She teases them back, knowing they're just joking around in a friendly way.

"Quit teasing me and start getting ready. I'd not like to get scolded, okay?" she says, her gaze shifting between her two friends.

"As if he's going to scold you!" Priyanka retorts, her laughter bubbling up.

In response, Ruhana playfully tosses a cushion at her friend, urging them both to prepare for the day. Akshara and Priyanka share a laugh but quickly move to prepare themselves, as they, too, wish to avoid any potential scolding from their professors.

*****

They start their trip by visiting the famous Ashtavinayak temple. Even though it's crowded, being together makes them feel safe. They enjoy their visit, finding peace despite the crowd. They've rented a tourist bus to see more places.

As they go on, everyone is excited about sightseeing. They laugh, talk loudly, and share joy while seeing different places. Some love the Queen's Necklace, others are amazed by the huge Arabian Sea. They're having a great time, with a few more places left to visit. They try Mumbai's famous street food and have a blast at the wax museum. Their final stop is Juhu Beach.

Ruhana really wanted to go to Juhu Beach. The professors relax with drinks while the students wander around on the shore. The guys run on the beach, and some girls stay to enjoy snacks at nearby shops.

Ruhana sits by the shore with her friends, feeling the water on her feet. She smiles a lot, enjoying the sunset and the fresh sea breeze. She seems lost in the moment, looking around as if searching for something.

She only notices her friends, Priyanka and Akshara, watching her when one of them nudges her. She looks around and she sees them staring at her.

"What's wrong? Can't you let me enjoy this beautiful view around me?" Ruhana says it with a hint of irritation.

"Enjoy it, and let Rhea do as she pleases," Akshara suggests.

"Rhea? Why is she coming between us?" Ruhana asks, visibly irritated.

Priyanka points to where Rhea is talking to Vineet. Even though Vineet seems uninterested, Ruhana feels really angry and sighs deeply. Why? She warned Rhea before, but Rhea doesn't seem to care. Ruhana can handle a lot, but Rhea is different. Why? Not because she's jealous, but because she feels Vineet isn't comfortable around Rhea. She's seen Vineet trying to keep his distance, but Rhea ignores it. Rhea tried getting his attention before, but Ruhana ignored it. Lately, though, it's clear Rhea's being more and more persistent, and it's bothering her a lot. She looks away. She doesn't want to make a scene right now. Her friends come closer to her.

"What's going on now? Why are you just standing there? I'm telling you, if you don't do something, Rhea might snatch him away. Then don't come crying," Priyanka warns.

"Cut it out! Nothing of the sort is going to happen. Obviously, Vineet isn't interested in her. Let her do whatever she pleases," Ruhana responds casually.

"Look, Ruhana, what if he actually is interested in her? It seems that way," Priyanka suggests, gazing at Rhea and Vineet, who stand at a distance.

Ruhana glances at them. Her friends might be right, but she knows that it's Vineet's responsibility to assist all the students, and Rhea is also a student and a fellow traveler on their trip. Vineet can't let go of his duty. Although Ruhana is irritated and angry at her friends' words, she maintains her composure.

She turns around once more and witnesses Rhea urging Vineet to accompany her, an invitation he politely declines. The girl remains stubborn, which triggers Ruhana's anger. She heads in their direction and offers Rhea a smile.

"Sorry, Rhea, for interrupting your conversation. But I really need to talk to Vineet. I'm so sorry. Could you excuse us?" Ruhana says it plainly.

In the process, she takes Vineet's hand and guides him away from Rhea. They stroll by the shore, and as the water touches Ruhana's feet, her smile returns.

"What did you want to talk about? Why did you appear so angry?" he inquires, breaking the silence.

Ruhana doesn't respond, but Vineet comprehends that she's upset with Rhea and her actions. She had warned Rhea earlier, but the girl paid no attention to her warnings.

"I know you don't like Rhea," he states softly.

"Yeah! Then why don't you stand up to her? Why do you let her have her way?" Ruhana vents her frustration at her best friend.

"She won't do anything. She's afraid of you!" Vineet responds softly.

"I don't think so. But you need to address her. Do you understand?" Ruhana glares at him.

Before Vineet can say anything further, the professors call them. It's time to return to the hotel. A long day has come to an end, and their conversation concludes.

Chapter 16:

The Trifle

The students make their way back to the hotel. They receive instructions to freshen up and then meet with their professors at the hotel's restaurant. The college administration has arranged for a buffet dinner throughout their stay at the hotel only. Ruhana and her friends take the opportunity to freshen up and change into comfortable nightwear. Afterwards, they join the rest of the group at the restaurant, where they have a great time savoring their dinner.

About an hour later, everyone finishes eating. Ruhana wants some quiet time, so she goes to the hotel garden. Some guests are walking or sitting there, enjoying the nice breeze. Ruhana's friends are tired and have gone back to their rooms, but she stays to enjoy the calm, soothing air. She also hopes to talk to Vineet, even though they've been together all day. They usually spend time together before going to their rooms, whether they're studying, talking, or just resting. She doesn't want to break this habit, even if it's just for a quick chat to say goodnight.

Ruhana sits on the swing in a quiet part of the garden. Vineet and Rohan join her for a walk. Rohan didn't expect to see Ruhana there. It's only 11 PM, but he knows Ruhana usually stays up late. He thought she'd be in her room with her friends. So, he asks Vineet why she's here instead.

"What's up with her? Why is she out here?" Rohan inquires, genuinely unaware that Ruhana has been taking evening strolls in the garden since their arrival.

Vineet pretends not to know, saying, "I have no idea, man. We're all here together. If I knew, I'd be here with her."

Rohan agrees and goes to Ruhana, who's sitting on the swing, humming her favorite song. It's a tune she often asks Vineet to play on his guitar. Vineet gives the swing a gentle push, interrupting Ruhana's thoughts. She looks up, sees Vineet, and smiles.

"Why are you here?" Rohan asks concernedly.

"Just enjoying the cool breeze here, for no particular reason," She responds with a smile.

Rohan watches her, and she smiles back. She blinks, trying to show Rohan that she's not tired and comes to walk in the garden because she's not sleepy.

"I'm okay, really. I usually walk after dinner. My friends were tired, and Vineet seemed busy, so I came here alone. It's actually nice to have some time to myself," she says with a smile, looking at the two guys.

Rohan gets a call from his mom, so he tells Vineet he'll meet him in their room. Vineet agrees, and Rohan goes off to talk to his parents.

Vineet sits next to Ruhana, who's still humming her favorite songs. They sit quietly until Vineet looks at her and speaks up.

"Are you still upset?" he asks.

"Upset? Why do you ask now?" Ruhana gazes at him, puzzled.

"I've never seen you so angry. I wanted to ask you about it. You were quite upset at the beach," Vineet recalls her anger.

Ruhana is upset with Vineet because he doesn't express his feelings. But when she asks him about it or tries to help, he gets angry. He talks to everyone, even Rhea, whom he doesn't like.

Ruhana wonders why Vineet doesn't talk to her but talks calmly to Rhea. She knows that the other day, if she hadn't been there, Rhea might have made him uncomfortable. But whenever Ruhana tries to speak, he tells her to be quiet. It seems like she's the only one he doesn't want to listen to, while he lets others do whatever they want without saying a word to them. Ruhana is extremely annoyed at this.

"Why do you listen to everyone else so nicely but not notice me?" Ruhana looks unhappy.

"Ruu..." Vineet tries to say something, but Ruhana cuts him off.

"Why should I always stay quiet? Rhea keeps sticking to you, and you don't stop her! Rohan asks you the same things, but you don't get mad at him. So why do you get upset with me? Why?" Ruhana remembers what happened at the beach.

"Why do I get scolded while Rhea doesn't? Why am I the one who gets told off for asking questions? Is it because I don't speak up much? Or because I take your words seriously? Tell me!" Ruhana looks at him, demanding an answer.

"I warned her to stay away from you! I told you not to talk to her, but you act like she's your close friend. And when I try to talk to you, you tell me to go away. Why can others ask questions, but not me?" Ruhana keeps talking, but Vineet stays silent.

"I might act childish sometimes, but it's to make you smile, not for me. I push you because I care, not because I need you," Ruhana says firmly.

Vineet says nothing. Everything she said is true. He gets upset with her because she doesn't argue back. She believes people should come to her with their problems, while others, like Rhea and Rohan, keep asking until they get answers. Vineet stays quiet. Ruhana looks at him and sighs deeply.

"Why don't you talk? Why is it always me you don't talk to, Vineet? I need to know. Why me?" she asks.

He stays silent. He doesn't know what to say. He's watched her try so hard, but he keeps his feelings hidden, not realizing she knows everything. She can tell when he's happy, sad, or stressed. She just wants him to open up to her. Ruhana turns to him and holds his face gently.

"Why, Vineet? I admit I was angry, but why do you always have to wear a silent face? Why, Vineet?" she asks.

She's heard lots of complaints from friends about Vineet being quiet and not talking much. She doesn't like it because she wants her lively friend back. But he doesn't have answers for her questions. He's been quiet for years, and now she wants to bring back his fun side. She moves closer to Vineet.

"Come on, Vineet. You've asked me so much, but now you're quiet. Please say something. Why can't you be who you used to be?" She asks, hoping for a response.

"It's late. You should go to your room," he says, changing the subject.

Ruhana sighs. She knows he's trying to avoid talking. She's getting frustrated.

"Vineet! You can't ignore these questions forever! It's time to find answers," she tells her friend firmly.

Vineet insists she go to her room. She sighs deeply. His tone shows he doesn't want to talk. She knows he's avoiding her questions. But she's determined to help him. Ruhana wants to talk to Vineet about why he's so quiet. She's tired of seeing him talk to everyone else—Rohan, his friends, even a girl named Rhea. Ruhana thinks it's time to have an honest chat with him about how he acts.

Ruhana isn't naive; she understands Vineet's actions well. She knows he often makes her quiet because she lets him. She sacrifices time with her friends, sleepovers, and shopping just to be with Vineet. Even though this causes fights with her friends, she only wants to see Vineet happy, like they were in childhood.

All she wants is to see Vineet smile and share his feelings, good or bad, with her. But she notices he talks to others, like Rhea and Rohan, freely. When she asks him things, he scolds her.

She thinks that, as close childhood friends, they should share everything. She doesn't want to force him to talk but she hopes he'll open up willingly. She believes that if she can share with him, he can too. She doesn't want to push him because that would ruin their special bond and make her like everyone else.

Even after being scolded, Vineet tells her to go to her room. Ruhana is tired of this. She wanted to bring back Vineet's fun side, but his behavior disappoints her. He promised to try to be happy, but it seems like he's not. When Vineet tells her to go to her room, she sighs deeply.

"Alright, Vineet. You can stay silent. You don't want to share something with me! You have other people with whom you can confide and share your heart and your problems. And I mean nothing to you, right? So, let's end it!" she says, looking at him.

"I won't bother you from now on. The last time, I forgave you, but this time, I won't. I had hoped this trip would be memorable. I promised myself that by the time we go back home, you will be the same Vineet who used to take care of me, tease me, and take me for ice cream at night," she says, her anger evident.

"But it seems like you don't want to do that. You said you would try to be happy, but you're not doing it. You don't like how Rhea keeps trying to get close to you, talk to you, cling to you—none of it. But you never tell her to stay away from you. I'm just asking you a simple question, and you not only push my hand away, but also scold me, and now you want to be alone! Why not do the same with Rhea?" She confronts him.

She's angry, and she's hurt. She's hurt that Vineet doesn't see her as mature as he is. She's hurt that he never shares his feelings with her. All she does to please him has made her seem like a child in his eyes.

"You don't want to break free from your own cage. I'm the one who's crazy for caring about you. I leave my parties, my friends behind for your sake because your presence brings me peace. But you don't want me to be at peace. You don't understand that I find my happiness in yours. That's why you don't feel the need to tell me anything. So, go ahead, talk to Rohan, Rohit, Rhea, and everyone else. I won't say a word to you. I won't coax you anymore. This starts tonight. Have a good night," Ruhana says firmly and heads to her room.

By now, her eyes are teary. She finds solace in Vineet, but he keeps pushing her away. He doesn't understand her feelings, as he's always preoccupied with himself. He knows Ruhana is upset with him, but he doesn't try to comprehend her emotions, the pain she feels when he doesn't treat her the way he should.

In her room, Ruhana unlocks the door with her keys and discovers her friends fast asleep. She, too, lies down on her bed and breaks into tears. Her patience has worn thin, and she can't take it anymore.

Meanwhile, Vineet stands motionless, trying to process what Ruhana had said a few minutes earlier. He knows she's angry with him, and it will be challenging to persuade her otherwise.

He can't deny the truth in her words. She's right. He never talks to her in detail. She's willing to forgo her friends to be with him, even if he doesn't communicate with her. She just loves having him by her side, and she's content with that. Even a small smile from him turns her into a bundle of joy.

On the other hand, girls like Rhea, Shriya, and even Rohan almost badger him to reveal everything. Ruhana is different from his friends, and she has the right to know everything. She is privy to every little detail, but she wants him to say it. She wants him to say that he's happy with her. Her family is his family as well. And now, he's hurt Ruhana again.

He knows she's his sunshine. When others walk away from him, she stands by him, holding his hand. Even Rohan, who claims to be Vineet's best friend, leaves him for his girlfriend. Ruhana leaves her friends, her parties, and her sleepovers just to be with him. He has heard Priyanka and Akshara telling him not to let Ruhana cancel the parties, but she remains determined. She never leaves his side, but today is different. She has made it clear that she won't coax andhim, that she won't chase after him.

Her words have hit him hard, and he doesn't know what to do. He tries to call Ruhana, but she doesn't pick up. It seems she's very angry with him. He sighs deeply. Now, all he can do is wait for morning and a chance to talk to Ruhana.

*****

Ruhana is in her room, lying on her bed, tears rolling down her cheeks quietly. She didn't expect Vineet to be so hard to understand. She never thought he would quiet her in front of everyone, even her friends and his. To her, they're like family, and no one else comes close to the bond she shares with Vineet.

She's tired and she has been patient for a long time. She's tried many times to get him to talk, but he never does. It's getting really hard for her to figure him out. She's exhausted from trying by herself because Vineet doesn't seem to try at all. He doesn't talk to her or share anything with her.

Ruhana and Vineet are very close. They've grown up together, and Vineet even calls Ruhana's mom "Ma" and her dad "Dad." Their families are like one big family. Ruhana's dad has taken care of Vineet since his own mom passed away, and Ruhana's mom treats Vineet like her own son.

But while Ruhana knows a lot about Vineet, she wants to see him talk and laugh, to see him happy without her asking. She wishes he would open up on his own. She wonders: if she can understand him, why can't he do the same for her? It's not as complicated as Vineet thinks. Just because she listens to him doesn't mean he can always silence her. That's not going to work anymore.

She's reached her limit. She's tired and can't take his silence anymore. To get through to him, she might have to become someone she never wanted to be, at least for Vineet's sake.

*****

The night passes, and Ruhana remains wide awake throughout. Early in the morning, she rises and takes a warm shower. Her friends are still sound asleep, so she quietly makes her way to the bathroom, hoping that the shower will help soothe her troubled thoughts. A half-hour later, Ruhana dresses in black jeans and a pink crop top. Glancing at the clock, which reads 7 AM, she decides to head to the restaurant for a cup of coffee. Leaving a note for her friends and securing her room with her keys, she departs.

Upon arriving at the restaurant, Ruhana orders a steaming cup of coffee in the hopes that it might offer some comfort. She occupies a corner window table, gazing at her phone while awaiting her coffee. Her thoughts dwell on Vineet, his words, and the different way he treats her compared to his friends. The only common thread is the repeated questions they pose to him, but when it comes to Ruhana, Vineet's behaviour takes on a distinct pattern. He refrains from sharing anything with her, even when she directly inquires.

Lost in her contemplation, Ruhana senses a familiar presence nearby. She lifts her gaze from her coffee mug to find Vineet standing there. Quickly, she averts her eyes and focuses on her coffee. Vineet takes a seat opposite her and regards her intently.

"Ruhana," he calls out, but she remains silent.

"Ruhana, I'm sorry," he says softly.

"No, don't apologize! You never meant it," Ruhana retorts.

"You know me, Ruu..." he begins, but once again, Ruhana interrupts him.

"I thought I knew you, but I don't. You've been treating me differently lately. You can talk to Rhea and Rohan, but not to me. Just because I listen to ou, and follow your instructions, it doesn't mean you can scold and silence me in front of others. They may be your friends, but they're not mine. I'm not just your friend; I'm family, your only family. But you're free to go and talk to those who coax you," Ruhana snaps at Vineet, her anger palpable.

Then, she adds something that takes Vineet by surprise, as he didn't anticipate her saying it

Chapter 17:

Her Anger, His Grief

Vineet is astonished by Ruhana's behavior. She didn't pick up his calls, and it has worried him. He sighs deeply as he sits on his bed in his hotel room. He doesn't know how to convince Ruhana. It seems hard at the moment.

He wanders over the words she said a little while ago. Maybe he should have expected this. Her words have told him that she has lost her patience. She has lost her faith and trust in him. He knows he's the reason for her tears. But he is unable to do what she desires from him.

The night passed in a blur, and Vineet couldn't sleep the whole night. He gets dressed and moves out of the room, leaving Rohan asleep. As he walks out of his room, he finds Ruhana running down the stairs. He tries to catch up with her, but she vanishes in a second.

Vineet sighs deeply. He had a good chance to talk to her, but he missed it. He moves into the garden in the hope of finding Ruhana, but she is not there. He looks at the swing on which she was sitting the other night, but she's not there either. He calls her another time, but there is no response. He closes his eyes for a brief moment and then opens them. He moves to the restaurant to have a coffee, and as he walks inside, his lips curve into a smile. He spots Ruhana sitting on the corner table.

He moves to her and calls her by her name, but the girl doesn't respond. He sits on the chair and taps on the table, but the girl doesn't respond. He then keeps his hand on hers. His touch breaks her trance, and she pulls her hand back; she's still annoyed.

"Ruhana,"

"Ruhana, I am sorry. I didn't mean to hurt you." Vineet says, he's guilty of his deeds.

"Don't say sorry! Don't say it ever again," she replies coldly,

"Ruu! You know me," he begins to speak, but Ruhana silences him.

"I thought I did. You know what? I was wasting my time behind you. And what do you give me? Your silence and your scolding when I ask you anything Why do I have to bear your silence, Vineet? I just can't understand you!" Ruhana blurts out her anger at him.

Vineet is astonished, and before he could speak further, Ruhana interrupts him another time and looks into his eyes.

"And as I mentioned, I won't try to persuade you. You're free to speak with Rohan, Rhea, or the professors, but not with me. And please, there's no need for you to stay calm in front of me anymore because I won't be asking you any questions. In fact, I won't even engage in a conversation with you. You're at liberty to talk to Rhea, the one who clings to you, and don't hold me responsible if she does something you dislike," Ruhana states softly yet firmly.

"Remember one thing, though. Not everyone in this world will be like Ruhana. Rhea, after all, tends to be quite clingy towards you. She doesn't understand your silence the way I do. She keeps on repeating things, but I can read your silence in a single glance. And not everyone will cater to your preferences. I was thinking of giving you time and space so that I could understand all your secrets. I thought you would trust me enough to share your pain and your suffering rather than turn to that model queen Rhea or that Rohan, who leaves you alone for his girlfriend. But I suppose I'm not capable in your eyes. You never considered me capable enough to understand your pain. I'm ruining my life like a madwoman just chasing after you. But that's not going to happen anymore. Now, you'll have to endure Ruhana's silence too. You'll have to bear the pain that I've been enduring every day when you scold me or ask me to remain silent," Ruhana says it sharply and departs from the cafeteria.

Vineet is taken aback by the choice of words. He follows Ruhana, wanting to talk, but she shoots him a stern glance and hurries to her room. They have only an hour before they must depart for another day of the tour, and Ruhana needs to regain her composure.

Upon entering her room, she discovers her friends getting ready. Priyanka gazes at her and playfully inquires.

"Did you go to see Vineet? Can't you go a few hours without seeing him?" Priyanka teases.

"No, I was just having coffee. And as for Vineet, let's put that topic on hold for now, okay? It might be better for us," Ruhana responds with a smile, or rather, a forced smile directed at her friends.

"What? Are you saying this? How did this happen?" Akshara joins the conversation.

"It just happened because I've made a decision not to be overly concerned anymore. Isn't that what you all have been wanting from me?" Ruhana says this as she grabs her sling bag and starts packing for the day.

Priyanka and Akshara exchange glances. They sense that something is amiss, but they choose not to inquire further. After getting ready, they head to the restaurant, where other students have already gathered. Ruhana and her friends have breakfast and prepare for another day of adventure. As they board the bus, Vineet attempts to talk to her, but Ruhana ignores him. He appears surprised, or one might say he's restless, as it has only been an hour since Ruhana stopped speaking to him.

He knows he must find a way to win her back and regain her trust.

Change is needed, no doubt.

*****

Vineet tries to talk to Ruhana, but she ignores him and walks away without looking at him. Later, they decide to explore Mumbai together. Vineet sees Ruhana getting on a bus with her friends and quickly joins them. Inside the bus, Ruhana is busy chatting with her friends and doesn't notice Vineet. Today, they plan to visit the Nehru Science Museum and the Nehru Planetarium, which excites students like Ruhana and her friends.

An hour later, they arrive at the Nehru Planetarium, and the professors emphasize the importance of staying together as a group. As the students disembark from the bus, Vineet tries to call Ruhana, but she disregards the call and joins her friends. Meanwhile, the professor summons Vineet, and he must respond to the professor's request.

*****

After a while, everyone met outside the auditorium. Ruhana, Priyanka, and Akshara were talking. The other two girls noticed that Ruhana wasn't talking to Vineet, which surprised them.

"Ruu, is everything okay?" Priyanka brings up the subject.

"Yeah, for now, I'm really excited about this star show," Ruhana chuckles.

"Alright, but why aren't you talking to Vineet? He was asking for you," Akshara says, telling a white lie in an attempt to coax Ruhana into talking.

"Can't we just focus on stars? You guys wanted me to experience something other than Vineet. You wanted me to move on from him and be with you. Now, when I'm actually doing that, why are you bringing him up?" Ruhana rolls her eyes at her closest friends.

"But you never do this!" Akshara looks at Ruhana.

"I have decided to stop worrying for him. I have freed him because he thinks I coax him into talking. If I have not done anything until now, it doesn't mean that I can't do it. I can't handle the guy who serves me silence. None of you really know me," Ruhana says before going to a nearby shop to get a water bottle.

Little did Ruhana know, everyone, including Vineet, heard what she said, especially the part where she called him "the guy who serves me silence." Vineet sighs deeply and watches as Akshara and Priyanka catch up with Ruhana. Meanwhile, he and the rest of the students are called, and the star show begins.

It's the start of an important day.

*****

The day quickly goes by. After watching the planetarium show, they have lunch at a nearby restaurant and go back to the Science Museum. Some students think it's a little boring, while others really like it. It's an educational trip, and there's still time to enjoy it.

As the evening falls, they return to the hotel. It takes about two hours to get back. The students are told to take it easy and meet up for dinner at the hotel restaurant, and everyone agrees with the plan.

Once again, Vineet attempts to call Ruhana, but she pays no attention to him and departs with her friends. Vineet lets out a deep sigh, overhearing the other two girls talking to Ruhana.

"Don't you think you're being a bit too harsh?" Priyanka inquires.

"Why do I sound harsh? He's harsh when he scolds me in front of you all. He has no right to do that," Ruhana says, coming to a halt.

"But he always listens to you," Akshara argues.

"Yeah, when he has no other choice! This trip, he didn't come because I asked him to. He came because the professors assigned him the responsibility. He spends time with me because he knows he has no one else, yet he doesn't trust me. But I'm the one who's being rude? What an observation, girls!" Ruhana speaks, her words dripping with anger, and Vineet clearly hears her frustration.

"Until yesterday, you all wanted me to be with you. Now, when I'm with you, you find me rude. Why? Don't I have a life? I used to stay with Vineet to ensure he doesn't feel lonely. I didn't want to leave him alone. I didn't want him to believe that friendship is a lie. But he's turned it into a lie for me. I used to be a crazy girl, following him. But that won't happen anymore! And if it bothers you too, then go ahead and befriend Vineet! Or stay alone!" Ruhana exclaimed before hurrying off to her room.

Why was she being so rude? It's Vineet who has been the source of her frustration, and he continues to be. Vineet watches her leave and lets out a sigh. He quietly goes to his room and changes his clothes.

He's lost in thought. Ruhana has always been there for him, by his side, and he has only repaid her kindness with scolding and anger. Why should she endure it? After all, she has her limits, and they've been crossed now.

Okay, he might not change completely, but he can at least make an effort to mend himself for Ruhana. She's given him everything he needs to shape himself into the person he is today. He may be older than her; he may hide his emotions, but he can't hide them from her. She knows him to his core.

Vineet sighs as he reminisces about how she used to encourage him to go out, laugh, and engage in activities that would at least make him smile. Today, the girl is not talking to him.

"Why should I care about the person who serves me silence?"

Yes, he has often responded to her with silence, but that can't be the norm. He needs to move beyond his past, but he doesn't know how. Then he recalls the advice his Ma (Ruhana's mother) always gives him.

He closes his eyes, takes a deep breath, and abruptly opens his eyes, only to see Ruhana's once-happy face now clouded with sadness. She has distanced herself from him.

He needs to bring her back, but how?

Chapter 18:

Whispers from the Past

Ruhana gets into a trifle with her best friends. She feels something suffocating her when her friends blame her for being rude to Vineet by not talking to him. Well, they ignored all those times when Vineet had been rude and harsh to her, prioritizing others over her. Why? Is she a toy to play with?

Ruhana freshens up and changes into a comfortable night dress. Her friends are still not in the room. She knows that Akshara and Priyanka may tease her, but they know that Vineet means the whole world to her. They may take her wrong, but she can't keep her self-respect at stake. She can't let Vineet scold her in front of everyone. Okay, he has a right over her, but she can't let him do what he wants. If he can't tell her anything, if he has only silence to offer, then she can do it too. She has prioritized him over herself; she thinks it is her duty to take care of him, to make sure that he is fine and not thinking of the traumatic past, but his silence towards her is no less than a trauma for her.

Ruhana moves into the restaurant and serves food for herself. She let her presence notify her professor, then took a corner table and started eating her food. Akshara and Priyanka sit beside her.

"Sorry, Ruu, we didn't mean to hurt you," Priyanka apologizes.

"I don't mind, Pree! I am used to false allegations. Anyway, take your dinner," Ruhana says it softly.

"Hey, We didn't mean to hurt you. You always go behind him; that's why we asked," Akshara says.

"It doesn't mean that I can't do without him. I don't go behind him for myself. It's my way to make him feel better. He's always alone, and I can't see him like that, which is why I used to follow him to make sure that he's fine. But I'm wrong. So I just stopped doing it," Ruhana says, her tone stern.

She's done with dinner. As she moves out of the restaurant, she bumps into Vineet. He holds her wrist, but she composes herself and jerks his hand. He calls her by her name.

" Ruhana! " he calls her name in a low tone.

" Vineet! I'm tired. I am going to my room. Also, don't think I will pull off by my words. I mean them," Ruhana says sternly while looking at Vineet and then leaves in a second.

Vineet is left disheartened. Well, he deserves this. He knows it. He knows that she is hurt. He watches her go away from him, and he feels restless and hopeless at the same time. He knows he is the reason for her sadness and the tears in her eyes. He wants to call her and talk to her but she is adamant enough at her place. His eyes are still glued to her until she disappears from his eyes. while a voice falls into his ears. As he looks around, he finds his own conscience in front of him.

"Why are you upset now? She's only returning what you have given her. And she is not at fault,"

"She has given her heart and soul to you and to your friendship. She doesn't want you to lose faith in friendship. She didn't want you to feel lonely; she didn't want you to stay unhappy! And this is

what you've given her? Silence! Scoldings, which she doesn't deserve. She just acts like a child because she finds you smiling at her stupid stuff! And you know it, you like it! Yet you ignore her while she has given her whole life to you,"

" You have taken her wrong! You know that she's emotional, and you take it as her weakness! And that's immensely wrong. When someone is weak for a certain thing or person, do not forget that person or thing becomes their biggest strength! And you are her strength and hope! But it's all shattered, Vineet! You're the one to do it,"

The conscience disappears, leaving Vineet thoughtful. Yes! He has taken her for granted. She is sad; she didn't even talk to him. The girl who can't sleep without spending some time with him is not looking at him. Vineet sighs deeply and moves towards his room. He's upset and so he just sits on the bed, staring at the empty wall.

He remembers all the times when she's been around him. Her giggles and her anger are what he can't forget. It's been a whole day that Ruhana hasn't talked to him. He trails down memory lane, wondering what made him like this.

His Dad! The person who never treated Vineet and his mother right. He even killed his mom! Remembering the incident still shivers him. He closes his eyes as the incident flashes in front of them.

Flashback Begins

It was the time when Vineet was just 6 years old. He's sitting in his room, playing the guitar. The boy had just started learning it. His mom entered his room and smeared his head. He jumped from the bed, stood near the wall and began to play the guitar. His mother smiled at him. Though he just started playing the tune of his favorite rhyme, he is all smiles to see his mom smiling. They were laughing around when a heavy voice echoed in the house.

It was his father who walked into his room. Little Vineet was scared enough and hid behind his mother. The man scolded his wife and asked her to lay the dinner table. Vineet's mom asked him to stay in the room only and come out only when she called him.

Vineet agreed and looked at his father scarily. He didn't behave well with his mom and Vineet wasn't an exception. Many times, when he'd ask to go for ride, his father would scold him or slap him. Vineet sat on the bed, hugging his toy, which is a small furry dog. His father left the room, eyeing him in anger. Little Vineet could not understand him and began playing with his toys.

Later that night, his mom made him sleep and then moved to her room. At midnight, Vineet woke up because he felt thirsty. He picked up his water mug from the table and drank some water. In the meantime, he heard some sounds. He recognised them; it's his mother. Though he's scared of his dad, he takes small steps towards his parents' room and peeps through the small creak of the door. As he looks inside, he's shocked and terrified at the same time, such that he couldn't control himself and a scream escaped his mouth. A call for his mom!

Inside the room, when his father feels a sound, he leaves his mom and walks towards the door. Vineet gets scared, runs back to his room, and closes the door. On the other hand, his father opens the door but finds no one. He didn't pay attention to the fact that his son might have seen him mistreating his mom. He closes the door with a bang and gets busy with what he is doing.

Little Vineet was still sweating. He was already scared of his dad, but he didn't know that he mistreated his mother, beat her, and caused her pain. He couldn't take it; after all, he's merely 6-year-old and he can't do anything for his mom.

Flashback Ends

He comes out of his reverie, breathing heavily. He hates his father. He hates taking his own name. He doesn't want to remember him. All he wants to remember is his mom, whom he loves dearly. All he's here for is his mom. Even Ruhana's mother tells him the same: his mom is watching him from heaven and he has to make her dreams come true. Vineet is immersed in his past. He's thrilled; his heart begins to beat at a fast pace, and he is shivering. Remembering the moment still gives him goosebumps. After that incident, he never saw his mom. Being a little boy, he was told that an accident at home took her life. But it didn't affect his father. When his father came to take him, he refused to go. He trails back into another bitter memory of the past.

Flashback begins

At the time of his mom's death, Ruhana's parents took care of him. It was another day and both Ruhana and Vineet were sitting in Ruhana's room. The girl was trying to cheer him up while he was sitting silently, staring into nothingness.

Meanwhile, a man enters the room. Little Ruhana thinks it is her dad.

"Dad! You say we should knock before we enter anyone's room. Why didn't you knock? This is my room." The girl says it innocently.

"I just came here to take away my son. Vineet, let's go." His father says it in a deep and dangerous tone.

"No! I don't want to go." Vineet shifts back on the bed with Ruhana by his side.

"You have to! We're leaving this city. Come on!" His father is adamant about taking him away.

"No! I don't want to go! You killed my mom!" Vineet shouted at his dad, and he is shocked.

"Beta! It was an accident." He tries to convince Vineet but the latter is not ready to understand.

" Noo! You killed her. You took away my mom; you used to fight with her. I will not go with you; I will stay with Ma and Ruhana," he shouts with all the energy he has and hides behind her mom.

Vineet's father gets angry and holds his wrist tightly. He is adamant about taking Vineet along with him. Though he knows that his son is right,. Due to extreme torture and all that he did with his wife, he took her life.

Vineet is too small to understand all of that but he knows that his parents don't share a good relationship. He has always seen his mother crying in his father's presence. For him, his father is his mom's murderer and he can't bear him in front of himself.

Meanwhile, his father is still adamant but Ruhana's dad somehow pushes his dad outside the house and warns him that if he tries to come near either Vineet or Ruhana, he will file a complaint against him at the police station.

Later, Vineet tells them that he wants to live with them and feels safe in their presence. Ruhana's parents didn't waste any time and took him into their care. Now, her parents were Vineet's guardians too and he started calling them Maa and Dad just like Ruhana.

Ever since then, they have been a small family of four people. Ruhana has been trying to cheer him on ever since she was four years old. It's been a long time since then.

Flashback Ends

Vineet snaps out of his daze, and his eyes are welled up with tears. Since his mother's departure, he's become a quiet and withdrawn person. It's Ruhana who's been making efforts to lift his spirits, doing things she knows he likes, even though he's been distant towards her. He recalls how she initially suggested the trip, which he declined. However, when his teachers assigned him the responsibility the next day, he reluctantly agreed.

Ruhana is constantly working to bring joy into his life, hoping to ease his pain and see him happy again. But he has consistently responded with silence. Today is no different. An entire day has passed, and she hasn't spoken to him. She's hurt, and he's well aware of it. She's never been this angry with him, and she's not just playfully pretending to be angry this time.

He had assumed she was joking, but now he realizes she's dead serious. He sighs deeply, feeling a void not just around him but also in his heart.

With a deep sigh, he decides to call Ruhana. He dials her number, and fortunately, she answers. However, before he can say anything, she surprises him with her words. It's clear she's angry, and he knows he needs to persuade her. No matter how challenging it may be, he's determined to do so.

"I asked you to leave me alone! I freed you; you can stay in your shell. Then why are you calling me now?" She asks angrily.

"Ruhana….I just wanted to talk," He says it in a low tone.

"Why now? I mean, when I look at you, when I ask you if you have any problems, then you scold me. You say that it is none of my business. You think that I can't understand your pain? And now you want to talk to me? Why Vineet? Why now?" She almost shouted at Vineet.

Vineet sighs; he knows he deserves her anger. She does everything to please him, to persuade him to share his pain and feelings with her, but he didn't give her a chance. She is super angry at him.

"And please, stop following me. My intention was simply to bring a smile to your face and share your pain. But you never acknowledged my efforts. And even now, you'll continue to hurt me, even if you say sorry. But I can't bear your silence anymore, Vineet. I just can't," she says with a pause.

"My reason for joining this trip wasn't just to spend time with you; I can do that at home. I wanted to change you. I hoped that in these 10 days, you would change. I know it's difficult, but I wanted my friend back. The friend who used to share everything with me, who took care of me, who would treat me to ice cream. I wanted you to share everything that bugs you with me, but maybe you don't think I'm worthy of it. I never understood why, and that's why I gave up. I lost. I couldn't break through your shell or your pain. And that makes me feel like a loser. I give up on you. You've thrown my twelve years of hard work away. Now, let me live in peace," she concludes before ending the call.

Vineet lets out a deep sigh. He realizes that Ruhana is deeply hurt, and he knows he must bridge the gap between them. This shouldn't have happened. He lies on the bed, her words reverberating in his mind. His eyes well up with tears; he never expected Ruhana to say such things. The girl is truly wounded, and he's the cause of her tears.

Wiping away his own tears, Vineet is determined to convince Ruhana to mend their relationship and bring her back into his life. It won't be easy, but he's resolved to do it. He can't bear the thought of losing her.

Chapter 19:

A Day Out - Solace in Chaos

In Ruhana's room, her friends are fast asleep, while she is wide awake. Her eyes are moist and she's looking at one of her pictures with Vineet. He's smiling in the picture and she has always prayed to God to keep his smile intact. But it seems like God has other plans.

She is tired of his silence, his habits of scolding her, of shushing her in front of others and his way of talking to the people who only take advantage of him, Ruhana decides to step back. However, her steps are neither working nor having any effect on Vineet. She puts her phone upside down in anger.

"I've done a lot for you, Vineet. And you never acknowledge it. I am not as weak or as childish as I show you. I do all that stupidity so that you talk to me; at least you smile. But my efforts are a waste. I'm not talking to you. I don't know if you realize it or not, but there won't be any efforts from my side. My dream is broken into pieces again, thanks to you. I won't forgive you. You have to realize my importance, Vineet. You have to!!"

Ruhana lies on the bed, trying to sleep, though sleep is far away from her eyes. All she can do is calm herself and not think about him, because she doesn't want to get hurt by his behavior anymore.

*****

Ruhana is exasperated. She's been managing to keep herself sane with Vineet around her. She knows that he has been through a rough childhood but she also knows that he is not leading his life in the right way. Living in a shell, keeping himself away from others, is not what will let him go forward in life. He has to take a break, take a deep sigh and begin from the start.

He has to move along the path that his destiny has chosen for him. He has to do something and change his destiny. But he is doing nothing to make his life better. He is just staying in the past and this hurts Ruhana.

They have grown up together. Vineet has been excited and protective from the day Ruhana was born. Their moms used to say that these two would share a pure and blissful bond of love, that is, friendship. They will set an example for the others to follow. Little did they know that there would be differences between the two childhood friends.

No, not this trifle, but as they grew up, Vineet distanced himself from Ruhana. She feels the distance, and when he doesn't share his heart with her, it increases the distance. Ruhana feels so and she is hurt and sad about it. She never wanted this; she doesn't want to part ways with Vineet. This is the reason that she does silly things and becomes the reason for gags in front of his friends and their common friends.

Her hope has completely shattered with the new trifle they had. She didn't think he'd scold her or shush her in front of many people on the trip. And it led her to lose her cool, to lose the sanity that she has been masking for 12 long years, living her life according to him.

Ruhana is exhausted from thinking and she didn't know when she fell asleep.

*****

It's early morning, and Vineet is sitting on the swing in the garden of the hotel. It's been two days since they sat here and chatted. She used to wait for him here and they used to spend some time together. But….

She's angry! Angry for the most obvious reason.

Ruhana! The girl is so tired of him that she has said on his face that she won't talk to him. Well, he has always given her pain and silence; how can he think that she will run after him after numerous insults in front of people she didn't want to become a laughing gag?

She has clearly stated that she'll not talk to him; she's mad at him and he has to convince her. He has seen her efforts, he has seen her trying hard to bring him back. She even dislikes Rhea and he remembers how she got angry when he talked to her. She simply dislikes the girl for her nature and her habit of showing off.

Ruhana's face flashes in his eyes. Her sullen and red eyes, her sad face, and her teary voice are all alarming. This is what he sees when he closes his eyes. And he's sad that it is all because of him. He's the reason for her tears and her sadness. And he has to make it right.

Vineet takes a deep sigh. What does the girl want? Only the smile on his face—she only wants to see him happy. All that she does is make him happy. Ruhana is the one who thinks about Vineet before herself. She cannot sleep before spending some time with him. Okay, they may not talk, but the silence is soothing to them. He looks at the stars and she looks at him. That's what she does. But that doesn't mean that she has kept her self-respect at stake.

He has realized that Ruhana has done a lot for him. Can't he smile for her? Can't he give her what she desires from him? Of course, she is not asking him to get the stars from the sky. She just wants him to move on. He can do that. Or, say, he should do that, in order to get back the girl who loves him dearly and is habitual of her; he can't stay even a minute without her.

As he's lost in thought, he is greeted by Rohan. The other guy is astonished but he knows that Vineet has been upset since the other day. He asks about Ruhana but Vineet denies telling him anything.

"You can't run away from the truth, Vineet. You know you like her; she means more than a friend to you," He says.

"What? I mean, it is not like that," Vineet nudges his best friend.

"If it is not that, then why are you worried? You should be happy that Ruhana is not talking to you," Rohan says tauntingly, as he knows that Vineet is feeling her absence in his life.

"You won't understand, Rohan!" Vineet sighs.

"The ones who want to understand, they do, unlike you," A feminine voice breaks their trance.

Vineet is surprised; well, it is Ruhana. He looks at her in surprise, so is she back to talk to him? A small smile lingers on his lips, yet he's left shattered.

"I just came to inform you that Professor Shah is looking for you two," Ruhana says it with a straight face.

Vineet looks at her for a couple of moments. There's no emotion on her face and she didn't cling to him, nor did she greet him. Oh! He needs to pacify her quickly.

He jogs to reach her and calls her name. She stops on her track and sighs. She turns back to him and smiles lightly. She's not the kind to ignore.

"Ruu, I am sorry," Vineet says It's genuine; it seems so with his tone.

"For what?" She asks simply, seeming oblivious to what happened the other day.

"I mean, I know I did wrong, but please don't be this mad. I know…." He says, but Ruhana cuts him in between.

"You don't know, Vineet. But, fine, I don't want to take grudges and ruin my trip," Ruhana says this briefly while Vineet looks at her.

"What? I am still on my word. I'll follow you like others do. Don't worry from my side. I just don't want to ruin my mood," Ruhana says as she feels his gaze at herself.

"But Ruu…." he tries to say; he wants to talk to her genuinely.

"We'll talk later, I think you should go and talk to the professors. Also, I don't want to talk about what will disturb me! Sometimes you are way too concerned for me, and sometimes, my simple questions raise your temper and you shout at me in front of those people, who later laugh at me. I don't know whom I should trust?" Ruhana says.

Vineet sighs and watches her go. She has said that she doesn't want to ruin her mood. Is she fine? Or is she masking her feelings?

Vineet doesn't know but he is well determined to convince Ruhana. He sighs and moves towards Professor Shah, one of the four professors who are accompanying them. There is a long list of places they have to visit. It has been 5 days of the trip already. Vineet and the class representatives take the charge. He heads to the bus, the same one as Ruhana. He looks at her, but surprisingly, the girl didn't pay any heed to Vineet.

He sighs. A long day lies ahead.

*****

The whole day passes quickly with lots of things to do, like going to different places, even going back to the planetarium and, of course, visiting Juhu Beach. They get back to the hotel at around 7:30 PM, feeling pretty tired. After taking a shower and having dinner, they're now relaxing on a swing in the garden.

The air today is cool and fresh, a change from Mumbai's usual humid weather. Even though they're tired, the girls are in good moods, sharing laughs. Right now, they're talking about the other people staying at the hotel. Apart from their college friends, only a few guests are around. Ruhana is having fun spinning on the damp grass."

"Girls, it feels like we've taken over this place, this hotel. I mean, we've been here for 5 days, and I haven't seen any new faces around," Ruhana remarks.

"I think all the rooms are occupied by our team alone. Haha!" Akshara chimes in with a giggle.

"Yeah, because we're always here after dinner, and I only see familiar faces. Thanks to Ruu," Priyanka says as she pushes the swing in a playful manner.

"Come on, both of you enjoy being here too. Don't blame me," Ruhana responds with a playful roll of her eyes.

Akshara and Priyanka giggle at her words, and then Priyanka looks at Ruhana, sensing her frustration with Vineet. She thinks for a moment and then gazes at her friend.

"We should blame Vineet, shouldn't we? You're always thinking about him, waiting for him, and you can't sleep without catching a glimpse of him," Priyanka suggests.

"Oh yeah! He's left no room for us. He's occupied both your heart and mind," Akshara teases, glancing at Ruhana.

Ruhana suddenly feels a surge of anger. Why do they always have to bring Vineet into every conversation? Weren't they the ones complaining that Ruhana wasn't giving them enough time? Now that she's here, spending time with her best friends, laughing, talking, and gossiping, they bring Vineet into the conversation.

Ruhana may be quick to forgive when Vineet apologizes, knowing his apology is sincere, but she can't keep forgiving him. She can't let him hurt her again. She looks at her friends.

"Why do you guys have to bring him into our conversation? Didn't I make it clear that I don't want to talk about him?" Ruhana asks, her tone laced with anger.

"But Ruu..." Priyanka begins.

"We were just teasing you. Of course, you can't do without him, can you?" Akshara rolls her eyes at Ruhana.

"I can, Akshara! It's been a long day. Besides, I can't let him do as he pleases, endure his scolding in front of others, or watch him talk to others and then go silent when I want to talk.," Ruhana says bluntly.

"But he's being genuine. He was sad, yaar. At least, listen to him," Priyanka pleads.

"Yeah, and then let him hurt me again. Just five days ago, he promised me he'd try to change. But he didn't. He practically ruined the trip. I got caught up in his words, thinking he'd keep his promise, but he didn't. In fact, he scolded me in front of other seniors. Don't I have any self-respect, or am I just a laughingstock?" Ruhana shouts at her friends.

Vineet did make promises, and he tried to keep them, but he failed. Ruhana's anger is justified, and she has every right to feel this way. She casts a last look at her friends and heads inside the hotel, her mood dampened once again. Sighing, Akshara and Priyanka follow her to their room, unaware that Vineet has overheard their conversation.

His eyes well up with tears. Yes, he couldn't keep his promise, and he didn't change. To win her back, he needs to mend his ways and open up to the girl who is his sunshine. He's determined; maybe this time he's truly sincere, and he gears up to apologize to her once again.

*****

Vineet bangs his hand in the air. He is angry with himself. His sunshine girl is upset all because of him. He has always taken her for granted because she's always been available for him. She does silly things and he mistook her for being a kid. He doesn't share his pain or his problems with her, and he diverts her towards other things. This is why Ruhana is upset with him. He remembers her words.

"I just wanted my best friend back. I wanted the Vineet who never kept secrets from me, who used to play with me, who would treat me to ice cream,"

"You—you enjoy talking to others but not me. Why not? I'm just a kid, after all. You only make fun of me in front of everyone. That's what you've been doing! You can talk to Rhea but not to Ruhana! Yes! Rhea might be more mature than Ruhana, and she gives you more space, right? You cling to her more, don't you?"

"You won't find another Ruhana, ever! Even if you search the entire world, you won't find her,"

Those were her final words. Since then, she has maintained complete silence towards him, not waiting for him in the garden after dinner, and avoiding any eye contact. It's been two days that she's been silent. However, he has been providing her with the same treatment for many years. She must be feeling it, but she hasn't uttered a word, allowing him time to heal. Yet, in return, he has only caused immense pain.

Vineet lets out a sigh, his eyes welling up with tears. He is also determined to win her over and regain her trust and affection once more.

*****

The next morning comes quickly. Ruhana wakes up right away as the sun's rays gently touch her head. She sits on the bed, feeling a bit tired because she stayed up late into the night and couldn't sleep. Thoughts of her best friend bother her, and she also feels guilty about how she treated Vineet recently, but she thinks it's necessary.

She wants him to understand how she feels when he ignores her, takes her for granted, and, most importantly, treats her with silence. It hurts her, and she wants him to realize it. For a while, she looks a bit sad, but then she smiles.

After all, it's a day for shopping, and they have a shopping spree planned. The teachers have thoughtfully included a day for shopping and some free time away from studies. They know that young people enjoy having some free time, even if there's some supervision. That's okay, right?

Ruhana smiles to herself because she doesn't want to hold grudges, whether against her friends or Vineet. She wants to enjoy this trip. While it would have been more fun if Vineet had kept his promise, she doesn't want to look sad and tired when she goes to RD's concert.

*****

Ruhana casts a glance at her friends and gently nudges them to wake up. She assures them that they'll have a great day together, filled with shopping. The girls take turns showering and getting ready for the day ahead.

An hour later, Ruhana, Priyanka, and Akshara are prepared to head out. They lock their room and make their way to the hotel restaurant. As they greet other students and sit down for breakfast, Ruhana's eyes inadvertently meet Vineet's, but she quickly averts her gaze and focuses on her breakfast.

There's a lot on her plate – steaming idli-sambhar, poha, and a red velvet pastry. While the treats are undoubtedly delicious, Vineet has also been a source of joy for her in the past, and yet, she's upset with him. She lets out a deep sigh and begins eating her breakfast while engaging in conversation with her friends.

Thirty minutes later, they are ready to depart for their shopping adventure. They have the entire day to themselves, and they plan to enjoy it to the fullest. Their shopping list is extensive, as girls never seem to tired of shopping.

Their first destination is Fashion Street.

*****

Upon arriving at their destination, the students formed their own groups. The girls, too, have created their own separate groups, comprised of students from different classes. It promises to be a fantastic day.

Fashion Street is a market that offers everything – clothes, jewelery, footwear, artistic pieces, and various handcrafted items. There are also numerous stalls serving delicious street food. Isn't it a delightful and vibrant place?

They begin wandering through the streets, pausing at chaat stalls and exploring shops selling imitation jewelery and clothing. No girl can resist the allure of jewelery and clothing, especially on the famous Fashion Street.

Akshara stops at nearly every jewelery shop, trying on various pieces and urging her best friends to join her. On the other hand, Priyanka keeps an eye out for footwear. Meanwhile, Ruhana looks a bit down, which prompts Akshara to ask, "Why the long face? What's bothering you?"

"You both have already done your shopping. I couldn't find anything," Ruhana replies, sounding disheartened.

"You're so choosy! I picked out those earrings for you, but you didn't take them," Akshara comments.

"I want a handbag, and I haven't seen a single shop selling handbags," Ruhana pouts again, eliciting laughter from her friends.

Ruhana rolls her eyes at them, but her two friends laugh, and Priyanka places her arm around Ruhana's shoulder, saying, "Relax, baby! We'll find a handbag for you,"

"Alright, buy me a handbag, you two," Ruhana concedes, rolling her eyes at Priyanka and Akshara.

Meanwhile, they reach the end of the street and come to an abrupt stop. The professors have called for them, and they've decided to meet at a restaurant on Fashion Street. A certain shop catches Ruhana's eye once more. It's a collection of handbags, and she excitedly informs her friends that she'll join them at the restaurant.

Akshara and Priyanka reach the restaurant, Cafe Latte. They take their seats, and Priyanka sends a message to Ruhana, urging her to arrive at the cafe soon. Vineet spots the two girls at their table but can't see Ruhana. He sighs deeply and inquires about Ruhana, to which they reply that she's still at a shop and will join them shortly. He nods and begins searching for other students.

More than half an hour passes, but there's still no sign of Ruhana. Akshara and Priyanka try calling her, but she doesn't answer her phone. They inform Vineet, who is now becoming anxious.

Not only is she not speaking to him, but she has also vanished. It feels like too severe a punishment for him. Now, he must locate her and offer an apology.

He can only hope that she might forgive him.

Chapter 20:

The Reconciliation

It's the day for shopping and as of now, Ruhana is missing. Priyanka and Akshara are in the cafe, worried about their best friend. Vineet is also worried about the girl. She has gone to purchase a handbag and now she's missing.

Vineet is already angry with himself, as he has hurt Ruhana. The girl is missing and this has doubled his punishment, he feels. It feels like she's doing this only to punish him. He is meddling with his thoughts when Priyanka breaks his trance.

"Vineet, please do something. Ruhana should have come by now," Priyanka says it worriedly.

"Yeah, I will see. You and Akshara, keep calling her," Vineet says, to which the girls agreed.

Vineet moves out of the cafe to look for Ruhana. He's panicked upon not finding Ruhana near the cafe. Well, for Vineet, he has promised her father to take care of her. But she is angry at him and now she's missing. He can't bear the punishment any longer.

"I just hope that she's fine," Vineet murmurs softly.

"She must be shopping. Relax, Vineet," Rohan comforts his friend.

"No! She's in some trouble, I feel. I am going to look for her," Vineet says so and walks ahead.

He's worried for her and he just wants to see her alright; only then will his aching heart find peace. He's constantly calling Ruhana but the girl is not picking up the phone. He throws his hand in the air, sighing deeply.

"Where are you, Ruu? I am sorry! Please don't punish me like this,"

Vineet murmurs to himself. He is missing her badly. He knows how it would have hurt her if he did not talk to her properly, even when she asked him. She always gets to know if he is upset, in pain, or happy. Yet he demands space and she readily agrees. But, since a day, he has been feeling emptiness, while she must be feeling it even when they're together. He sighs again; he has to apologize to her. He just needs to find her—his sunshine—Ruhana.

*****

Ruhana purchases a handbag from the shop and moves ahead. She's in a hurry to reach the cafe but it seems like the stars are not in her favor. She's walking until she finds a bakery, and that too is one of a kind. It's named RDz and it is famous for its cupcakes. Though they can get it at the cafe where they are having lunch, out of her excitement, Ruhana runs inside the bakery and purchases some cupcakes and chocolates. As she steps out of the bakery, it starts to drizzle. The shopkeeper allows her to stay inside the shop until the rain stops. But the case is different. The rain doesn't stop. Ruhana decides to walk to the cafe. What else can she do? Maybe she will go back to the hotel and change her clothes. It won't harm them, as its shopping day for them.

Making up her mind, the girl thanks the shopkeeper and steps out of the shop. The rain is always dear to her but today the case is different. As she moves ahead, she trips and falls on the road, spraining her leg. She sighs deeply, as there's no one to help her out. All she can do is help herself.

*****

Vineet is searching for Ruhana frantically. As he moves forward, he hears some giggles from the street. Vineet looks around and he finds a gang of boys he encountered earlier in the day while strolling around. He had scolded them for teasing girls and also asked them not to cross their limits. He feels that Ruhana might be having some sort of problem.

He walks speedily but doesn't find anyone or doesn't see anyone due to heavy rainfall. He stands in a shade to save himself from the rain.

"Where are you, Ruhana?" he asks himself, clenching his fists.

"It is because you feel it. She might be okay, but because you are worried for her, you are having bad thoughts. Maybe she is in any shop, saving herself from the rain," Rohan says.

Vineet looks at his friend and agrees. Yes, it is raining, and she might be in the same shop where she went to buy a handbag. He should keep looking, and she will take care of herself, obviously. He should not worry so much.

"You should not hold your feelings, Vineet. She is special to you. And you're being strict—not only to Ruhana but to yourself, too. Just drop it, befriend her, and love her like she does to you," Rohan says and Vineet is surprised.

Okay, she is someone he can't imagine his life without! But he doesn't want to hurt her. He might not be able to love her back. He's afraid to lose her—to lose her love. He can't let her walk away. He has to find her now.

As the rains subside, Vineet begins to look for Ruhana. They walk into the market and meanwhile, familiar sounds reach his ears. It's like someone is in pain. Vineet walks ahead and is astonished to find Ruhana sitting on the stairs of a shop, completely drenched in water. He rushes to her.

"Ruhana, where were you? Do you have any idea how stressed I was? At least you could call. I told you to be in the group; why did you leave Priyanka and Akshara? And what happened?" He asks all questions in one go.

"Nothing Vineet. My ankle got twisted and I lost my path because of the rain. You should not worry," Ruhana says, her tone still blunt.

Vineet massages her ankle and asks her if she can walk. She agrees and then Vineet helps her to walk. He stops an auto and they head to the cafe. Informing the teachers, Vineet takes Ruhana to the hotel, though there's a silence prevailing between them.

After reaching the hotel, Vineet takes Ruhana to her room and they change into a fresh set of clothes. Ruhana finishes dressing up when Vineet enters the room and begins to apply an ointment to her leg. She tries to stop him but he continues doing the task—he applies the ointment and wraps her ankle with the crape bandage.

After finishing his task, he looks up, and the words that leave his mouth leave Ruhana surprised.

"Ruhana!" He takes her name first; he wants to make sure that she is listening to him and as she looks into his eyes, he gets his answer.

"I'm sorry, Ruhana. I know, I have hurt you a lot," Vineet says and these words leave Ruhana surprised.

"Really! You took so much time to just say sorry. And will it heal the pain that you have given me?" Ruhana says her eyes never leave his.

"I know, Ruhana! But all of these days have been stressful without you. I promise, I will try to be the person you want me to be," Vineet says and she's more astonished.

"Vineet, you promised me this before we commenced the trip. You promised me again two days ago too. And then you broke your word. How can I believe you?" Ruhana looks at him.

Vineet is perplexed. The girl is right. All these years, she has been trying to please him. She has always given him time and he has asked for more time in turn. He promises her but breaks them in an instant. It'd be hard for anyone to believe a person who breaks their promises every now and then. Vineet looks at Ruhana and she is already waiting for his answer.

He walks near her bed and sits on his knees. He holds her hands in his and looks into her eyes. He's guilty of hurting her and he wants to clear it for the final time.

"I know I have hurt you. But I mean my words this time. Please don't get angry like this. Your anger is no less than a punishment for me. Ruhana. I cannot see you stepping away from me. Please forgive me!"

"I assure you, I'll be completely open with you. You have the right—you have the right to know everything about me!" Vineet declares, leaving Ruhana in astonishment as she gazes at him.

"Do you think so? I mean, will you abide by your words?? I don't doubt you, Vineet. Because, for me, your words are the decisions that you make for me, but for you, you never tell me what you feel! So, I am just curious!" Ruhana asks; she knows he is apologising genuinely, but she wants to make sure that he will not back off his own words.

"No! I won't back off my words, Ruu! These two days were a hell of boring without you. You do so much for me, and I haven't done anything for you. But, now, it would be different. I will try to be the person you want me to be. Promise!" He says and there is a smile playing on his lips.

Ruhana looks at him for a few seconds while he blinks his eyes in affirmation. A smile forms on her lips and she hugs him instantly. He's surprised but he hugs her back. After all, he's getting it after two days and he wants to take in all her warmth.

"I'm glad, Vineet. I know it is not easy but please know that I am always there. Mumma and Papa are there too. Remember, you address them as Ma and Dad too. Then, please consider it for your family only," Ruhana says as she parts the hug and looks at Vineet.

"You know what? Seeing you in pain is very painful for me. You're my best friend and I always wish the best for you. But you need to come out of your shell and live your life. You cannot ruin your future because of your past, Vineet," Ruhana says.

"If you're willing to give it another shot, I'll support you. I'm ready to sacrifice anything except you in this world. Please, just inform me, okay? I sincerely hope you won't break this promise again—because if you do, I'll shatter too," Ruhana declares, locking her gaze onto his.

Vineet knows that she is right. He has to leave his shell. He may not have his own mom beside her but Ruhana's mom has always been his mother figure. She has always fulfilled his wishes when his own mom didn't. This girl is also working hard to bring him back to life and he has to take a step. If not now, —when?

Vineet sighs deeply. He holds her hands in his, and he kisses her knuckles gently.

"I know, Ruhana. And you know, you are my sunshine in the dark. I cannot lose you. I will try my best," Vineet says, making her smile.

"You keep your promise and you will always find me near yourself. I just need you, and I want you to try. I hope I can rely on you to bring my best friend back?" She questions.

Vineet says nothing but nods his head positively. This is all he can do for this lady in front of him. She has done only good to him and he has to become better for her. This is the only thing Vineet can do for Ruhana. She smiles and hugs him tightly once again.

Vineet has a relieved smile on his face; He's glad that she's happy and no longer angry with him. And now, he needs to work on himself, he can't lose her again.

Chapter 21:

The New Beginning

Ruhana and Vineet resolve their differences, with him vowing to transform into the person she desires and promising to open up his heart to her. For a few hours, when she was away from his eyes, he turned restless, and he realized her importance in his life. She smiles as he makes the promise but she also warns him that if this time he breaks his promise, she won't forgive him.

He's already terrified by the thought of loneliness he bore for the last two days. He won't be able to handle it one more time, so he readily agrees and assures her that he won't break his promise this time. She gazes at him hopefully, she wants to believe that Vineet is saying it genuinely and won't go against his own words. She holds on to the hope that he will indeed keep his promise.

Ruhana smiles at him, while Vineet sighs deeply. He is glad to have her back in his life. He makes her sit on the bed comfortably and makes an order at the room service. He orders a plate of pasta and a chocolate waffle. He knows that her favorite food always cheers her up. Ruhana is surprised, she feels this would lead them to hear the scoldings from their professors but Vineet convinces her that this order won't be a problem. Of course, they have some extra money to use in case of emergencies.

"Relax! Nobody is going to say a word to you. Trust me! Anyway, you will have the food and take a painkiller, okay?

I don't want any tantrums from you," He rolls his eyes at her.

"I am hurt, and you're scolding me? I am upset with you and you're again in your bossy shoes," She makes a face while he just smiles.

He chides her by taking the name of her favorite musician. Her eyes twinkle with joy.

"R.D!!!Are we going? Really?" Ruhana chuckles loudly.

"Indeed, you have those VIP passes, and I assume you won't abandon me, will you?" Vineet asks, a smile playing on his lips.

"Absolutely! I adore him, Raj D'sena! His voice is so soulful," Ruhana chuckles, grinning widely.

"Oh, I didn't realize you were such a big fan. I thought I was the only one on your mind," Vineet teases her.

"I'm a huge RD fan. And, well, you're always on my mind. But my admiration for RD is different. And I love him, but I can't compare you to him. You two have different places in my heart and life," Ruhana says, sending a teasing glance his way.

"Oh, true! But I do play the guitar quite skillfully, you know," Vineet mentions, emphasising his own talents.

"Yeah, but you can't outshine my RD. No more comments about RD! Or I might just have to take extreme measures. Got it?" Ruhana rolls her eyes, while Vineet laughs in response to her words.

He's not making fun of her, her admiration has always brought a smile on his face. It's her nature - she can't bear to hear anything negative about the people she loves or likes. She may not know RD, short for Raj D'sena, the singer and musician, but she adores his voice, perhaps feeling a soothing connection. With Vineet, she always finds peace. Her interaction with Vineet has always been surreal and she loves it. When they sit on the terrace at night, they rarely exchange words; it's the silence and their shared emotions that communicate. He respects this habit of hers, yet occasionally, her annoyed expressions amuse him.

Vineet snaps out of his reverie upon hearing the doorbell, which signals that someone is at the door. He opens the door to find their order. Vineet receives the delivery and expresses his gratitude to the delivery person, then returns to where Ruhana is seated and places the tray on the table. As they uncover the dishes, she is excited.

"It smells absolutely delicious! I can't wait to dig in," Ruhana exclaims with excitement, her laughter filling the room.

"It's all yours. Enjoy your meal, and don't forget to take your medication," he says, placing the painkiller on the table for her.

"You're leaving? There's no need to go. Come join me for a meal. I know you must be hungry too, and this is way too much food for one person," Ruhana insists, her warm smile inviting him to stay.

He might be trying to make amends for his past actions, but she continues to call him over, just as she always has. She gestures towards her bag, asking him to fetch it, and he obliges, not wanting to upset her by disobeying her request. Ruhana takes out a paper plate and serves a meal for him.

"Mom packed this. She knew we might get hungry. There was no room in your bag, so she put it here. We didn't think we'd need it, but fate had other plans. What can you do?" Ruhana giggles, making him smile.

"Your mom always knew. I just didn't understand. I'm sorry, Ruhana," Vineet apologises once more.

Ruhana raises her eyebrows, showing that she's not upset with him, and asks, "Sorry for what?"

"For not treating you, your mom, the way I should have. I know she was always there, but..." Vineet pauses, unwilling to finish the sentence.

"Vineet, as long as you realize that you are important to us, it's enough for us. She wanted a son like you, Vineet, and see, her wish came true," Ruhana says sweetly

"You're like a godchild to them, Vineet. You made them experience what it's like to be parents. Aunty used to leave you at our house for hours. You used to help Mumma keep me occupied. She's like your mom. She'll forgive you even if you don't say sorry to her; she won't wait for an apology," Ruhana adds, her words filled with meaning.

Vineet smiles lightly, appreciating the words that have the power to uplift his spirits. He nods in agreement, and they both indulge in their delicious meal. For the next few moments, the two friends are immersed in their food before playfully bickering over a waffle.

"No, that's mine. I won't share," Ruhana insists grumpily.

"Hey, no! That one deserves a share too," Vineet responds with the same determination.

"Nope, the chocolate waffle is all mine. You can order another one," Ruhana retorts, rolling her eyes at her best buddy.

"No way! I want it from that batch. You said everything you have is mine too," Vineet playfully teases, winking at her as he takes the plate from her.

In the end, he offers the first bite of the waffle to his sunshine girl, and they share the rest happily. Ruhana is content and happy, silently wishing that this moment could last forever. She wants to see that joy on Vineet's face every time they interact.

A little later, Priyanka and Akshara return, finding Vineet with Ruhana. They can tell that the two have made amends, and all is well between them. After making sure Ruhana is safe and sound with her friends, Vineet leaves the room, promising to meet her at dinner in the restaurant.

The day ends on a happy note, and Ruhana is filled with excitement. She hopes that things will change now.

*****

The next day marks the second last day of their trip and finally the trip is coming to end. They are sad that the trip has come to an end. They've explored new places, learned new things, and had new experiences every day.

Ruhana is eagerly waiting for the concert of her favorite singer, Raj D'sena, aka RD. Her friends tease her with RD's name, and she can't help but smile. When they meet for breakfast, Akshara decides to playfully tease her.

"What's so special about RD? I thought Vineet was special," Akshara teases.

"Oh, he is! But RD is special too. I love his voice," Ruhana replies dreamily.

"You're really obsessed, Ruu! It's like you're about to meet him. Will he even meet you?" Priyanka playfully knocks on her head, snapping her out of her daydream.

"He's humble and sweet; he'll surely meet his fans," Ruhana says dreamily.

"Yeah, yeah! Leave some cute and hot guys for us too. You already have a long list. Manage with Vineet for this lifetime!" Akshara teases.

"I can do that for the next seven lifetimes," Ruhana says, glancing at her best friends.

"Why are you two jealous? Don't roll your eyesat my men, okay? Find someone for yourselves," Ruhana says, rolling her eyes at her best friends. They all burst into laughter.

After breakfast, some students decide to explore the local market, while others opt to relax at the hotel. They learn that RD's concert is scheduled for 5 PM at the same hotel they are staying in. Ruhana chooses to stay back and rest since her foot is still bothering her. Priyanka and Akshara want to go out, so they leave Ruhana in the garden and promise to return soon.

Vineet comes to her aid and offers to help. Ruhana asks him to take her to her room, as she needs someone to support her. Vineet agrees and accompanies her to her room. Along the way, he surprises her by blindfolding her.

"Vineet! What's going on? What are you doing?" Fear creeps into her heart.

"Relax; I'm here with you," Vineet reassures her, holding her hand tightly for comfort.

"But why did you blindfold me?" Ruhana asks curiously.

"It's a surprise! Come with me," Vineet says, and they take cautious steps in a specific direction.

After about ten minutes, they stop, and Vineet removes the blindfold, leaving Ruhana astonished by the sight before her eyes. She's overwhelmed, unable to speak a word.

Chapter 22:

Surprising Her: Meeting her Rockstar

Ruhana is in awe that Vineet has planned a surprise for her. She accuses him of abducting her while he laughs. He teases her that kidnapping her won't benefit him but he adds that she will be grateful for his surprise. They stop after a while and he removes the blindfold. Ruhana closes her eyes and opens them to adjust to the light in the room. She sees it and recognizes it as the auditorium of the hotel. The hall is empty but decorated beautifully. Colorful balloons, dim lights, and a light fragrance are in the air. She is mesmerized by the view. As she turns towards Vineet, he signals her to look behind her. She is astonished but follows his lead.

In the next instant, her eyes widen, seeing the person before herself. It's the man she adores- Raj D'sena. Ruhana looks at the new person and then at Vineet, who smiles lightly. She's unable to react, finding her favorite singer in front of her.

"You were talking about him. Go and talk to him!" Vineet whispers in her ears and slightly pushes her towards him.

He's no one but, RD, aka Raj D'Sena, about whom Ruhana is excited. She loves music and wherever she finds something that touches her heart, she loves it. And with RD, Ruhana is in love with his music and singing. Ruhana looks at him, unable to process that she's standing near the man she admires. More than that, she's elated that Vineet did it for her.

"So, you're Ruhana! Your friend told me that you're very excited to meet me!" It's RD, who breaks her trance.

"Yes— yes I wanted—but I didn't see it happening soon," Ruhana stutters at the moment, causing RD to laugh.

"Some things happen unexpectedly, Ms. Ruhana," He says.

"And I believe it now. I just need to believe that this isn't the dream, but reality," Ruhana chuckles.

At the same time, RD holds Ruhana's hand and she's startled by his touch. He then places a slim book in her hand and asks her to hold it. She obeys him and he actually signs on the first page of the book—to be precise, his autograph—and she didn't even ask for it. She's looking at him while he smiles at her.

"It should be enough for you to believe that it's not a dream," He smiles at her.

"Wow! This is more than I could think. Thank you so much!" Ruhana shook hands with him.

RD and Ruhana share a quick hug and even Vineet joins them. After a little chit-chat with RD, Ruhana and Vineet move out of the auditorium, thanking him for his time.

*****

As they move outside, Ruhana jumps to her place and hugs Vineet in an instant. She's super thrilled to have met the singer himself. She never thought it'd happen. She's glad that Vineet is there to help her with it.

"Thanks, Vineet! Seriously, this is the best surprise ever," Ruhana says, chuckling as she finishes her sentence.

"Anything for you," He says that because he's trying to be the one she wants and she knows it well.

"I understand, and I'm pleased that you're making the effort. Meeting RD is one thing, but this is even more significant to me. You planned all of this, spoke to RD, and brought me here. I'm elated that you've fulfilled my dream, the one I've always longed for. Thank you, Vineet," Ruhana says with a soft tone, her smile never fading.

"I realize that I've hurt you deeply, Ruhana. This is nothing compared to what you do every day," he admits, and he's correct.

"I'll do it. You can't stop me from doing anything for you. And I'll never forget this, especially since my favorite people are involved," Ruhana smiles.

"I'm glad, Ruhana. Maybe my guilt will diminish a bit now," Vineet says.

"No! Don't say that. I'm thrilled to see you changing. I've always wanted to see you like this, and you're doing it. I can't express how happy I am today. Thank you!" She chuckles and hugs him once again.

Vineet smiles, happy to be the reason for her smile. He then takes her to her room and tells her to rest, also mentioning that he'll take her to the concert. His only concern is her sprained leg, and he wants her to be well. She assures him that she's fine and will take care of herself. She asks him to rest too, and he agrees, nodding.

The afternoon passes quickly. Ruhana wakes up from her nap and attempts to move her leg, feeling some relief from the pain. She smiles and gets ready for the event. True to his promise, Vineet arrives on time. At the same time, Priyanka and Akshara return. Ruhana tells them to get ready, as they're all going to the concert. Akshara assures Ruhana that they'll join them shortly.

Vineet takes Ruhana with him, checking her foot, which is now much better.

"Hmm! I think the surprise worked; your leg is in better condition," he teases her about meeting RD.

"So, don't be jealous, okay!" Ruhana glares at him while Vineet laughs.

He continues teasing her until they reach the auditorium. As they enter, they are captivated by the beauty of the setup. Shimmering lights, a decorated stage—everything exudes elegance, creating the perfect concert atmosphere.

Ruhana scans the hall in hopes of catching a glimpse of her superstar, RD, but doesn't spot him. However, Vineet taps her on the shoulder and smiles.

"Don't be upset. Your RD will be here shortly," he teases.

She playfully slaps his arm, asking him not to tease her, but he just laughs. Today, he seems more interested in pleasing her.

"Don't stare at me, or you'll fall in love," he winks at her.

She playfully stares at him, knowing she's already in love with him, even though he may not want it, and she slaps his arm.

"I love my RD, you know. You don't poke your nose in between," She says it teasingly.

He looks offended a little which she notices. He doesn't respond back and instructs her to take a seat. Meanwhile, the concert begins, and it's announced that RD will take the stage soon.

Ruhana gazes at the stage, she's thrilled and excited to watch him live. She knows that everything seems beautiful with Vineet by her side, but she's uncertain about his feelings for her. Lost in her thoughts, Vineet leans towards her and says something.

"Please don't faint while watching RD. You're too heavy for me to carry," he jokes.

"What do you mean?" she turns to him, slightly annoyed.

Vineet stares at her for a moment, then bursts into laughter.

"I mean, if you faint, how will I take you back to your room?" he says, earning a playful slap on his arm.

"Shut up, Vineet! And be quiet, okay!" she says, irritated.

"Oh yeah... RD is here," Vineet says, pointing to the stage.

Ruhana turns to the stage but doesn't see RD. She looks back at Vineet and finds him laughing; he's been pulling her leg.

"Oops! I didn't expect you to be so angry!" he feigns a sad face.

Ruhana looks at Vineet and he's laughing. Seeing him laugh is a pretty sight to her eyes. And she is content. She's glad that he's trying. She turns her focus back on the stage. RD is still not on the stage, but she is enjoying the light music around her.

*****

Vineet glances at Ruhana and finds her lost in the music echoing in the hall. He smiles. She is an innocent soul who loves to be the way she is. She always wants the people around her to be happy. Vineet knows that she is the genuine soul and she has always wished for his wellbeing. He's glad that she's smiling because of him, and this is a great deal to him. Today, he has served her with happiness, not silence. She won't be mad at him, and he's glad about this.

Meanwhile, it is announced that the singer and his band will arrive on the stage in a few minutes. He finds Ruhana stirring in her seat; she's ecstatic; this is the first concert that she is attending. He feels her holding his hand and she chuckles as she spots RD stepping onto the stage. He knows that she's happy.

"He'll not go anywhere without singing your favorite song," Vineet teases Ruhana, at which she glares at him.

"Shut up, Vineet!" Ruhana glares at him while he laughs.

" What wrong did I say?" He raises his eyebrows at Ruhana

" Stop teasing me! Let me concentrate on the concert," She says, slapping on his arm.

"Yeah yeah! Concentrate on your RD!" He emphasises the last word, making Ruhana glare at him.

He laughs, while she just stares at her for some good seconds. Okay, if teasing her makes him laugh, she can become the laughing gag, but only for him. He shouldn't make fun of her in front of others. She smiles and chuckles suddenly as RD's voice falls in her ears—he is singing her favorite song. She chuckles at the moment, cupping her own face. She is thrilled to see his smiling face, as he's looking at the crowd and singing.

Vineet smiles at her act; he knows she's happy and so, he doesn't say anything; he just watches her enjoy the music of her favorite singer.

"Oh my god! He sings beautifully! You know, that is why I love him. I am so happy I can watch him directly in front of my eyes," she chuckles, holding his hand in hers once again.

Vineet just stares at Ruhana, nodding her head in agreement. She is indeed right. RD's voice touches the heart and Vineet cannot deny the fact now. He is mesmerized as well. Meanwhile, Ruhana glances at him, feeling his stare on her. She raises her eyebrows at him, asking him about the matter. Today, Vineet is smiling, and it is a big deal to Ruhana. He asks her to enjoy the concert; he knows she is excited about it, but at the same time, she is highly concerned about him. But, he doesn't want her to miss the concert. Ruhana agrees; for her, he's by her side, he's smiling, and there is nothing more that she can wish for at the moment. She is happy —soul-ly happy.

*****

Around 9 p.m., the concert ends, and Ruhana once again runs to him, asking for another autograph in her personal diary. Well, she got it unasked and she owes it to Vineet. RD smiles affectionately at the girl and signs her diary. Ruhana is happy. She hugs Vineet as they walk out of the auditorium and her friends tease her with RD's name.

Ruhana asks Priyanka and Akshara to reach the restaurant for dinner and tells them that she will join them shortly. The girls disperse; they know Ruhana wants to share a moment and have a talk with Vineet, her best friend. As the two girls leave, Ruhana glances at Vineet, and she thanks him again, to which Vineet says something that leaves Ruhana touched, and she ends up hugging him.

Chapter 23:

The Journey Back Home

Ruhana is glad as the concert ends and she asks for another autograph from her favorite artist and he obliges. After that, she moves out and tells her friends that she will join them in the restaurant soon. It's enough for them to understand that Ruhana wants to have a conversation with Vineet in person. As they disperse, Ruhana looks at Vineet. She's thankful to him for arranging her meeting with RD.

"Vineet, thank you so much. I am truly grateful," Ruhana says it softly.

"This is the least I could do for you, Ruhana," Vineet says it smilingly.

"I'm glad you did it. Otherwise, no one does it, not even the ones who are close to you," She says that and hugs him tightly.

"I had to do this, Ruhana, because you've done so much for me. I often overlook the things you do, and I should be grateful to you, which I haven't been. This wasn't difficult, because you never ask for anything. You only want my time and companionship, for which I struggle. You find your happiness in my joy. I'm truly sorry, Ruhana. This is the least I can do to earn your trust," he says, wrapping his arms around her petite waist and pulling her in a warm embrace.

"Great! I'm delighted, Vineet. I'm even happier now that I've heard you. You've kept your promise, and that gives me hope," Ruhana replies, glancing at Vineet.

"I'll do my best, but I can't bear to lose you. So, please stay by my side," he emphasises, looking at her.

Ruhana holds Vineet's hands and reassures him that he's not alone, that she'll always be there for him, and that she won't stop teasing him. He chuckles at her words, and she admires him. Holding her hand, he guides her to the restaurant, making sure she doesn't get hurt.

Ruhana is moved, knowing he cares for her, but she wishes for him to move forward. Now that he has made an effort, she hopes he continues to do so. She wants him to break out of his shell and become the man he was meant to be.

The day concludes on a joyful note, and everyone retreats to their rooms. It's their last night in Mumbai, and the next day, they'll be heading back to their hometown.

*****

The following morning, Ruhana wakes up and realizes that it's their last day in Mumbai. She wakes up Akshara and Priyanka, and they start packing their stuff. They will be heading back home in a few hours and they need to pack first. They've decided that after packing and freshening up, they will have breakfast and stroll in the huge gardens of the hotel.

"Ah, ten days are coming to an end! Back to that usua routine," she exclaims sadly.

"And exams! We have to start studying," Akshara remarks.

"But after that, we'll plan another trip," Priyanka adds with enthusiasm, jumping on her toes.

"Oh yes! But to do that, we'll have to bid farewell to these wonderful memories," Ruhana says, her face reflecting a hint of sadness.

The girls share a heartfelt hug, and then they depart. They have a flight at 12:30 PM, and since the professors mentioned it would take an hour to reach the airport, they plan to leave the hotel before 10 AM. Every student feels a brief moment of sadness as they've enjoyed their trip, and it's coming to an end.

Soon, they'll return to their hometown, and everyone is excited to be back home. Isn't it the case for all of us? We often grow weary of our monotonous routines and crave something refreshing. This trip to Mumbai has certainly rejuvenated them for their everyday lives back home.

A few hours later, they arrive in their hometown, Delhi, and Ruhana's father picks them up from the airport. They're delighted to be home. Vineet and Ruhana both seem relaxed and a bit tired. Ruhana's mother suggests they freshen up and she prepares coffee for them.

After freshening up, Ruhana rushes out of her room and takes her place next to her dad, while Vineet sits beside his mom and rests his head on her shoulder. Ruhana quickly grabs her mug and giggles before Vineet has a chance to do so. He smiles at her playful gesture.

"Vineet, I hope she didn't trouble you, did she?" Ruhana's mom asks, looking at the young man.

"Huh! He troubles me every day. And you don't say anything to him? Very bad, Mom!" Ruhana pouts at her beloved mom.

"Who said you're not a kid? You just acted like one," he says, smiling broadly.

"I have to do that. I can't stand your silence, you know. Remember, you promised me something, and to make you speak, I have to speak, right? You don't say much," Ruhana says innocently, reminding him of his promise.

"But that doesn't mean you're going to trouble my son, understood?" her mother says, looking at her daughter.

"Mom's on my side! You won't be able to do anything," he teases her.

Vineet is grateful to have this lady by his side. She has always treated him like her own son, shielding him from loneliness. He has always been a part of their family. Though she scolded him when he was a child, she loved him even more. Ruhana would get annoyed sometimes when they were kids, and Vineet used to convince her. He wears a small smile as he thinks about the lady who is now his mother, and no one could ever take her away from him. He watches as Ruhana makes a face.

"I won't trouble your son, but I will ask him to be happy. Otherwise, I'll trouble him even more than he can imagine," she says before taking a sip of her coffee.

He chuckles because he knows she won't do anything to hurt him. She sometimes makes mistakes just to hear his scolding or to receive his care. Despite her occasional irritation, she loves being around him, no matter how angry or annoyed he may be. He listens as Ruhana's mother continues speaking.

The lady asks them to relax while she sets the dinner table. Ruhana's dad inquires about their trip, and Ruhana starts sharing every minute detail while Vineet becomes a silent but attentive listener. Meanwhile, her mom calls them for dinner. This small family enjoys their meal with casual conversation, and Vineet participates, making Ruhana happy.

*****

Later that night, Ruhana is in her room, preparing her backpack for college. Her phone rings, and her face lights up as she hears the caller. It's Priyanka, and Ruhana eagerly answers the call. Her excitement is clearly visible on her face.

"Are you serious, Pree? Is it really going to happen?"

"Wow! That's fantastic! Let's definitely check it out, and I'll also ask him!" Ruhana exclaims with a chuckle.

"You don't know, Pri. He plays the guitar so well. I'll ask Vineet to participate in the festival. He promised me he wouldn't let me down," Ruhana says, her happiness evident.

Indeed, Vineet vowed to be the kind of friend Ruhana wants him to be—her best friend. He already cares for her, but he understands that her level of care and love for him exceeds his own. Ruhana ends the call, and at that moment, Vineet knocks on her door. She takes his hand and pulls him inside, urging him to sit on the bed.

"Vineet, do you know our college is organising a festival?" She inquires, aware that he probably has the information.

"Yes, I came to tell you about that," Vineet responds.

"Yay! I'm going to participate. You should too, please," Ruhana pleads, holding his hand.

"No, Ruu! I'll be in the audience to cheer you on," Vineet replies softly.

"Why not you? You promised me something, remember?" Ruhana tries to convince him.

"No! It's getting late; you should go to sleep," Vineet says, changing the direction of the conversation.

"Okay, you have until tomorrow to decide. Time is running out. Let me know what you decide. Come on, go and get some rest!" Ruhana playfully taps his cheek.

Vineet simply smiles at her and exits her room, suggesting that she get some sleep. But Ruhana can detect a hint of sadness in his eyes. She understands that he has committed to change and that breaking out of his shell will take time, but she can sense his current sorrow. She quietly follows him to the terrace.

Vineet is sitting on the swing, gently playing a soft tune on his guitar. This particular tune is his mother's favorite, and she used to love it when he played it as a child. Now, Ruhana often requests that he play this tune. As she watches him, she realizes that Vineet is pained while playing the tune, perhaps missing his mother.

Ruhana approaches the swing softly and sits beside him on thes wing. He didn't realize her presence and kept on playing the tune, while she closed her eyes, haring him. He stops playing the guitar when he realizes her presence and she looks at him. She knows he's teary eyed and when he blinks his eyes, she holds his hand.

"You don't need to hide your tears from me, Vineet. You know you can't," she says gently.

He offers a faint smile in response. Deep down, he understands that she's right. She sits beside him, holding his hands. Vineet knows Ruhana is correct, but emotions, especially those concerning loved ones, can be difficult to control.

Vineet and Ruhana sit in silence for a long while, gazing at the twinkling stars in the night sky. They don't need words to communicate; this silence is what they needed. They allow the silence to convey their feelings, letting their heartbeats speak for them.

His reverie is interrupted when Ruhana falls asleep on his shoulder. She appears peaceful and serene while asleep, which brings a smile to Vineet's face. He carefully lifts her in his arms and carries her to her bedroom, gently laying her on the bed. He kisses her forehead softly and adores her for a few minutes.

Indeed, she is the reason he lives, and their relationship is simple. She may argue with him, irritate him, and even fight with him, but she also cares deeply for him. She can't stand to see him sad and is willing to do anything to uplift his spirits. She is his beacon of light.

Vineet has come to realize that she means more to him than he thinks. During their time in Mumbai, she was upset with him and refused to speak to him for two days, leaving him feeling restless. She gets upset every time he withholds information from her. She is his sunshine, and he acknowledges it.

As he turns to leave, she holds his hand. He glances at her sleeping form, gently releases his hand from her grip and leaves the room.

Vineet then retreats to his room, where he sits on his bed and his gaze falls upon a photo frame resting on the side table. It contains a picture of him with Ruhana. She has been extraordinarily kind to him, and Ruhana and her parents are his only family. He's not a stranger; they consider him their son, as her mother often reminds him. A sweet memory from their past crosses his mind.

Flashback Begins

It was a sunny winter afternoon when he was 8 years old, and Ruhana was 6. After school, they decided to play at Ruhana's house. Ruhana sat grumpily on a swing in the garden, ignoring her mother's calls to come inside.

Vineet noticed her and pushed the swing gently. Her lips curled into a smile. He asked about her mood, and her face turned gloomy.

"I want to go to the circus, but my mom won't let me," she said sadly.

"She will take you to the circus," Vineet reassured her.

"But I want to go with you," she said grumpily.

Vineet smiled. Their city had a circus, and their schools were taking the students there. Ruhana learned that Vineet's class was also going, and she insisted on going with him.

"My class is going, and I can't take you," he explained.

"But I'll go with you!" she insisted.

"Your class is also going," he tried to convince her.

However, the determined little girl wouldn't disturb him. Vineet sighed, and an idea struck him. He rushed home, leaving Ruhana feeling dejected.

"Vineet isn't listening. I'm angry with him," she muttered to herself.

Her mood changed when she heard music. Looking up, she saw Vineet playing the guitar, her favorite tune. She couldn't help but smile. He promised to take her to the circus, but she had to be a good girl and not complain. She agreed and rested her head on his shoulder while he continued to play the song.

Flashback Ends

Today, the situation is different. Ruhana doesn't demand anything but answers. She asks him to smile, as his life has been painful from a young age. Ruhana has always understood his silence, and with these thoughts in mind, Vineet falls asleep.

Chapter 24:

News about the Fest

The next morning, Ruhana wakes up to find herself in bed. She smiles thinking about Vineet; he must have tucked her in bed last night. He cares, and she knows it. She decides to make Vineet participate in the annual festival. Yes, he has promised her and he has to listen to her. She hops out of bed and moves into the bathroom. She takes a shower and gets ready for the day. She has to do a lot of work—there are projects and examinations, and finally the annual festival. None of these things can be dumped and Ruhana has made it clear in her mind that she will do everything; after all, she is a girl who loves to do new things. Moreover, things will go as she plans with her friends.

She gets ready, makes her hair, and packs her backpack with the required things. There is no chance to make any delay; she has to finish her project and assignments as soon as possible. She walks out of her room and finds her mother brewing coffee in the kitchen. She keeps her bag on the couch and moves into the kitchen.

"Good morning, Momma! Where's that quiet fellow of yours?" " Ruhana inquires about Vineet.

"He does have a nice name," her mother responds with a smile.

"Yeah, yeah, but he's always so quiet. He's the 'silent boy,'" Ruhana remarks with a playful expression.

"Why do you call him that?" her mom inquires, looking at her.

"Because I find it amusing. At least he responds to me when I give him nicknames. I bet he'll argue that he's not silent, but he is. He rarely talks, and you support him, so he's your silent boy,'" Ruhana adds, casting a glance at her mother.

"Alright, now you relax. Your dad and Vineet have gone for a morning jog," her mother says, playfully shushing her.

"Okay, let me enjoy my coffee. You can wait for your 'silent boy,'" Ruhana teases, while her mother simply smiles.

She understands that Ruhana is just joking. Vineet also calls her "clumsy" and "talkative," but it's all in good fun, and they only do it within the walls of their home. Outside, Vineet and Ruhana truly look out for each other.

Ruhana sits on the couch, savoring her morning coffee, and her mother sits beside her, placing the tray on the table. The tray contains two cups, probably one for Vineet and the other for Ruhana's dad.

She listens to the song and rests her head on her mom's shoulder, and the lady pats her cheek.

"Get up, sleepyhead! I don't want Ma to suffer," a teasing voice falls in her ear.

"Hey, I'm not a sleepyhead! Be quiet!" Ruhana scowled at Vineet.

"You are! You always make me run late," Vineet pouts.

"No, you're late. You haven't even taken a shower yet. You—you, silent boy—go freshen up; you're starting to stink," Ruhana playfully taunts him.

"Hey, I'll be ready in no time. You're just lounging on Ma's shoulder with your heavy head," Vineet teases.

"Hey, be quiet! If Mom doesn't mind, why do you?" Ruhana narrows her eyes at him.

"Because I'm concerned about Ma. But you, clumsy girl, you'll trouble her," Vineet teases back.

"That's right! That's why I call him 'Silent Boy.' When he should speak, your silent boy remains quiet, and so do you," Ruhana says, making faces at her mother and Vineet.

Vineet giggles at the moment; his titter is like a refreshing sound to her ears. She smiles at him, losing herself in the moment. She then asks him to get ready and he agrees. After half an hour, they leave for college.

*****

The day has begun on a happy note. After a lengthy ten-day tour, some students are feeling sad about their holidays ending, while others are happy to be back home. During the break, Ruhana sits in the cafeteria with her friends when one of them approaches and shares the details of the festival.

"Wow! Are they also planning a prom?" Ruhana inquires with enthusiasm.

" Yes, we'll have contests in singing, dancing, music, drama, and even a fashion show," her friend responds.

"Fashion show? Really?" Ruhana exclaims.

"Yes, indeed! It's going to be a lot of fun. Let's go and see what contests they have," Akshara suggests, persuading her friends to join her.

Ruhana is quite excited about the upcoming festival, and after college, she eagerly tells Vineet about it. He smiles at her enthusiasm but shakes his head when she asks him to participate in the music competition. She knows he's not easy to convince, but she's determined to persuade him.

Later that day, Ruhana is silently sitting on the living room couch when Vineet comes out of his room and sits beside her. She's upset with Vineet's silence on the festival's participation. She starts channel surfing, ignoring him. Their mother notices the unusual quietness.

"What's going on? Why are both of you so silent?" she inquires.

Their home is usually filled with laughter when both of them are around, and she loves that about it. But today, her two children are unusually quiet. Vineet shrugs before responding to their mother's question.

"Ask Ruhana. She's the quiet one today, even though she's usually the talkative and argumentative one," Vineet says, looking at their mom, who smiles.

"That's very true, Vineet. Well, can you help me for a bit?" She asks her son.

"Of course," he nods and follows her into the kitchen.

After assisting his mother in the kitchen, Vineet returns to the living room to find Ruhana engaged in a phone conversation, shouting at someone. He smiles, knowing that she's likely upset with her friend. He glances at her as their mother enters with two glasses of cold coffee. He takes the tray from her and moves towards Ruhana, placing the tray on the table and sitting beside her, observing the changing expressions on her face.

Ruhana eventually ends the call by shouting at her friend once more and tossing her phone on the nearby couch. She mumbles something in irritation, which brings a smile to Vineet's face. He picks up his cold coffee glass and looks at her.

"What's bothering you?" he asks, although he anticipates her scolding.

"Nothing! And even if I told you, what would you do?" She responds irritably.

"If you don't tell me, how will I know what's bothering you, Ruhana? Come on, share it with me!" He tries to convince her.

"Huh! As if you'd listen and agree to what I say?" She glances at him.

He gazes at her for a moment, then says, "We'll think about it, princess. Tell me what's wrong,"

"No, no, you forget it. I know you'll disagree," she says sadly and begins to walk to her room.

Vineet smiles at her antics and follows her.

"Alright, fine. But don't say I didn't try to help you. Don't disturb my mom," he says, holding their mother's hand as she approaches.

She glances at him and says, "What's going on?"

"Look at him. He always finds ways to tease me. First, he doesn't agree with me, and now he's insisting I tell him what's bothering me. How is that fair?" Ruhana complains to her mother.

"You should be glad, he asked. These days, you can't trust anyone," her mother comments.

"But she doesn't believe me, mom," Vineet says with a touch of sadness.

"As if you're going to help me, are you? Because once you agree, you'll have to follow through," she warns him with a stern look.

"We'll think about it, as I've already said," he clarifies.

Ruhana stomps her foot in frustration. "How can I expect anything from you? I hate you, Vineet!" She playfully slaps his arm and storms out of the house.

Vineet laughs as he watches her leave and turns to their mother. "Oh God, who knows what she will do in future? She's still such a child!"

"And you love the child in her, don't you?" their mother asks, giving him an inquisitive look.

He glances at her briefly, unable to grasp her words, or perhaps unwilling to do so. She pats his cheek.

"Don't overthink it, son. I know you love Ruhana just the way she is. So why don't you accept it? You know what she wants, so why do you resist?" she says.

He remains silent, as always. She kisses his forehead.

"Okay, I won't say anything more. Just think about what you're doing. You'll find your answers. Now, go to Ruhana. She must be feeling down," she advises.

He nods and heads out, reflecting on his mother's words.

*****

After his conversation with Rekha, Vineet walks out of the house and finds Ruhana sitting on the swing in the garden. He gives the swing a gentle push, bringing her back to the present. She glances at him but opts to remain silent, aware that he is unlikely to listen to her. Vineet takes a seat beside her and gazes at her.

"What's bothering you? I'm not used to your silence, you know!" He attempts to cheer her up.

"Yeah, yeah, and you serve silence to me, isn't it?" She responds sarcastically.

"Why are you upset?" Vineet inquires.

"Choices change, Vineet. And you must reconsider your choices. If you can't do things for others, why does it bother you that I'm silent?" she questions.

He's at a loss for words. Standing up, he tries to leave, but she catches his wrist and looks into his eyes.

"Ruhana, I can't," he says softly.

For him, changing his nature is a tough task. Over the years, he has grown accustomed to being silent, and he can't easily trust every person he encounters. She gazes at him.

"You're running from yourself, Vineet. Please don't do that. You know it may not be easy, but it's not impossible. We can make it happen. I'm always here for you, and you know that," she says, taking his hand in hers.

He listens to her in silence, realizing deep down that what she's saying is correct, even if he doesn't want to believe it. When he doesn't respond, she looks up at him.

"You know, these days, I hear people say that you're living in the past, and it's true, Vineet. We can't forget what happened, but we can start a new chapter. I don't like it when someone says anything negative about you. You're capable of anything you set your mind to. People want you to participate in the festival," Ruhana says emotionally.

"The guitar competition! Why don't you join when you're so talented? Mom would be delighted to see you pursuing your passion. Please, Vineet, don't hide in your shell. The world is beautiful. Let's explore it, Vineet, please!"

He looks at her, realizing that she's hurt. Perhaps someone from her circle criticized him, and this girl always wanted to be there for him, unable to bear anyone saying anything negative about him. In addition, he had refused to participate in the festival, and she wished him to return to his true self.

He eventually agrees, making a promise to her, once again pledging to be the person she desires him to be. She can't believe her ears as he makes this commitment to her. She holds his hand and asks him to keep his word. He agrees, and they walk home hand in hand. When they arrive home, they find that her father is back. Ruhana rushes to greet her dad, and Vineet smiles as she embraces her parents. Her father calls out to Vineet, hugging him and giving him a paternal pat on the back. Vineet is grateful for having them as his family, even though he misses his own family.

Later, the family of four enjoys dinner, and Vineet heads to the terrace, while Ruhana hurries to her dad. She hugs him and spends some time with her parents. As she exits her parents' room, she hears Vineet playing an emotional tune, aware that he plays it when he's feeling down.

She places her hand on his shoulder, and he hugs her within seconds. She pats his back and smears his hair. "Calm down, Vineet," she advises.

"I miss her, Ruhana! I miss Mom. If she were here, I wouldn't be the way I am now," he says despondently.

She releases the hug and cups his face. "Vineet, Mom is up there in the sky, always watching over you. I know you miss her, and I miss her too. But can't we be happy for her? Vineet, I know who you were and who you are, but I want my best friend back. Will I get him?" she asks.

He turns his gaze toward the sky, and she stands beside him, pointing to the brightest star. "Look, those are the people we love. Mom must be looking at us and wanting us to be happy, isn't she?" she says.

He nods in agreement, still holding onto her. "Vineet, I know that life dealt you a severe blow, and it still hurts, but we can't stop living; we have to live and create our own identity. I believe we can!" she says.

He looks into her confident eyes, which seem more certain about him than he is about himself. He holds her hand and interlaces his fingers with hers, assuring her that he will give it his best shot. She smiles and rests her head on his shoulder.

Chapter 25:

Profound Conversation

Ruhana understands that Vineet is trying to become the person she wants him to. But she wants him to try a little more, to push himself a little more. She's aware of his past and the happenings. Nevertheless, Ruhana yearns for him to move beyond those hurdles.

Vineet makes promises to her, but somehow he falters and fails to follow through on the things he should do. They're again at their safe place, the swing ont he terrace. This place holds special significance for them since their childhood

Today is no exception, but their routine has undergone a transformation. Vineet is no longer the same person he was in his youth. He now seems to seek answers in the dark sky, while Ruhana remains committed to her habits. She keeps talking, and he responds with soft hums. He recognizes the immense efforts Ruhana has invested in their relationship.

Once again, she becomes his anchor. Vineet gazes at Ruhana and clasps her hand. She returns his gaze, aware that he is struggling to express himself. He's no longer the outspoken boy from his childhood. She looks at him and lightly squeezes his hand.

"Vineet, please don't keep your thoughts locked in your heart. Say something. I know you have much to share, and I'm all ears," she emphasizes the last three words.

"Ruhana, I'm not sure how to thank you. You've done so much for me. You've been my friend since the day you were born, but I haven't reciprocated. I'm sorry," Vineet confesses.

"Vineet, I'll be content if you simply keep your promises," Ruhana smiles.

Vineet is astonished by Ruhana's simplicity, as she has always been gentle and patient with him. In recent days, she has been upset with him, resorting to the silent treatment. She's weary of trying to persuade him to move forward, as his promises often go unfulfilled. Despite this, she remains composed, patient, and gentle when dealing with him. Currently, she sits across from him, quietly listening. Their nighttime meetings have become a routine, where they may not exchange words, yet the silence between them conveys everything. She tenderly kisses his temple.

"Vineet, you're my first and dearest friend. I'm willing to do anything for you. I can't bear to see you unhappy and distressed. Your pain pains me deeply. That's why I'm here, sitting with you. All I want is for you to progress and shape your own identity," Ruhana softly expresses.

"I'll keep trying, Ruhana. I want to become the person you wish for," Vineet responds softly.

"You can do it, Vineet. I know you can. I'm here to support you, always by your side. We'll work on it together," Ruhana reassures her best friend.

"The past may have been difficult, but the future holds beauty. We'll make it, won't we? You'll help me, won't you?" Ruhana gazes at Vineet.

"Yes, Ruhana. I can— I want to do it for you. I'll strive to become the person you envision," Vineet says, holding her hands.

"That's all I want. Thank you, Vineet. We'll grow out of this together," Ruhana says.

Vineet entwines their hands and kisses her knuckles, knowing she'll always stand by his side. She smiles at him, and they spend a long time on the swing. Eventually, Ruhana falls asleep with her head on Vineet's chest. He gazes at her peaceful face and smiles. She is his source of sunshine, guiding him towards the life he truly deserves. He acknowledges his stubbornness and reluctance to move on but realizes it's high time to do so.

With Ruhana asleep, Vineet lifts her into his arms and takes her to her room. He gently lays her on the bed and covers her with a duvet. After one last glance at Ruhana's serene face, he leaves her room.

Ruhana's words resonate in his mind, bringing a slight smile to his face. However, before long, Vineet drifts back into his painful past.

Flashback Begins

Vineet had a strained relationship with his father. On a pleasant day, a young Vineet is in his room, engrossed in playing the guitar he's been learning. His mother sits beside him, listening to the melody he's producing. The boy flashes a smile at his mother, who admires the skills he's starting to acquire. Although it's just the beginning of his musical journey, he's overjoyed to see his mother's happiness and knows he's the cause of it. She pulls him into a warm hug, and they share a brief laugh when a loud voice startles them.

Vineet's father has entered the room, and the boy is filled with fear. He instinctively seeks refuge behind his mother. His father is inebriated, and Vineet has witnessed his dad berating his mother, which is the primary reason for his resentment. The young Vineet watches his dad grab his mother's arm and scold her.

"I told you to have dinner ready! Why don't you ever listen to me? You're wasting your time here, and Vineet is wasting his time with this useless guitar," he angrily exclaims and throws the guitar, shattering it into pieces.

"Dad!" Vineet almost shouts, but his father silences him.

"Quiet! You're just wasting your time on this useless thing. And your mom doesn't have anything better to do," he berates Vineet, seizes his mother's hand, and forces her out of the room.

"One day, you'll regret your actions!" his mother says with resentment before leaving the room.

The young Vineet hides behind his pillow as his father exits the room, his mind filled with memories of times when his father would scold or even physically harm him unnecessarily. The little boy is compelled to witness the troubled dynamics between his parents.

Flashback Ends

Vineet snaps out of his trance, clutching his mother's photograph close to his chest. He doesn't know when he fell asleep, but the painful past continues to haunt him, and he struggles to push it away.

*****

The following morning, Vineet awakens to a gentle touch on his head. He opens his eyes and finds Ruhana's mother seated beside him, softly stroking his hair, with a warm smile on her face.

"Ma! Good morning," he greets her, and she reciprocates with a kiss on his head.

"Is everything alright, son?" she sweetly inquires.

"Yes, Ma. But why are you here?" Vineet asks, curious.

"Not much, dear. You didn't wake up at your usual time, so I thought I'd wake you up," she explains while continuing to caress his hair.

"Oh," Vineet begins to search for his phone, realizing that his alarm didn't go off.

"Oh, relax, my child! It's alright. I know you were up late. It's good to get some rest. Now go and freshen up," she advises before leaving the room.

Vineet smiles and hurries to get ready. As he steps out of his room, he finds Ruhana enjoying her breakfast. He takes a seat beside her, and she looks at him. While he's pouring juice for himself, he hears Ruhana asking a question.

"Did you cry last night?" she asks, studying his face closely.

He's taken aback. Yes, he's been feeling down lately and remembering the past, tears have welled up in his eyes. But Ruhana has noticed. He doesn't respond, but she gently turns his face toward her.

"Vineet, how many times do I have to tell you that you can't hide anything from me? I might be younger than you, and you might have more life experience, but no one understands your feelings better than I do. Even Ma says that I know you better than she does, and she agrees that you listen to me more than you listen to her," Ruhana says while maintaining eye contact.

"I'm fine. I was just missing my mom," he says, trying to change the subject.

"Alright. Tell me about it when you're ready. You know I've promised to support you. We need to grow while preserving Aunt's memory. Our parents are always there for us, and we're here for them," Ruhana reassures him, and her mother arrives with breakfast for Vineet.

They finish their breakfast and head to college. It's the week to register for the annual fest, and everyone is excited about it. Ruhana decides to talk to Vineet again about participating in the Music competition that's part of the event. During a free lecture, she's in the cafeteria with her friends, enjoying some coffee. One of Ruhana's classmates approaches them and shares some surprising news, leaving Ruhana and her friends astounded. They also need to register for this event. Ruhana is thrilled and contemplates discussing it with Vineet.

Later that day, when they return home, Ruhana discovers Vineet playing a tune on his guitar. She sits beside him and listens to the melody. Vineet is unaware of her presence until he finishes the song and spots her, flashing a smile.

"Vineet, you play so well. I love it when you play the guitar. We have a competition in the fest... Why don't you participate?" she suggests.

He remains silent, and Ruhana looks at him, understanding his emotions.

"I know you already have many responsibilities, but you should take part. I know you'll win. You should showcase your talent as well," she encourages, boosting his confidence.

However, Vineet doesn't respond and exits the room, leaving Ruhana worried. She's concerned that he might make a hasty decision or once again refuse to go against his promises.

Chapter 26:

Healing needs Time

Ruhana and Vineet talk with each other and the former insists on taking part in the annual fest. But he didn't reply to her. She understands that he has a lot of responsibilities on his shoulders; after all, he is the head boy of the college. He has to manage a lot of things and with the festival coming up, he has to do a lot of things. Also, they have exams coming up and they have to prepare for the exams as well. She looks at Vineet, who's lost in his own thoughts.

"Okay, Vineet. You take your time, and I will be glad if you agree with me. If you'll do it for me, I will believe that I am important to you. I will wait for your reply. For now, we should concentrate on our studies," Ruhana says it softly.

Vineet smiles at Ruhana; they finish their breakfast in silence and later, Ruhana's dad drops them off at their college. Though Ruhana and Vineet say that they can go to the college by themselves, Ruhana's dad insists that he loves to drop them to their college, and the two respect his love.

Once they reach the college, they part ways. Vineet moves to his class while Ruhana looks for her friends who are waiting for her. They move to their class and are discussing their upcoming exams and the annual festival. The three girls take their seats in the class and begin to talk. Their teacher hasn't arrived yet.

"Hey, Ruu! Did you ask Vineet about the festival?" Akshara asks while looking at Ruhana.

"Yes! I did. But he didn't agree. I mean, he didn't reply instantly. I know what is bugging him. So, I gave him time," Ruhana says this while looking at Akshara and Priyanka.

"But he should agree, Ruhana. Until when is he going to stay in his shell?" Priyanka looks at Ruhana.

"I don't know, Pri! I mean, I am always trying to get him out of this but things aren't falling into place. I hope that he agrees because he has promised me," Ruhana says it softly.

" I hope he does, Ruu. You are doing so much for him. He must understand this and do the things that he should be doing," Priyanka says it softly.

"I hope and wish the same," Ruhana says and meanwhile, their teacher enters the class and everyone falls silent.

The class begins and three hours later, they get free from all their lectures. Priyanka, Ruhana, and Akshara move out of the building, and they find Vineet and their other friends in the garden of the building. They meet each other and after talking for a while, they leave for their respective homes. Ruhana assures Priyanka and Akshara that she will call them later in the evening.

*****

Ruhana and Vineet reach their home and find their mother waiting for them. They greet her and move to their respective rooms to freshen up and change. On the other hand, the lady prepares coffee for them. She sets the coffee and snacks on the table and at the same time, Vineet and Ruhana join her in the living room. They tell her about their day at college and ask about her wellbeing. Ruhana tells her that she'd be going to college for this week only. Her mother acknowledges this, and in the meantime, Vineet says that he needs to finish his assignments by next week.

Ruhana's mother asks Vineet about the festival, to which he turns silent. The lady knows that he's still in a dilemma. Ruhana cringes at him.

"Huh, see, this boy is silent again. That's why I call him Silent Boy. He can only talk about work," She says, her tone irked.

"Yeah! I do not pass the time!" Vineet replies, making a face.

"Hey! That's showcasing the talent. I asked you to take part in Music-that is not for myself; it's for you!" Ruhana says.

"But you are the "Silent boy". You won't listen!" Ruhana says it teasingly.

" I will! But first, do your exams! We have ample time to think about the festival, you know," Vineet winks at her.

Ruhana is astonished. Will he really think about her suggestion? The mere thought excites her. She looks at him and he smiles at her, acknowledging her thoughts. She smiles—maybe he will change his mind after their exams. Maybe he is trying to change. She smiles, and Vineet moves to his room to finish his work. Ruhana's mom keeps her hand on her head. She gives a meaningful glance to her daughter. The girl knows that it will take time for him to open up and she now knows that Vineet is trying hard to be the man Ruhana wants him to be. She hugs her mother tightly. The lady pats her back and head softly. She knows that she needs support in order to stand strong for the guy who is their family.

"Everything will be fine, beta. Just believe in God and in the love and care you have for Vineet. Just like those days in your childhood passed, this shall pass soon," her mother says, comforting her.

Ruhana nods and moves to her room as her phone rings. She talks to Priyanka as the ladies discuss the assignment, after which, Ruhana gets lost in the past.

Flashback Begins

It was the worst day of their lives. She was playing with him at his home. She was sitting in his room and playing with him when they heard a harsh voice. Vineet got scared by the voice, as if it was his dad. His father entered the room, glaring at the boy. Vineet stared at his father while the man scolded them for playing and making noises. The man was drunk and didn't know what he was doing. He scolded Vineet for playing with Ruhana and he scolded her as well.

His father was a different being who never liked him being with Ruhana, or you might say, he didn't like kids. Ruhana looked at him scaredly, and the man shocked her by holding her wrist tightly. The little girl pleaded with him, but he didn't listen and pushed her out of their house. Vineet tried to save her but, in turn, his dad slapped him.

Little Ruhana rushed to her home, crying. She blurted out everything to her mom, who was not shocked because she knew about the problem between her friend and her husband. She calmed her daughter and tried to cheer her up.

Flashback Ends

She comes out of her trance as she feels wetness on her face. Tears are trickling down her eyes. She's still feeling goosebumps from that harsh touch. She wipes her tears and remembers how rude Vineet became to his father. She looks around her room and pens a diary entry in her diary.

"Vineet was so scared of his father. He didn't let him speak. How could someone be so harsh with their kids? And why was he angry with Vineet? Was I the wrong one to enter his life? But Vineet still cares about me. I will heal all his wounds,"

She caresses the words and closes the diary. She just wants Vineet to be happy. Meanwhile, she hears Vineet calling her and she rushes to his room. A smile makes its way onto Ruhana's face and she rushes to Vineet's room and finds him busy on his laptop. She also finds two coffee mugs on the side table. She looks at him.

"Hey! What happened? And why do you need two cups of coffee," Ruhana asks, raising her eyebrows at him.

"One's for you, Ruhana. Sorry, I had a call so I called you here. Maa made for you too, obviously," Vineet smirks at Ruhana.

"Hey! She has to make it for both of us. She has to take care of both of us," Ruhana makes a face, causing Vineet to laugh.

"Yes! And you're a kid," He says it teasingly.

"Yeah, and you're the silent kid because mom says we are still kids for her. If she could manage, she'd have not let us grow," Ruhana says softly, at which they stared at each other for a moment but then broke into laughter.

They sit and enjoy their coffee together. Ruhana is actually staring at Vineet, who's working on the laptop. He's a serene sight to her eyes and his voice is music to her ears. She can stare at him all day, leaving anything that comes her way but not Vineet. All she wants to do is to be by his side and help him come out of his shell and live his life to the fullest. That's the only thing she wants from her life now.

Soonish, they call it a night and Ruhana runs to her room. She latches the door and lies on the bed, finishing her work. She's glad to have spent some time with him. There's a smile on her lips and she knows that he may change his mind and do what she wants but she has to keep bucking him up. She has to cooperate and assure him that things will be fine soon. She has to take the leap, as she knows that he won't do it.

Amidst all the thoughts, she falls asleep. She hopes that the new day will be surprising and that things will eventually fall into their place.

*****

The next morning seems to be a chaotic one. Ruhana and Vineet get ready for college. It's the day of submission of their projects. Vineet is doing some last-minute work on the project while Ruhana is checking her report. Their mom looks at them, chiding them for not finishing the work last night. Both of them smile at her; they know she will say so, but she also knows that some things are left to be checked at the moment. They're engrossed in their work when the lady calls them.

"Come on, have some breakfast, and do not panic. It will be all good," She talks about the projects.

"I hope so, Ma. I am almost done. But I don't know, why is the model so problematic?" Vineet makes a face.

"It will be fine, Son. Come on, have breakfast," She calls him, smearing his head.

"Yeah! That's what I told him last night. But he doesn't listen to me," Ruhana makes a face.

"You don't listen to me either," Vineet rolls his eyes at her.

"Hey, I do. You don't listen.. You always do things as they please you," Ruhana says it teasingly.

Before Vineet could reply, Ruhana's mother barges into the conversation, stopping them and asking them to have breakfast. She looks at them and pretends to scold them as well.

" What's this with you two? You two tease each other and then you can't live without each other. I mean, you two can't do without each other. Why so? What's the use then??" she says.

" That's the friendship and the love that we share. But your silent boy doesn't understand anything. He loves to love his silence," Ruhana says this while looking at Vineet and her mother.

" Ah! I am trying," He makes a face.

" It's time to act, my son. Not to try. It's been many years already," her mom says while looking at both her kids.

Vineet sighs, he knows it. He knows he needs to crack the shell that he's in, but it's hard. Of course, everything is hard but you need to try and act. Ruhana's mom adds something more, to which Vineet couldn't say anything but ends up embracing the lady in his arms.

Chapter 27:

Life Goes On

Vineet and Ruhana have a banter and Ruhana's mother pacifies the two souls. The lady tells Vineet that it is time for him to act and not just keep trying. Vineet agrees with her. She is right and he knows that what the lady is saying is for his own good. Both of them are her kids and she knows what's best for her children. How can she let them go on the wrong path? She has to pave their way and make them realize the reality that life throws at them. Vineet ends up hugging his mother, who pats his back.

"I know you will do the best. You already know what's best for you and for your best friend too," Rekha says, smearing his head.

"Uh! He doesn't know anything. Your boy is not too good to understand. He never listens to me," Ruhana barges into the conversation.

"Hey, don't speak too much. It's between me and Ma. Stay out of it, okay?" Vineet rolls his eyes at Ruhana.

"I will! I am already between you and Ma. Actually, Maa is between us. Haha! I'm not going anywhere," Ruhana clicks her tongue out at him.

"And you're stuck with me in this lifetime. You've got no lease, you know!" Ruhana rolls her eyes and slaps his arm lightly.

"So bossy you are! Ma, see, she teases me like this," Vineet tends to complain to the lady, who just smiles.

"So what? You're the same, Mister!" Ruhana glares at him.

Vineet glances at her and she glares back at him, telling him that he's always irritating her and never listens to her. He makes a face but Ruhana is adamant about teasing him. Meanwhile, her dad joins them and kisses Ruhana on the head. The girl complains to her dad about Vineet but he only praises the young lad. Ruhana makes a face but soonish, they finish the breakfast and Ruhana's dad drops them at their college. He wishes them luck and kisses their heads softly.

*****

The day has started off with banter between Ruhana and Vineet and the former is happy for the latter. She knows that things will be better today. The rest of the day passes in a blur. Around 4 p.m., they meet on the college premises. Ruhana rushes close to Vineet and hugs him.

"How were your projects?" Ruhana asks Vineet.

"It was good. Ma was right; things can be better if we try," Vineet smiles at her.

"Yay! Finally, you got it! I am so happy, Vineet. So, it's time for a treat," Ruhana chuckles.

"Of course, Ruu! Let's go! There's a Baskin Robbins parlor nearby," Priyanka chides them.

"Yes yes! Today's the last day of college! Let's go!" Ruhana says and entangles her one hand in Vineet's.

Vineet can't deny the fact that it is the last day of their college and they should enjoy it. This time, it won't turn around again. The group reaches the ice cream parlor with a lot of hustle and bustle. They are happy and sad, both at the same time. They got to go through the examination now. But they are glad to have the festival and the prom after that. This is enough to keep them perked up.

Maybe this short break and the joy of meeting again is keeping their spirits up and they'll gather with extended enthusiasm and make their festival, a highlight of the year. Ruhana also hopes to keep up her spirits and bring Vineet out of his shell.

Maybe, this time is worth it.

*****

It is a fine day—a holiday. Ruhana is up early; she has showered and is dressed in a casual tee shirt and pants. She is having her breakfast while scrolling through her phone. Vineet follows her shortly; he is back from his morning jog along with dad. He taps Ruhana's head in order to tease her and she glares at him.

"Hey, don't touch my hair. And what are you doing here? Go and shower! You're stinking," Ruhana makes a face at him.

"Let me have some coffee," He says this and sits on the chair beside her.

"Noo! Have your coffee later!" Ruhana makes a face at him.

"Noo! You go and study! You're always chatting on your phone., Vineet says it teasingly.

"Shut up, you silent boy! You tease me but when I talk, you stay silent. Mumma! See, your silent boy is teasing me and then he will say I am bothering him," Ruhana complains to her mom, who's in the kitchen, preparing coffee for Vineet and tea for her husband and daughter.

"You are bothering me, let me concentrate on the newspaper," Vineet says, picking up one of the newspapers lying on the dining table.

"Yeah, yeah! That's what you do? But let me remind you, if you will not talk to me, then I will not come to you! Do your things alone," Ruhana reminds him of his promise.

He smiles; he knows she is very particular about things that are related to him. She can leave anything for him. For her, he is her ultimate universe and for him, the case is the same. Though Vineet refuses to accept reality, he assures Ruhana that he will remember his promise and won't break it at any cost.

She looks at him, as if, she's asking for his assurance and he assures her with his eyes. He also flashes his cute smile at her, which is enough to melt her. Yet, she signals to him that his soft traits won't work and that he has to abide by his words. He agrees, this is the least he could do for his forever best friend.

Ruhana smiles as soon as she gets reassurance from Vineet. She keeps her plate in the sink and rushes to her room. She has a lot to study and she also asks Vineet to concentrate on the forthcoming exams.

Vineet watches her as she runs to her room after hugging her parents and telling them that they can call her if they need any help. He is famished by her ways; she can help anyone, keeping her tasks at stake. She can lose her moments or things but she is always willing to help people around her, especially the ones whom she loves and the ones who hold a special place in her heart.

Vineet also finishes his coffee in the company of his guardian and then his Ma asks him to freshen up and study. Her only motive is that later, they can enjoy some family time during lunch and dinner times. And other than that he can spend time with Ruhana on the terrace. He smiles lightly. He knows all of them love him, care for him and are his family. He can only stay happy for them and look after them by reciprocating the love they hold for him.

He hugs his Ma and moves into his room. Yes, he has a lot of work to do and he has to also spend time with his best friend — His Ruhana. He smiles at his thoughts and gets busy with his studies. It's going to be a long day for the two of them.

*****

The day whizzes by, and Ruhana and Vineet find a moment to unwind before dinner. While their mother, Rekha, prepares dinner and their father attends to some official matters, Vineet is explaining something to Ruhana. She watches him, she's amused at the moment and can't understand anything.

"Ugh, this is too much! Let's talk about it later," Ruhana declares, pulling a face.

"Come on, try to understand," Vineet pleads.

"No, I can't grasp it now, and I'm famished. Let's continue tomorrow," Ruhana insists firmly.

"But it's important," Vineet argues.

"I know, but I'm not getting it now. Let's call it a day. I'm exhausted," Ruhana maintains her stance.

"Lazy girl! You make a drama even in studying," Vineet teases.

"As if you don't! Stop teasing," Ruhana retorts.

"I don't tease you. You provoke me," Vineet jests.

Ruhana grumbles and throws a cushion at him while he retreats into the kitchen, seeking solace with Rekha, complaining about Ruhana. Yet, a smile never leaves his face. Ruhana steals a glance at Vineet and her lips curve into a smile. Despite the banter and disagreements, if he's smiling, she feels content.

Ruhana finds her happiness in Vineet's joy. Her sole wish is for him to break out of his shell and become an even stronger individual than he already is.

Chapter 28:

Love of a Family

Ruhana and Vineet share some moments together. She refuses to study as he is explaining something to her. She whines at the moment and the two buddies get into a banter. Vineet teases Ruhana and she responds back gradually. He runs into the kitchen, where their mom is preparing dinner. He hugs her, locking his arms around the lady's waist. He casually complains about Ruhana and the lady smiles at his silly complaints. These two often do this. Sometimes, it's Ruhana who's complaining about Vineet and sometimes, it's Vineet. They tend to complain about each other but within a few moments, they get back together. *Again, in the teasing mode.*

Ruhana looks at Vineet, who's giggling at the moment and is complaining to their mother. There's a contented smile on his face and that is the reason for her happiness. She sets the dining table and her eyes are constantly fixated on Vineet. Meanwhile, Vineet notices her gaze on him. He continues to tease her, telling her that she shouldn't ogle at him.

"You're an antique piece. And I can stare at you forever!" Ruhana winks at him.

"Hey, Noo! I'm not some showpiece!" Vineet glares at her.

"Haha! But you've got a beautiful smile. And look, even Maa is staring at you. You can't say anything to her," Ruhana teases him.

Vineet turns his gaze towards the lady and finds her staring at not only him but at Ruhana as well. She's a mother and no matter what, her kids may outgrow her lap but never her heart. She loves them immensely and Vineet knows that her love for him has always increased. He immediately hugs her, hiding his face in the crook of her neck. The lady pats his back and Ruhana begins to tease her best friend. The healthy banter continues until Ruhana's dad enters the scene. Ruhana rushes to hug him and kisses his cheek.

"Dad, you see, your son and wife have teamed up," Ruhana says, pointing towards Vineet and Rekha.

"We're a better team than you and Dad," Vineet teases her.

"Hey! Noo! We're better than you," Ruhana makes a face at the guy.

"No! You're an antique piece! You annoy everyone," Vineet makes a face.

"You're an annoying and silent boy," Ruhana makes a face.

"Oh! Enough of both of you! Let's have dinner," Ruhana's dad says.

Vineet and Ruhana agree and the family of four has their dinner together. The dinner table is full of laughter and banter between Ruhana and Vineet and the older couple is just smiling at them, watching them argue and play. They know that until Ruhana and Vineet are together, they'll always be happy.

The dinner ends on a happy note and Ruhana helps her mother finish up the kitchen chores. She offers to make coffee, to which her dad and Vineet agree at once. Ruhana and her mom are astonished but they let it go. She asks her mother to go and relax in her room. Rekha agrees and moves to her room while Vineet and her husband are playing a game of carrom. Ruhana prepares instant coffee for her family and everyone gathers in the living room.

Ruhana's mom also joins them and the little family relishes the coffee amongst light chitchats. Vineet and Ruhana tell them about their busy schedules, and the elderly couple tells them to give their best. A little while later, Rekha and her husband retire to their rooms. Ruhana's dad kisses their foreheads and asks them to rest well. Rekha turns to them.

"You know what's good for you. So, just do your best! If you're happy, things will automatically fall at their respective spaces. You guys get what I'm saying? Think about it," Rekha says softly and walks to her room.

Ruhana and Vineet share a glance and they run up to the terrace, next to Vineet's room. She sits on the swing and Vineet begins to play a tune on his guitar. She closes her eyes to feel the crisp wind and hear the soulful tune that Vineet is playing. A couple of minutes later, she opens her eyes and then hugs him, clinging to his shoulder. He's astonished at the moment.

"Thanks, Vineet," She says it precisely.

'Thanks? Why? What did I do?" Vineet asks, clueless about her words.

"For doing what you did today,. Mumma already said that if we stay happy, things will fall into place. You've done it today," Ruhana says this and again embraces him in her arms.

"That's the least I could do, Ruhana," Vineet says softly.

"And that's enough for me. Your smile makes me happy, Vineet. I feel as if things are actually falling into place," Ruhana smiles at Vineet.

"I'm not able to return what you do for me, every single day," Vineet says he's guilty that he can't return back the love he's showered with.

"As long as you try, I am good, Vineet. I just want you to open your heart to me and be the person you were in our childhood. I miss all the things we used to do in childhood. It's been years since we went to have an ice-cream," Ruhana says it softly.

"If we try, things will get better. I know you can. You'll do this for me, or at least for Ma. I trust you!" Ruhana looks at him and smiles.

Vineet looks at Ruhana for a few seconds and then embraces her in his arms without saying anything. For them, silence does all the talking and all this while, Ruhaan has a smile on her face.

Maybe, she'll soon get what she wants — her best friend back to life and she can only hope at the moment.

*****

Ruhana and Vineet share some time on the terrace. They do not need words to converse; instead, silence does all the talking. Ruhana's sitting on the swing with her head resting on Vineet's shoulder. They're staring at the night sky, maybe, searching for something—maybe the answers that are not visible to their bare eyes. It seems like they are just lost in the beauty of the night sky. Meanwhile, Ruhana's trance is broken and she checks her watch. It's been a long time since they've been together and now they must call it a night. She looks at Vineet, who's still staring into the darkness. She nudges him and asks him to rest. He nods and they walk to their respective rooms silently, bidding good night to each other.

*****

Ruhana assures herself that Vineet is fine and tucked in the bed, and she walks into her room. She sets her study table, locks the room from the inside and climbs on her bed. She's got a habit of reading something before sleeping, so she started reading a book and that's her favorite.

She is touched by a line from the book — *Everyone has a story*. She believes every word of this line and for herself, she knows that she and Vineet have an amazing story and there's so much to tell the world. She's famished to learn how one character in the book, Meera, wants to become a well-known author. Her determination to do something in her life is what keeps her going.

Ruhana feels the same for herself and Vineet. They only need the determination to pull themselves out of their shell. As she's reading, her thoughts settle on Vineet. She's thinking about him—he's her best friend. She only wants good for him and she can do anything to make him do what's best for him.

For a few days, Vineet has been trying to be happy. She is elated by the same. His smile is the reason for her happiness. She can do anything and everything to see him happy. They're on leave from college as they have to prepare for exams. They've been getting into banter every now and then and her parents adore them. Today, they've gotten into banter many times; they tease each other, and they love teasing each other. Vineet ends up hugging his Maa and complaining about Ruhana while she does the same with her father.

Today has been better than other days. Vineet has started to keep his words and promises. Ruhana is glad that the guy has started being happy. She's elated by the very fact. She smiles to herself and thanks God for the good change that Vineet has brought into his life. Life seems to be better now. She also feels that she will get her best friend back.

Ruhana closes the book and keeps it on the study table. She gets down from the bed and walks towards Vineet's room. The door is not locked from the inside so she pushes the door lightly and peeps inside. Vineet is asleep on the bed and the bedside lamp is still on. She enters the room with cat paws, stands near the bed and begins to adore him. He looks calm in his sleep, as if there's no pain in his life. She knows that once he wakes up, he will take up the silent avatar and she doesn't want it. She wants him to stay happy forever.

She feels as if her attempts are succeeding now. He's beginning to come out of his shell. He's trying, and it is enough for her. He's smiling, he's talking to her, and, he's doing every little thing that he used to do, well, that is not an exception, but he's trying to smile and is spending time with her. It is the most beautiful thing that has happened in the past few days.

Ruhana looks at Vineet; she smears his hair and kisses his forehead. Well, she has finally done it. Every time she watches him sleep, she thinks of kissing his forehead and letting him relax. But she's never done it. Today, she doesn't stop herself and does it as she desires. She smiles to herself and watches his serene face for a couple of minutes more.

She just wishes the best for this guy who's asleep in front of her. She turns off the lamp and, stroking his hair for one more time, leaves the room, silently closing the door.

*****

She reaches into her room and closes the door. She picks up her diary from the drawer of her study table and sits on the bed. She pulls a cushion from her lap and begins to write a diary entry. She smiles at the action she took a couple of minutes ago. She begins to scribble some words in her diary.

"Waqt har ghaav bhar deta hain, agar koshish shiddat se ki ho."

Truly, my affirmations are coming true. He's healing. That's what I have been trying for so long. His smile is beautiful; all I want to do is see him smiling. He's trying and I am glad about it. I wish he healed soon; my wait would be over then. He'd heal up and I would share my feelings with him.

Oh yes! I love him. I don't know if he feels the same but I do. Maybe infatuation but the more I know him, the more I know his persona, and I fall for him.

And I wanna tell him that "Falling for you" is the best ever thing that has happened to me.

She ends her diary entry with a small smiley and keeps it back in its place. She smiles at the mere thought of them confessing, but it has a long way to go. She lies on the bed and soon falls asleep, only to dream of a beautiful life ahead.

Chapter 29:

Healing Each Other

Ruhana and Vineet enjoy some time together before bidding each other goodnight. Later, unable to resist, Ruhana quietly enters Vineet's room to observe him as he peacefully sleeps, a faint smile gracing his face. Hopeful for a brighter future, she envisions Vineet overcoming his pain and revealing his authentic self.

Morning arrives swiftly, with Ruhana awakening first. Swiftly refreshing herself, she changes into a fresh outfit and joins her mother in the kitchen, assisting in breakfast preparations. Soon after, Vineet and her father join them. Ruhana playfully teases Vineet, who responds with a playful click of his tongue.

Their playful banter turns comical, drawing hearty laughter from their amused parents. Ruhana's mother nudges the two...

"You both have upcoming exams. Shouldn't you be studying?" she remarks.

"Yes, so much to cover. Your silent boy seems to be in a mood today," Ruhana teases.

"Hey, stop using that term," Vineet retorts.

"Why? You respond when I call you 'silent boy' Otherwise, you're mute," Ruhana pulls a face.

"Understand his silence, sweetheart," her dad advises.

"See, I've got Dad on my side! Haha! It's a win-win for me," Vineet quips.

"Yeah! Silence is challenging, Dad. It's better to talk. But it's fun to tease him," Ruhana giggles.

Vineet just smiles, shaking his head, and they both retire to their rooms to study. With only a week left before their exams and a festival to organize, they delve into their studies diligently.

*****

As the day unfolds, Ruhana's father heads to the office while her mother tends to household chores. Vineet and Ruhana immerse themselves in their studies within their respective rooms. However, Vineet eventually takes a break and passes by Ruhana's open door, where she sits on her bed, engrossed in writing in her notebook. Numerous books are scattered around her, along with an open laptop.

Vineet sighs, recognizing Ruhana's habit for spreading her study materials while learning. She often utilizes multiple books and the internet simultaneously, asserting that learning encompasses various resources. He pauses, observing her as she speaks what she's writing, though inaudible to him. His reverie is interrupted by Rekha's voice.

"Your coffee is ready, Vineet," she announces with a smile.

"Coffee? How did you know?" Vineet expresses surprise, having not requested it.

"You're my son, not by birth, but I know your needs. Ruhana will ask for something to munch on soon. She always does when she studies. You're a coffee person," Rekha explains, just as Ruhana voices her request for a snack.

"You're truly the best, Mom," Vineet responds, embracing her warmly.

Rekha smears his hair affectionately while Vineet begins to drink the coffee. She moves into the kitchen and fries some potato fingers giving a bowl each to Vineet and Ruhana. After a brief break, Vineet hurries back to his room, needing to resume his studies.

The day rushes by, with Ruhana idling in the foyer, nervously awaiting her father. Her mother senses her scheming nature, while Vineet joins in and taps her head playfully.

"What's up, little miss?" he teases.

"Shut up! You go sit over there," Ruhana retorts, pointing at the couch.

"Why? What's on your mind? Don't overthink; you'll forget what you've studied," Vineet jests.

"Stop it! I don't forget. You're annoying. Go annoy your mom. Let me wait for Dad," Ruhana complains.

"Hey, that's rude!" he exclaims.

"Yeah, yeah, you and Dad team up to tease me. But today, Dad's on my side," she quips.

"We'll see when Dad arrives," he replies softly.

Later, when her father returns home, Ruhana clings to him, asking for the things she desires. After a playful exchange, they sit down for dinner. Post-dinner, Ruhana assists her mother before retiring to her room. As her parents slumber, she sits on the balcony, engrossed in sketching with canvas and colors, while Vineet peeks into her room, discovering she is focused on sketching their night scene.

He enters quietly and is surprised to see Ruhana sketching their night-time schedule. The canvas depicts a starry, moonlit night with a swing on the terrace, where two figures, likely representing themselves, sit. She hums while sketching the serene scene.

Lost in the moment, Vineet realizes Ruhana's thoughts about him, capturing a cherished moment between them. She draws a girl leaning on the guy's shoulder, unmistakably portraying them.

She's offered him so much, expecting nothing in return, only desiring his time. Despite his avoidance, she consistently supports him, a realization dawning on him as he emerges from his trance, stirred by her unexpected words.

Life's challenges seem easier with her presence. Since their return from Mumbai, Vineet's thought process has changed. He notices a positive change in himself and is elated to witness Ruhana's happiness. Their recent playful exchanges have lifted her spirits, evident in her gleaming eyes.

Despite feeling inadequate in comparison to Ruhana's unyielding support, Vineet acknowledges the pain he caused her in the past. Yet she stood by him, solely seeking his happiness. Overwhelmed by his contemplation of Ruhana, his trance breaks when she addresses him.

"What are you doing at the door, Vineet? It's just us awake at this hour," Ruhana calls out.

"How did you know?" Vineet queries, finally entering the room.

"I know you well. You're my best friend. Who else would?" Ruhana chuckles.

Vineet joins her on the floor bed and Ruhana shifts the canvas towards him with her drawing, which is far more intricate up close.

"This is beautiful, Ruu," he admires.

"I'll make a colored picture This is just black and white. We'll each hang one in our rooms," she plans enthusiastically.

"That's a great idea! I'll take this!" Vineet attempts to claim the canvas.

"Hey! Put it back; it's not finished yet. Place it back on the board," she insists, lightly slapping his arm.

"See it through my eyes, Ruhana. It looks complete," Vineet suggests.

"But you're not taking it now. We'll frame them after exams. Until then, you can come to my room and see them," Ruhana announces.

Vineet smiles, acknowledging Ruhana's attachment to her belongings. She shares everything with him, unlike with others, setting boundaries. His reverie is interrupted by her warm touch on his shoulder as she leans her head on his shoulder.

"It's so beautiful, Vineet. Things become beautiful with you. After sketching this, I feel so peaceful," Ruhana smiles, focusing on the sketch.

"I know! It's beautiful, and I've learned this from you. Thanks for always sticking by me. I've annoyed you so much, yet you're here, holding on," Vineet expresses, tilting his face towards her as she grasps his hands.

"Vineet! I've told you many times. You're my best friend, maybe...maybe more. I'll always be here. I just want us to be like the old days. I know life hasn't been easy for you, and it's not. But we'll pave our way. I'm glad you're doing that," Ruhana says with a smile.

"I wish I could do more. Maybe you're healing me," Vineet says, his gaze fixed on her.

"I'm glad, Vineet. I've always prayed for you, and I always will," Ruhana says, embracing him in a side hug.

Vineet reciprocates the embrace, and while she whispers heartfelt sentiments, inaudible to him, she holds his hand. As midnight approaches, Vineet suggests they both get some sleep for the looming exams. They part ways, and as Vineet leaves, Ruhana locks the door and settles onto her now-empty bed. Retrieving her secret diary, she documents the day's events, recalling their banter and mutual reassurances. The diary entry concludes with a poignant note:

Falling in love is simple, but preserving that love and its essence is challenging. Falling for you has been my greatest joy. Perhaps, one day, you'll feel the same about me.

Chapter 30:

Planning for College Festival

Ruhana is elated that Vineet is trying to break his shell. He has begun to share things with her. They spend ample time together and she is happy with the development. Her mother has also signaled to her that he's healing in some way. Maybe the upcoming festival will help.

Ruhana finishes her diary entry with a quote. She confessed in her diary that she loves Vineet but is unaware of his feelings for her. She can wait, though. It's better to make him realize his importance in her life and to let him confess his feelings. She calls it a night and drifts into her dreamland.

To be precise, a world where she's happy. Vineet is by her side and there is nothing else that she desires. Her parents and Vineet - - - it is all that Ruhana wants in her life.

She's laughing and he's staring at her. She throws questioning gazes at him while he shakes his head simply. He might not express his feelings or love but his eyes say it all. They say correctly that eyes speak more than words and in their case, it's true.

*****

Ruhana is still lost in her dreamland when her mother calls her. She opens her eyes and finds her mom sitting beside her. The lady smiles at her daughter and asks her to wake up. Instead, Ruhana keeps her head in her mom's lap and hugs her. The lady smears her head softly and Ruhana looks at her.

"Mumma, things are getting better," She says it softly.

"I told you, honey. Things take time to happen. And healing takes time," Rekha says it softly.

"Yeah, mom. I understand. It's just that I can't see Vineet in pain. I can't bear his silence. I get impatient, Maa. But, I think, it is getting better. Vineet is healing," Ruhana chuckles softly.

"He will heal. We are helping him and he will heal up soon," Rekha smiles at her daughter.

"Yes, Mumma, and I hope it happens soon after our exams," Ruhana chuckles and rushes into the washroom.

Her mom shakes her head and walks into Vineet's room. She knows that the boy needs some attention too. She ruffles his hair and he wakes up, greeting her. He hugs her and stays in the same position for a long time. He mouths a word of gratitude to the lady and sits up on the bed. Rekha asks him to come for breakfast and leaves the room. Vineet smiles as the lady moves out of the room. She's been with him for many years and is like his own mom. She's been very considerate of him and cares for him as a mother.

This family has always given him love, joy, smiles, and blessings. They care for him like his own parents would have done for him. And he didn't fail to notice the excitement in Ruhana's eyes and his mama looked happy as well. It may take some more time for him to heal.

And he will heal—heal for Ruhana and her parents.

*****

The days pass and soonish, it's the week of their exams. Ruhana and Vineet are all set to go to college. Rekha and her husband wish them well for the exams. They're excited enough, for as the exams will end, they will be able to celebrate the festival and enjoy the prom. Ruhana is excited that she'll talk to Vineet and persuade him to take part in the cultural program of the fest.

Since Vineet is trying to heal, Ruhana feels that he will agree with her. He already said that he'd do everything that he can for her. And Ruhana hopes that Vineet will not back off now. Soonish, the days pass and they finished with the exams. And it's time for the fest.

Ruhana is elated and she's all set to converse with Vineet. Things will change for sure, she hopes, and she's all set for it.

*****

Life seems good. Ruhana is elated that Vineet is healing. They have finished their exams and now they're ready for the festival. Just a few days and there will be a festival in the next week. She's elated and planning festival. She's on the call with her best friends, Priyanka and Akshara. The girls are chiding Ruhana as she's filling them with all the information.

Akshara and Priyanka know about her feelings for Vineet. They keep teasing her as she stays by his side instead of being with them. They also know Vineet, all that Ruhana has told them. They also know him personally, as they keep visiting her home and he stays close by.

"I am glad he's changing," Ruhana chuckles on the phone.

"Yes! I am going to ask him. He said that he would think about it," Ruhana says this on the phone.

"He will agree; I know him," She chuckles again.

Ruhana laughs at something that her friends say and then pretends to scold them.

"Shut up, you two! Nothing will happen. Vineet will get out and do everything. He promised me, so you people stop intimidating him," Ruhana says over the phone.

They talk for some more time and she cuts the call. She smiles to herself and looks at the message that Akshara sent her. This is the list of programs that will be held at the annual festival. There's also a fashion show, which is exciting to many people in the college. Ruhana and her friends are also planning to participate in the fashion show. They have also decided to visit the college to acquire the required knowledge about the festival.

She sits on the bed when her eyes fall on Vineet, who's standing at the door of her room. He's leaning on the wall and his eyes are fixated on Ruhana. She raises her eyebrows, asking him the matter at which he smiles.

"What are you up to, silent boy?" Ruhana asks teasingly.

"Hey, stop calling me that!" Vineet sounds a little irked.

"Noo!" She begins to tease him.

"You're no longer a kid, Ruhana," Vineet says making a face.

"Yeah, I know. But I want to be a kid. You're enough to be mature," Ruhana makes a face.

"But, grow up! You'll be a graduate soon. You should learn," He says but Ruhana cuts him as he begins to lecture.

"You should learn to act childish sometimes. Life is not a straight line, Vinu. There are different small lanes, different visuals, and different emotions that we should imbibe in ourselves," Ruhana smiles softly.

"It's not that easy, Ruu. Life is not so easy that you take it for granted," Vineet says.

"Who says we are taking it for granted? I am not taking it for granted; in fact, I am grateful that I have you as a friend in this life. I am glad to have my parents; I can't get any better than them. Vinu, I'm just saying that life is difficult but we make it complicated. And you've started to untangle all the complications; I am glad for that, Vineet," Ruhana says it softly.

Vineet stays silent at the moment. He knows she's right and he's been trying hard to come out of the shell that he has created around himself. Ruhana looks at him.

"Vineet, I am glad you're trying. Remember that life is hard, but we can make it easy by living it fully. You've got to try and I know you can do it," Ruhana says and cups his face softly.

"Thank you for trying, Vineet. And believe me, things will be fine soon," Ruhana says this and smiles at him.

"Why are you so sure?" Vineet asks softly.

"I trust you, Vineet. You know that life is a maze. And we need to look at the bright side. You've started to come out of your shell and I am glad about it. So, you have to keep trying," Ruhana says it softly.

"I am trying my best, Ruhana" He says and pauses while Ruhana looks at him.

"Things will happen eventually, Vineet. Also, I wanted to ask you something. Will you take part in the guitar competition?" Ruhana looks at him.

"I don't know, Ruu. I also don't want to disappoint you. But, I can't decide myself," Vineet says it honestly.

"You have to decide, Vineet. And you should do that. You can't live in a shell. You can't let the past dawn upon you. You should try more," Ruhana says she's concerned about her best friend.

"Ruu, you are right. I've realized that you're the sunshine of my life. You're the only one who keeps me sane all the time. Maa, dad, and you are the only ones who've always stood by my side. You were right, Ruu. We have to be happy for the people whom we love, we should be there," Vineet says this and pauses at the moment.

"I was there, but not fully. It felt like a responsibility but you did everything for me. You left things that you love only for me. That's a late realisation, Ruu, but I am glad I could realize. Maa does the same. And she told me the same," Vineet says, boring his eyes into Ruhana's.

"I am really happy to hear that. You are trying and it matters to me. Your friends, my friends do not see it the way we do. I am happy that you have started to look at our relationship like I do. Thank you, Vineet," She says and hugs him, embracing him in her arms.

Vineet tightens his grip around her waist. These two share a special bond that their parents also know. Ruhana is delighted to learn that Vineet thinks in the same way right now. They remain in the hug for some good minutes. Ruhana wants this moment to never end, but everything has an end.

"You've granted the biggest happiness to me, Vineet. I am just so happy that you've come out of your shell. I know, in no time, things will fall into places. It will be easier for both of us," Ruhana chuckles.

He smiles and he knows that she's being honest. He holds her hands and squeezes them lightly.

"I will try my best to not let you down. I have done it in the past, Ruu, but not now, I promise," He says.

Ruhana smiles and assures him of his decision and further, Vineet adds something that leaves Ruhana touched and astonished.

Chapter 31:

The Musings and the Fest

Vineet opens up about participating in the college fest and it makes Ruhana happy. She jumps on her toes happily and pulls him into her embrace.

"Are you sure? I don't want to force you, though. But I'm glad to have you participate. I will make me happy," Ruhana chuckles.

"I know, Ruhana. You have never forced me. You've given me the liberty to be the person that I am. This is the least I can do for you," Vineet says it genuinely.

"That's more than enough for me, Vineet. I am glad that you're trying to move ahead. And it only makes me happy," Ruhana says.

"Only for you! Because no one has been on my side the way you have. You were right, Ruhana. Even Rohan left me at the times I needed," Vineet says softly.

"I know, Vineet. I am glad you're on the right path, now. I can't be happier," Ruhana exclaims softly.

"Yeah! I will abide by your words. I will take part in the fest. I'll play the tune that Mom used to love. What do you think?" Vineet asks.

"That's a great idea, Vineet! She's looking at you from the heavens. And she'd be the happiest," She agrees with a smile.

"Since you've been with me forever, this is the least I can do and you deserve even more," Vineet says he's guilty of not giving her importance.

"Don't be sad, Vineet. Everything is fine. I am glad for what you're doing. I know it's difficult but I am there with you. Do you think that you're alone? I am always there, in this life, you're not getting rid of me, at least not so easily," Ruhana says so and threatens him.

"I am really glad, Ruhana. Things have become easy with you by my side. I know I am bad at expressing my thoughts, but yes, I mean all the words that I've said," Vineet says it genuinely and gracefully.

"I know, Vineet. You're the man of your word. I don't need anything other than your happy self. And I know things will get better with time. Trust me!" Ruhana assures him.

Ruhana and Vineet share some moments as they talk further. The former is glad about Vineet's decision and in the meantime, they hear their mom calling for them. They run towards the lady and hug her.

"Woah! You two are so happy! Hmm, what's the reason?" Rekha asks them.

"Your silent boy is coming back on track. And I am happy," Ruhana chuckles.

"Maa! Tell her to stop calling me a silent boy!" Vineet whines.

"That's what you are! But yes, we can compensate and think of a new name," Ruhana teases him.

"Noo! I have a good name! Start taking that, you little girl," Vineet teases her back.

"Yeah yeah! But I love it in a short way! Vinu! Isn't it cute?" She says.

"I know I am cute! Rhea used to say that too," Vineet says teasingly.

Hearing Rhea's name, Ruhana glares at him. She's already frustrated with the said girl and now. Vineet is again bringing her in between. She hates her, or maybe she's jealous, but she hates the fact that Rhea tries to approach Vineet and she can't bear him. Though she knows that Vineet doesn't like Rhea, the girl is always saying foul words, just because she's the daughter of the college's trustee.

"I hate her! And why are you so concerned about Rhea?" Ruhana makes a face.

"She just compliments me, Ruu! Why are you so angry?" Vineet asks, pretending to be unknown.

"Yeah, and you take it very seriously! What I say doesn't matter to you! This is why, you remembered Rhea, huh!" Ruhana glares at Vineet, who's suppressing his laugh.

"Oops! What did she do that you're so angry?" Vineet asks her softly.

"She's the reason, you know. Huh! I just hate her!" Ruhana makes a foul face.

Vineet breaks into laughter at her reaction, while Ruhana sends a fiery glare his way.

"You taught her a good lesson last time. She's scared of you, even I am," Vineet says, making a scared face.

"Shut up! Go and practice for your competition! And stop talking about Rhea!" She warns him, causing him to smile.

Ruhana makes a face while Vineet brings up his guitar and begins to play the tune, actually playing it for his Maa. The lady is listening to him with a smile while Ruhana begins to hum the song that he's playing. Vineet looks at her and smiles. He can tell how happy this young girl is to see him playing the guitar.

As their eyes meet for a fraction of a second, Ruhana smiles at him while Vineet promises himself not to let her smile diminish ever.

*****

Ruhana is glad that Vineet has decided to take part in the annual fest of the college. She is elated and her happiness is visible on her face. As Vineet's eyes meet hers while playing the guitar, he silently promises himself that he won't let her smile ever diminish.

He can do this much for the girl who cares for him so much. This is the least — keeping her happy is his only concern. When she can leave her friends for him why can't he be happy and mingle with her? Well, he has decided to open up, to be the man she wants him to be — her one and only best friend.

She is excited and she wants to tell her friends that Vineet has decided to take part in the fest and he will play the guitar. She's elated and excited, such that, she is not able to hide her excitement. They reach the college as the fest preps have begun. Ruhana has decided to do a skit with her friends and the girls are going to take part in the fashion show as well. The students are excited to have a fashion show which is unusual at the fest this year.

As they reach college, they rush to their respective groups of friends, and he needs to meet the senior professor regarding the responsibilities for the festival. They part ways and decide to meet at the main gate in the afternoon again.

*****

Ruhana gets busy in discussions with her friends. They choose a theme and begin to plan the skit. Also, they have to choose dresses for the fashion show. There's a lot of work to do for them. Annual fest, fashion show, and Prom — everything is in line and they're excited.

The day passes in a blur and it's already afternoon. Ruhana parted ways with Akshara and Priyanka and they headed out of the college together. She finds Vineet at the main gate with Rohan and soonish everyone leaves for their homes. Ruhana and Vineet walk together as they have to buy a few things for the home that their mother told them to buy.

*****

Ruhana tells Vineet that she's taking part in the skit and the fashion show as well. She's excited that she and her friends are going to design dresses for themselves. Vineet teases her a little but then tells her that he has got his name enrolled in the music competition and it makes the girl jump on her toes happily. Her happiness seems no bounds. She holds his hand and squeezes it lightly.

"I am so happy, Vineet. You know, it seems like my efforts are paying off. Thank you!" She says, showing her gratitude towards her best friend and she's being genuine.

"Ruhana, I already told you, this is the least I can do for you. Because of all that you do for me, I haven't done it ever. But I want to do it now," Vineet says genuinely and it brings a smile to her face.

"That's enough for me, Vineet. I am eager to hear you on the stage," Ruhana jumps on her toes.

"That will be for you only!" Vineet says this while looking at her.

She smiles big at him as they arrive at the marketplace – The D-mart shopping mall. They get the required things, Vineet gets the things billed up and they carry the bags and walk towards home.

The home is near the mall and they reach home in less than 15 minutes. Rekha's been waiting for them for lunch. They quickly change into casuals and the three of them sit for lunch. They tell her about the fest and they discuss the events. Ruhana also tells her mother to come for the annual function, to which the lady readily agrees.

"Silent boy is changing!" Ruhana comments, a smile playing on her lips.

"Hey! You're still stuck with that! So mean!" Vineet makes a face.

"I'm stuck with you forever! Yeah, we can think of a new name, Musical Boy!" Ruhana clicks her tongue out at Vineet, who whines at her words.

"It's not a thing to make face, such a good name. Now that you're playing guitar, you're the musical boy!" Ruhana winks at Vineet.

"Maa, tell her not to do this!" Vineet complains to his mother.

"Ah! In your case, she doesn't listen to me, Son. And I won't stop her now, she's already waited for a long time," Rekha says it meaningfully.

"Yay! Mumma is on my side. No one can save you from my wrath! And," she says but pauses.

"And? What are you up to?" Vineet raises his eyebrows at Ruhana.

"And Rhea! She'll face my wrath. Huh! She was again arguing with me!" Ruhana makes a face.

"What did she say now?" Vineet asks.

"If she again does something, I'll teach her a lesson." Ruhana says angrily.

"Calm down, Ruhana! She won't do it. And why are you focusing on her? You should focus on your work. Rhea doesn't have any work, and even if she has, she has people to do it," Vineet says, he is not pleased with Rhea.

"He's right! Why do you get so hyper when it comes to Rhea?" Rekha asks.

"I hate her! And the way she sneaks near people! And I dunno, what is her problem?" Ruhana exclaims.

"Concentrate on your work, Ruhana. Come on! Grow up! Rhea doesn't stand near to you in any way," Vineet tries to cheer her up.

Ruhana looks at Vineet and he assures her with his eyes. She smiles, calming down a bit. Meanwhile, Vineet's phone rings and he attends the call while Ruhana helps her mother wind up the chores. As Ruhana stands near Vineet, finishing her work, he says something that leaves her worried as well.

The Heated Argument

Vineet and Ruhana finish lunch and are talking to each other when his phone rings. He takes the call and turns worried as he hears the caller. He cuts the call and looks at Ruhana and their mom together. Rekha asks him about the matter. He tells the ladies that the annual festival of their college will take place at the Heritage Resort, which is on the outskirts of the city. The students, especially the ones who are taking part in the festival, are required to stay at the resort only. It worries Ruhana; her parents may not allow her. To her surprise, her mother pats her cheeks and permits her to go. She holds their hands in hers—both Vineet and Ruhana.

"I trust you! It starts at home. I know you two are very excited about this festival, so you can go. I will talk to Papa. He will agree. And yes, we will be on time as well. These are the only memories that will make you laugh in the future," Rekha says it meaningfully.

"Thanks, Mumma! It means a lot. Don't worry, we will not do anything that will be problematic for us or for you and Papa," Ruhana assures her mother.

"I know! I am already so proud of you and Vineet. But, yes, both of you need to be in contact with me. Yeah, you two are grown up but you're still my kids," Rekha says, her voice filled with warmth.

"Yes Maa! We will call you. But there's still time; we have to move in there the day after tomorrow. Rest details will be told in the college tomorrow," Vineet says.

'Yeah, I have rehearsals for skit tomorrow, Mumma!" Ruhana informs her mom.

"Okay! It seems like you two are going to be super busy. But go and rest for a while," Rekha taps their heads.

Ruhana and Vineet agree and move to their respective rooms to get some much-needed rest. Ruhana falls asleep but Vineet isn't able to sleep. He's tossing and turning in the bed and thinking about the happenings in his life. Lately, he's trying to mend things with Ruhana. Well, it's always sorted, but he's trying to do things her way. Obviously, he can't do things the way she does, but he can always try. He only wants his Sunshine Girl to be happy. Soonish, sleep overpowers him, and he falls asleep.

*****

The days pass in a blur and soon it's time to head to the Heritage Resort, a day before the annual festival. Ruhana's mom packs some snacks for them and instructs them to share them while Vineet and Ruhana share naughty glances. Rekha shakes her head and then the two of them leave for the resort. Their dad offers to drop them and they agree. Ruhana and Vineet also remind them to come to the resort for the annual festival. Rekha and her husband agree and instruct them to keep calling them. Vineet and Ruhana nod and they take their leaves.

*****

An hour later, Ruhana and Vineet are dropped off at the entrance of Heritage Resort by Ruhana's father, who embraces them and reminds them to look out for each other before departing. Upon entering, they encounter some teachers whom they greet warmly. Ruhana eagerly seeks out her drama teacher for a chat, while Vineet assumes his responsibilities for the upcoming festival.

The resort sprawls expansively, boasting two grand buildings surrounded by picturesque gardens. The primary structure houses a vast hall designated for the cultural programs, while nearby rooms are utilized for rehearsals. These facilities occupy the ground floor, while upstairs rooms have been reserved for student accommodations. The arrangements appear promising. Ruhana heads to her assigned room accompanied by Akshara and Priyanka, while Vineet shares that his room, where he stays with his longtime best friends Rohan and Abhinav, is conveniently located opposite Ruhana's.

Ruhana finds comfort in Vineet's presence, and together they settle their bags in the room before rehearsing their lines on the bed. Meanwhile, Vineet invites her for lunch, prompting the girls to convene at the resort's restaurant. Laughter fills the air as everyone relishes these joyful moments. The teachers have announced that rehearsals will commence at 4 PM, allowing everyone to rest after the tiring journey to the resort, especially for those students who travelled long distances.

Deciding to gather in the rehearsal hall at 4 PM, Ruhana and her group plan to tackle various tasks before the festival begins the following day. After lunch, everyone disperses to their rooms, recognizing the need for proper rest.

*****

As evening falls, students start gathering in the hall, where refreshments like tea and coffee are available. Some indulge in these treats while others engage in discussions about their performances. Ruhana focuses on tweaking the dialogue for the skit she's written, absorbed in her work.

While engrossed in modifying the dialogues, Ruhana recognizes a familiar voice as she looks up and spots Rhea entering the hall. Despite finding Rhea bothersome, Ruhana suppresses her annoyance, channeling her attention back to refining the play's dialogue.

The play holds immense significance for Ruhana, and she meticulously reviews it aloud, seeking feedback from her friends. However, as they concentrate on their work, they overhear Rhea making cringe-worthy and inappropriate remarks to others.

Initially attempting to ignore Rhea's behavior to avoid a confrontation, Ruhana knows Rhea's penchant for stirring up trouble. Eventually, Ruhana loses her composure, lashing out at Rhea in frustration, shocking her with the sudden outburst.

"Ah! The fluffy love story!! Didn't you get anything better? Well, you can't think of anything beyond love and fluff," Rhea comments.

" Then why don't you think it, Ms. Rhea?"" Ruhana says, trying to sound casual.

" Yeah, I could, but I thought you'd do it well, but you didn't," Rhea comments sarcastically.

"Everything is opposite of what I expected. Huh! Silly fashion ideas, fluffy love stories, and whatnot," Rhea cringes her nose. She thinks that she can do things better than what's going on.

"Enough Rhea! Shut up! If you can do better than us then why didn't you take responsibility? You and your silly girls can do everything but not work. Your dad is the trustee of the college so you're poking your nose in matters about which you don't know anything," Ruhana shouts, losing her cool.

"Behave, Ms. Ruhana! Vineet won't come here to save you," Rhea snaps at Ruhana.

"You need to learn how to behave, Ms Rhea! And please! Don't drag Vineet in between. You know, he's far better than you. And no one needs you here! Did you get it? Just get out!" Ruhana shouts and pushes Rhea so that she stumbles a few steps but glares at her.

"How dare you push me? Do you even know who I am? You're ruining everything around the festival. Don't you know who gave you all these responsibilities? You're ruining it all. And your best friend! Vineet!! He doesn't even have good taste! I don't know how does he tolerates you. You're so annoying!" Rhea comments, unknown of the wrath she'll face now.

" I've tried to persuade him, but he's ever so silent and sticking to you. Ah! Neither good taste nor good company I feel pity for him," Rhea says and this angers Ruhana.

Within a fraction of a second, Ruhana slaps Rhea hard on the cheek, shocking her to the core. Rhea looks back at Ruhana who just slapped her. Ruhana holds Rhea's wrist and twists it hard.

"Stop the nonsense, Rhea. As a fellow girl and a student of the same college, you're embarrassing those who are putting in hard work. Just because your dad is a trustee of this college doesn't give you the right to insult everyone. We're better than you! At least we're doing something productive. You and your followers seem to have nothing better to do than make fun of others,"

"And yes, about your fondness for fluff and romance! Yes, I love it too. But at least I don't cling to everyone like you do. Maybe you've forgotten, I warned you to stay away from Vineet! But you persisted, being stubborn and arrogant,"

Ruhana's voice grows intense as she releases Rhea's hand, causing her to lose her balance and fall to the floor. Ruhana stoops down to her level, gripping her face firmly with her fingers.

"I feel like dragging you out of this resort, but I won't. I'm not like you. And just because someone stays quiet, it doesn't mean they're weak. Not everyone is as disrespectful as you. My silence doesn't signify my inability to act. You've said enough; now it's time for you to face the consequences,"

With determination, Ruhana delivers another slap to Rhea, causing her to collapse to the floor once more.

"This is disrespecting others' hard work, and also for disrespecting my best friend. I have stayed quiet, but you haven't changed. I don't fear any punishment, Rhea, but I can't bear you badmouthing Vineet or any other student present here. If you can't do anything, sit back at home,"

Ruhana firmly grips Rhea's hand and forcefully guides her out of the auditorium, leaving Rhea stunned and unable to resist. Spotting the college trustee nearby, Ruhana directs

Rhea towards her father, who is taken aback by Ruhana's visible anger.

"Sir, please ask her to leave the campus immediately. She's disturbing everyone around here. She's not doing anything productive, but she is pointing the flaws out from everyone who are working hard. She's not superior just because she is your daughter. Because of people like her, the students who work hard are overshadowed. She gets more recognition than students like me, and it's unfair. I can't tolerate her presence here. If she can behave respectfully, she can stay. But if she speaks ill of anyone, especially Vineet, I can't predict my reaction. I know you're not like her," Ruhana expresses urgently.

"You'll regret this, Ruhana," Rhea retorts through clenched teeth.

"No! You'll face consequences beyond just slaps and pushes, Ms. Rhea. Leave now. And don't you dare come near me or my friends," Ruhana warns firmly before departing from the scene.

Vineet is awestruck by her anger, while the trustee feels embarrassed hearing negative remarks about his daughter. He escorts Rhea away, fuming anger, knowing Ruhana has exposed the truth and every word of it holds weight.

On the other hand, Vineet is spellbound and astonished to see Ruhana in so much anger. She's always a calm soul. Yes, she hates the wrong happenings and she's always annoyed with Rhea. But today, she's saying things in front of the trustee and her anger is unbounded. Meanwhile, his trance is broken when his friends call him. Others also come out and Priyanka and Akshara tell everything to him and the other people.

Vineet is astounded at the happening of events and meanwhile, Rohan says something to him that now makes some sense to Vineet.

Chapter 33:

Contemplating Thoughts

Vineet stands rooted at his place as Ruhana leaves the auditorium in anger. Rohan pats his shoulder.

"Didn't you hear her, Vineet? She's more concerned about you than herself," Rohan says it softly.

"Ah! She's concerned for no reason." Vineet wavers his words.

"No, she's fighting for your self-respect. She's arguing for you, Vineet. No one does it for anyone else. She's not as selfish as Rhea is. Try to understand; she can't take any bad words for you, and she's waiting for you to be the way you were," Rohan tries to convince him.

" He's right, Vineet. Ruhana answered back to Rhea when she spoke badly about you. There are ample feelings that she's hiding in her little heart. But she doesn't say it, because you mean a great deal to her. She doesn't want to lose you, so stays silent," Priyanka says as she looks into Vineet's eyes.

" Yeah! I think you must go and have a word with her. She's hurt and she'll only talk to you," Akshara says it meaningfully.

Vineet nods his head thoughtfully and runs out of the auditorium but doesn't find Ruhana around. He runs to her room and knocks on the door.

" Ruhana, open the door," He calls her.

"Vineet, just leave me alone," Ruhana shouts from behind the door.

"Please relax, Ruhana. Rhea is nowhere around. You don't need to stress yourself for her," he says, persuading her to open the door.

"Vineet, please. What she said may not offend you, but it did to me. She's no good. She's no one to judge me, you, or any of us. Just leave me alone. I don't want to talk to you," Ruhana shouts and asks him to leave.

Vineet sighs deeply but understands that Ruhana is in deep agony. She can't take the wrongs happening anywhere around her. She answered back when Rhea said bad words for Vineet and having someone say awful things about her best friend, Ruhana feels as if someone is piercing her heart. He lets it go and decides to talk to her when she calms down once. It may be easier then.

*****

The evening passes in a blur. It's night and thankfully, Ruhana comes into the restaurant for dinner. Akshara and Priyanka rush towards her and ask her if she's fine. She agrees and silently acknowledges the concerns of her friends. She serves dinner for herself and occupies a table. Priyanka and Akshara join her at the table. As they settle down, Priyanka again asks Ruhana if she's fine to which she smiles.

"I'm fine! You know what? I can't tolerate Rhea! And yeah, sorry for all the nuances I created, but I was in a bad mood," Ruhana apologizes to her friends.

"We understand, Ruhana. We want you to be fine. We can discuss the script post-dinner," Priyanka suggests.

"Yeah, we can. At least that bitch won't be there," Ruhana makes a face, she's still upset with the evening incident.

"Relax, Ruhana. She's nowhere around. She won't be here after what you did with her today. Calm down," Akshara bucks her up.

"Yeah, I don't wish to see her anytime soon. Well, let's get going. I am done!" Ruhana says and gets up from her seat.

She asks her friends to meet her in the room and moves out only to dash into Vineet. They share a glance and he holds her hands.

"Are you okay?" Vineet asks softly.

"Yeah! And sorry for being harsh with you. I didn't mean it but I was upset and shouted at you," Ruhana says.

"It's okay, Ruhana. I get it. And I also got the gist of it. I only want you to be fine. Girls like Rhea deserve what they got from you," Vineet smiles at her.

"Really? I wish you could understand all the emotions a little deeply, Vineet. But, I am glad that you understood what I felt at that time," Ruhana smiles at her best friend.

Vineet looks at her and nods, he knows what she's talking about. He needs to understand the minute details of life, the emotions that everyone feels. He neglects them for himself. For all the pain that he undergoes, he neglects others. No, she's not complaining. He's trying and she knows it. She only wishes he had known how she feels for him. That's been her dream for a long time. They part ways and Ruhana makes her way to her room with Priyanka and Akshara.

*****

They enter the room and Akshara locks the door. The three of them plop down on the bed, hiding beneath the duvets. They read the script and made all the changes. And then they lie down on the bed. It's a bit cool on the outskirts of the city.

"Ruhana, why don't you tell about your feelings to Vineet?" Akshara asks softly.

"But I don't even know about his feelings," She replies sadly.

"What if he feels the same for you?" Priyanka asks while looking at her.

"What if he doesn't? " Ruhana cross-questions her.

"We're best friends, I know. But I don't know what he feels about me. I agree that he cares about me. He takes care of me; he's always there when I need a friend. Yeah, he's become harsh and sometimes he becomes hard to understand, but I don't know if he loves me or even if he holds any kind of feelings for me," Ruhana says this as she looks at her besties.

"Just go and tell him. Or at least ask him for prom night. You two can talk then," Akshara suggests, reminding her about prom night.

"But will he agree?" Ruhana asks.

"He will; just talk to him, Ruhana," Priyanka chides her and Ruhana agrees.

They discuss a little more and then drift into sleep. They need a lot to do the next day.

On the other hand, Vineet is in the garden of the resort when Rohan shows up near him, asking about his well-being

"Dude, are you okay? I mean, I know you like Ruhana, but what made you take part in the contest? As far as I know, no one can make you change your decision. Then how?" he asks.

Vineet just smiled and threw the ball into the basket and sat on the bench.

"Yeah, I decided to take part because it'd keep her happy and our parents too," Vineet smiles softly.

"She's no more your best friend Vineet. She's more than that. Believe me!" Rohan says with a smile.

"It's nothing like what you're thinking Rohan. You know, I don't believe in Love," Vineet says in order to deny the fact that he doesn't believe in love and it's not love that he feels for Ruhana.

"You're fooling yourself Vineet. I mean agreeing to something, getting worried for her, caring and then scolding her, is not what is done for friends. She's worried for you, she can't bear bad words for you, she can fight with anyone for you, Vineet. It's a whole lot of difference that she feels for you," Rohan pats his shoulders and move inside the resort.

Vineet is lost in thoughts. Yes, Ruhana is different. He has recently been doing things that please his sunshine girl. She's always been there when he needs him, like, right now, as well. He remembers her words from earlier.

Yes, he needs to learn everything that makes her happy. Vineet has to act precisely and be the man she wants him to be. He sits on the bench and remembers all that happened between them. She's his solace and he's hers. She's at peace when she's with him and even he feels at peace when they are together. Every time when he cried, remembered his mother, she has been his pillow to cry on. She's been there convincing him, is it just what a friend does?

In Mumbai, he did find time to stand in silence with her. When she got lost, he was the most panicked person. And when she was found, he was relaxed. He did agree to her, and only for her.

He just sits still analyzing his deeds and actions towards her and calls it a night soon.

Chapter 34:

The Confession

The next day rises early. Ruhana is the first one to wake up. She finds her friends still sleeping. She freshens up and dresses up for the day. She ponders over what her friends said the other day. Yes, she dismissed the thought, saying that she doesn't know if he holds the same feelings. She's unsure of what he feels about her. He never confesses his heart, he's scared of love but he always cares. Ruhana's lost in her thoughts when her phone pings. She checks the phone and there's a message from Vineet. She checks it and a small smile appears on his lips.

"Good Morning, I hope you're not angry now. Meet me in the resort garden in thirty minutes. - Vineet."

She smiles lightly, okay, she's been harsh with him too. And maybe, she can talk to him. Yeah, this may be a good chance. Also, her friends are asleep. She can go. She ties her hair, wears her jacket and leaves the room clutching her phone in hand.

*****

Ruhana reaches into the resort garden and finds him near the swings in the corner. As soon as their eyes meet, he signals her to sit on the swing. Ruhana rushes towards the swing and takes her seat. Before she could greet him, he pushes the swing and her lips curve into a smile. He comes towards her side and looks at her.

"Are you okay?" He asks softly.

"Yeah, seems so," Ruhana replies lowly.

"You were very angry yesterday. Please let it go," Vineet says, very much concerned for her.

"Yeah, that girl got on my nerves yesterday. I wish to not see her face today," Ruhana says ruefully.

"Rhea is not your worth, not even for your anger," He says in a convincing tone.

"Well, I know that. I am glad you understood what bothers me. Anyway, I don't want to talk about her," She says, her tone thick with emotion.

"Okay, how's your skit going?" He asks as he gives another push to the swing.

"It's fine. We will get to practice after breakfast. And what about your practice?" She asks him.

"It's going fine. You want to hear?" He asks her hopefully.

Vineet knows that when he will play the guitar, it will boost her mood and he only wants it at the moment. She gazes at him and nods her head positively. He smiles lightly and begins to play his guitar. Ruhana smiles as a familiar tune falls in her ears. She looks at him and he smiles at her. Well, he knew that it will make her smile.

He plays the guitar for a little more time until her phone rings. It's Akshara calling her. Ruhana attends the call and her friend asks her to come for breakfast. She agrees and tells her that she will meet them in the restaurant in a few minutes. After that, both Vineet and Ruhana head towards the restaurant and he asks her to be happy. It's the annual fest tonight and he wants her to be fine.

*****

The day passes in a blur. Ruhana has called her parents and they have assured her that they will be on time. They are also excited to see both Ruhana and Vineet performing. It's the first time that Vineet is doing such a thing and for them, both of them are their children.

Ruhana is ecstatic and excited at the same time. She's happy at the moment and doesn't want anyone to ruin it. She's in the auditorium with her friends and practising for the last time. It's going in the same way as she thought. She jumps on her toes happily. After that, they disperse to their room to get ready, it's going to be a great night and they've got to make the most out of it.

Ruhana gets dressed in a black full-length dress with golden borders. It's perfect for her look in the skit. She makes her way into the main auditorium when Priyanka informs her that they should take a look at the resort from outside. Ruhana agrees, they have heard that the whole resort is decorated beautifully with lights and other decorative pieces. The girls head out, truly, the resort is decorated beautifully. There's a carpet aligned from the main entrance to the auditorium entrance. The girls are mesmerized and the others are too.

Ruhana is surrounded by her friends when that familiar, annoying voice falls in her ears again. She looks up to see Rhea along with her two friends standing before her. She's smirking and Ruhana sighs. Ah! She's still hungry for some more slaps. Rhea looks at her from top to bottom.

"Hey, what did you think? You'd keep me away? No, you can't!" She smirks at her.

"Please get going, Rhea," Ruhana snaps at her.

"Ah, did you get to persuade Vineet? Well, you can't! Haha, he's neutral. How can anyone be with him?" Rhea jokes about and it rages Ruhana.

"It's better than being with someone like you!" Ruhana slams the girl.

"Oh, just shut up! You're crossing your limits," Rhea shouts at Ruhana, as she never thought that this girl could use such words for anyone.

"You cross your limits every day, Rhea. No one would ever love you. You're not worth the love and I am least interested in putting my energy into you. Please leave!" Ruhana says it coldly.

"Oh please! You leave from here! You're not needed anyway!" Rhea says sarcastically.

"Yeah, you're right. Even god can't make you respect your elders and friends. You're not worthy to be born as Trustee Sir's daughter, you may be a good friend but you're a ridiculous woman! And yes, you don't deserve the man you're talking about. Vineet is way better than you and you're not worthy of anyone standing here. But you won't understand," Ruhana spits all her anger in her words and runs out into the garden.

Rhea is offended by Ruhana's words, moreover, she's shocked because Ruhana has always been a kind soul. She never uses bad and foul words for anyone, even if she doesn't like the person. Rhea moves into the auditorium while Ruhana rushes into the garden of the resort.

Vineet comes to the place and is astounded to hear everything. Yes, he heard what Ruhana said to Rhea. He looks at Akshara, Priyanka, Rohan and Abhinav.

"She still cares for you, Vineet. She isn't doing it because she's your friend, you mean more than a friend to her," Akshara says.

"Yes, Vineet. I already told you. The way Rhea speaks for you, boil her blood. She cannot take anything against you. And yes, she's far better than the girls who drool behind you," Rohan says.

"Yes, Vineet. Please! Go ahead, voice your feelings for her and please, listen to her. She's in the back garden of the resort," Priyanka says and moves inside the auditorium with Akshara and the two guys follow them.

*****

Vineet runs towards the back garden of the resort and finds her standing on a platformed area from where the sunset is clearly visible. He stands by her side.

"It looks beautiful, right?" He says, trying to initiate the talk.

"Yes, but not as much as sunrise. And it wasn't beautiful until you weren't here," Ruhana looks at Vineet.

"Why are you crying?" Vineet says, noticing her teary eyes.

"Nothing. Just watching the sunset. There's still time until the fest begins," She says, looking at the sun.

"I heard what you told to Rhea. Why do you fight for me?" Vineet says softly.

"Because you mean a great deal to me, Vineet," she says softly while he gazes at her silently.

"I don't know why you keep silent always, but I can't hear if anyone says bad about you. You mean the world to me," Ruhana says softly, along with teary eyes.

He's touched at the moment. She's been fighting for him ever since his mom left her. She's been there almost every day. He looks at her and she continues.

"It hurts me when people put blame on you. I can't take any wrong against you. That Rhea was again saying bad about you. I couldn't hold it," Ruhana says.

"I — I don't know…. What to say? But, this is too much that you do. I never knew that I will be this important to anyone," Vineet says.

"You are! You just don't want to understand it. You're caging yourself. But please don't do it, for my sake. And please know, you're the most important and most valuable to me," Ruhana looks at Vineet.

He slides his hand around her waist at which she flinches for a moment. He's feeling the same, he knows she's important to him and he can't survive without her. Well, her words have touched her heart. He's lost in thinking about what all she's done for him when he feels her hand on his cheek. He looks at her and is lost in her black orbs while his touch feels like peace and serene to her. He can read her eyes and all the love is hidden beneath them.

"I don't know what you feel, but I think, it's better that I tell you what I feel. You may say, I am being kiddush, but it is my love for you. I love you, I really do! If it's not love, then I'd be not affected by it. I just don't want to lose you and your friendship. But it's better I say it out," Ruhana says and down her gaze.

Vineet is surprised and touches. He pulls her close, his hand still around her waist. He tilts her face to make her look at himself.

"I know it, Ruu. It's just that I was running from it. You're always annoyed with Rhea and then your gestures. Maa also said that you've waited enough. And now I know how it feels like," Vineet says.

"You're getting it right, I had been running away, from you, from all the love. But, I can't deny that you're the sunshine that I need. You're my peace, Ruhana. Your anger, your tears, everything affects me. Your smile is the key to my happiness. I am sorry for the mess. It won't happen again," Vineet says genuinely.

Ruhana is looking at him and he keeps one hand on her cheek, making her believe that this is not her imagination but reality. He kisses her head and she closes her eyes to feel his warmth.

"You are the only one I need, Ruhana. And yes, Falling for you is the best thing that has happened. I mean, I was already inclined, but realisation dawned today. I love you, I really do," He whispers softly, while Ruhana is stupefied and takes a few moments processing her words.

"It's what I was dying to hear, I love you, too, Vineet," She says amidst tears.

She looks at him, it seems her dream coming true. She's looking at him with teary eyes while he rubs her fresh tears with his thumb. She holds his hand and kisses his knuckles and rises on her toes, pecking a small kiss on his lips. She pulls apart, but Vineet pulls her close again, and kiss on her lips deeply. Their hearts feel full after the confession and the small kiss turns into a passionate one.

Ruhana's heart feels full of what just happened a moment ago. She breaks the kiss, looks at him and then hugs him, thanking him for making her life brighter with just his presence. They stay in the hug for many moments, smiling to have each other.

Until the eternity, now!

Chapter 35:

A New Beginning

It's the day of the annual fest and Ruhana is quite ecstatic. She has opened her heart and told her feelings to Vineet; it happened right after the fight she had with Rhea. She won't forget that moment in her life.

Ah! He loves her too; he holds the same feelings for her.

They've shared their feelings and shared a passionate kiss. Ruhana finds herself blushing after the moment and so does Vineet. His gaze is fixated on her as they walk towards the auditorium. He knows that she's still in the stance and he wants to make her believe that their confession and their love are real. They're holding hands all the while and then Vineet side-hugs her as they enter the auditorium and whispers in her ears.

"It won't change ever. I promise. I've said, I will be an open book to you. Go ahead; I know you will rock it," Vineet motivates her.

"I am glad for that, Vineet. I knew you always felt it but you never said anything. I wanted to but at the same time, I didn't want to lose you. I am glad we are still the best of friends," Ruhana beams at him, her tone laced with excitement.

"Maa says friendship is the base of everything, and so is ours," Vineet says, still side-hugging her.

She says nothing but hugs him for another time, surrendering herself in his warm embrace. Meanwhile, Vineet's phone rings and they part ways towards their friends, Everyone is near the stage and the show has just started. Vineet and Ruhana spot their parents in the front row and are glad that they will watch them clearly when they perform on the stage.

Soon after the prayer, a set of awards is distributed, after which the skit is numbered. Ruhana, Priyanka, and Akshara look at each other and wish luck to each other. They signal their partners and they head backstage. Ruhana looks at Vineet once and he also wishes her the best for her play. Beaming at her companion, Ruhana disappears backstage.

Soonish, the play started. It's something usual and serene, but what hits the hearts of people is the ample amount of humility, affection, and love portrayed in it. It hits even harder because it's based on friendship. It's about how three friends overcome the problems that life is throwing at them without breaking the friendship.

As the play comes to an end, everyone in the hall is teary-eyed. Yep, the relationships that come from the heart are more heart-touching and endearing; they make their own impact on anyone's life. That's the beauty of friendship. Everyone's emotional and it seems that the plan has worked. The girls share a group hug and exit the stage. They're happy that the plan worked and everyone loved it.

After the skit, Ruhana joins her parents in the audience, as do her friends. They witness many students showcasing their talents and many awards are given. Ruhana's got the award for the best skit that they played. Vineet is awarded for his prefect duties. He's a great student manager. Also, he performs beautifully in the contest. Ruhana's heart feels full to see him perform.

There's a small smile on Vineet's face while he's playing the guitar. Well, it's the same tune he plays when he misses his mom. Ruhana loves it too, therefore, he plays it when she's sad or upset. Also, there are tunes that are their favorites as well. Ruhana is pretty happy to hear him. While he was on stage, Ruhana felt that their eyes met quite a few times, and she always cheered for him.

Soonish, the event comes to an end. Everyone is happy. It's the end of the year and the beginning of something new. They'll have holidays and later, their new classes will start. But there's something left for the fest to end - - the prom night. It's yet to happen.

Ruhana's parents meet Vineet and Ruhana and then leave for home while the other two stay at the resort. As the others spread to their rooms, Vineet and Ruhana sat on the swing where they spent time in the morning.

Vineet gives swings to Ruhana and they look happy. She asks him to sit with her on the swing. She holds his hand and thanks him. He has finally done something that has made her happy. He sets the strand of her hair behind her ear, and asks her a question.

"Why do you love me so much, Ruhana? I mean, you have always been there. I've hurt you many times, yet, you stood there like a rocks beside me, why?" He asks gently.

"I cannot measure my love for you. I can do anything and everything for you, Vineet. It hurts me when you're in pain and your happiness makes me happy. It's simple, after my parents, you're my entire world. Maybe ever since we became friends. You've been my priority and will always be.

I LOVE YOU!" She says and keeps her head on his shoulder.

He kisses on top of her head and they stare at the moon. Meanwhile, Ruhana stands up from her place and then sits on one knee before him.

"Will you come to prom night with me? " she asks him.

"Yes! I don't want to lose you again. I can't. There's no reason I can deny the lady I love. Thanks for everything, and thanks for bringing me back, Ruhana. You won!" He says and gently kisses her forehead.

They just stare at the night sky—it's beautiful and infinite --just like their LOVE.

*****

They part ways when he checks his watch and it shows 1 AM. Oh! It's too late and they should hurry to their rooms. If any professor sees them outside, they'd be punished, and they don't want it, especially when they've justgottent together. Vineet walks Ruhana to her room and kisses her forehead softly before walking into his own room across hers.

She watches him go — he's the peace of her life.

*****

Ruhana enters her room and finds that her friends are still awake. They already know that things are fine between her and Vineet. Also, Ruhana has told them that they have confessed their feelings to each other. Priyanka is the first one to send a tease her way.

"So, are you happy? I mean, things are going fine; he has told you how he feels," Priyanka says.

"Yeah, he said that he'll be how he is right now," Ruhana chuckles.

"Ah! That's great. So, if you hadn't said, how'd he realize? See, I was right, he felt the same," Akshara says.

"Yeah! And that was beautiful." Ruhana says, blushing to remember the confession they made and her first-ever kiss.

"Well, I am glad! I thought that this story would die in the infinite emptiness, just like in the dark. But there's a meaningful end to it," Ruhana says it softly.

"Every story has an ending, Ruu. I knew you'd achieve it," Akshara side-hugs Ruhana.

"I am glad it happened. He's healing, and there's nothing more that I demand," Ruhana says.

"I knew, you'd do it. You love him so much," Priyanka hugs her best friend.

"I do, and now that he knows it, I wish this story flourishes forever," Ruhana says.

She looks at her friends who are happy and they assure her that everything will be fine.

*****

Ruhana lies on the bed yet sleep is away from her eyes. She's happy. For now, she knows that Vineet loves her too. He's trying to open up, he's accepted her love and admitted that she's the only sunshine in his life. He loves her dearly and knows that her love is helping him heal, she's on cloud nine. With him near, she's elated. And for the prom night, she's elated that he's her partner — what more does she want now?

She falls asleep amidst the thoughts of prom night. Tomorrow will be a beautiful day again.

*****

The next day rises early. Ruhana is the first one to wake up, though she didn't sleep for a longtime, due to her joy. She just spent the night thinking that how her life would be with Vineet beside her. She dresses up and rushes out into the resort garden. As expected, Vineet is there near the swing. She smiles to herself and runs towards the swing and takes her seat. He smiles and gives a push to the swing and she squeals in joy.

"Wow! Today is a beautiful day. And do you know why it is more beautiful?" Ruhana gazes at Vineet.

"Just because we're together," Vineet beams at her.

"So true, Vineet. I am glad that we're together. It's like a dream come true," Ruhana smiles at her best friend.

"Is it your only dream?" He asks softly.

"Yes! To bring you back was the only dream I had. And you're back now! So I am the happiest!" She says joyfully.

"I can see it in your eyes. I want to thank you for making me realize that the world is still beautiful," He says, the smile never leaving his face.

"It is beautiful, Vineet. You should look with your heart. You will find the beauty hidden beneath. Love is really beautiful," She says this while thinking about the moments they spent together.

"It is! Thank you, Ruhana. For making me realize that friendship and love —both are beautiful. And when it is in one face, life is more beautiful. Nothing can be so serene like this," Vineet says and kisses her head softly.

Ruhana smiles at Vineet. She doesn't say anything, instead, they look at the sun rising. The orange-hued sky is serene and so is his presence –Ruhana feels so. She rests her head on Vineet's shoulder as they watch the sunrise. Life seems good to them.

*****

The day passes in a blur. Soonish, it's night, the time for the prom. The same auditorium is beautifully decorated. There are teachers and many students standing in pairs. Ruhana enters the auditorium with Vineet followed by other students. The ceremony begins and some awards are given. And there begins the prom.

Selective soft songs are being played and the couples begin to dance. Some of them seem to be in love, while some of them look friendly. They seem to enjoy themselves. Vineet holds Ruhana's hand as her favorite song rings in. They begin to dance and time passes by.

Ruhana is the first one to stop dancing and she's panting heavily. Vineet holds her hand and makes her sit on the tables set on the side. Even Priyanka, Akshara, and their partners join them. The guys get drinks for the girls and soonish they move to have dinner.

It's a great night out, and the prom ends at midnight. Though tired, Ruhana wants to hang out for a little while. Some more time won't hurt, right?

*****

Ruhana and Vineet spent some time on the swing again, relishing the cool breeze. Ruhana keeps her head on his shoulder and Vineet holds her hands. It seems like he wants to say something and she allows him to speak.

"Ruhana, I know that you've tried your best. It's just that I never thought of it this way. You always tried to make me happy, and you always helped me heal. Your care when I am sick, your understanding when I am upset or sad, Your sadness because of me, and your anger when Rhea is around. I never felt it this way —the way of your love. You always accepted and understood my silence, but I could not ever understand your words. I'm sorry!" he says, boring his eyes in hers.

"I know Ruhana; I've done many wrongs. I never understood the intentions behind your naughtiness and your anger when I overwork. I just thought that even you'd be taken away from me if I loved you. It has already happened, Ruhana. Mom left me alone. And I didn't want to lose you," he says tearily.

Ruhana's eyes are teary as well. She knows he's being frank and genuine. She rubs off the fresh tears that trickle down his eyes. She cups his face.

"Time isn't the same every moment. Love isn't always bad. Yes, I know that what happened was terrible. But it will not repeat. Let's begin again," She says it softly and places a kiss on his forehead.

Vineet looks at Ruhana with teary eyes. They're experiencing the same feelings that hey hold for each other. He again apologizes to Ruhana.

"I'm sorry, Ruhana. I never meant to hurt you. I really love you," he confesses his love for her.

Ruhana is happy she's happy to know that she's loved back in return. When you love someone, it is equally searing and magnificent to learn that your special someone loves you back with the same amount of passion that you hold for them.

Ruhana hugs Vineet, resting her head on his chest, as they let the silence do all the talking. They know they will be happy together.

Epilogue

Time passes by — it's five years since Vineet and Ruhana confessed their love for each other. It's been two years since they got married. Ruhana's parents got elated to learn that their kids are together and they want to spend their lives together. Her parents got them married.

Ruhana is now working as a fashion designer. She is hoping to start a fashion boutique of her own. Vineet has established his own business and Ruhana has helped him. Their parents are also happy with the progress of both their kids. Now, Ruhana and Vineet are expecting a baby.

It's a fine day, Vineet is sitting in his living room, reading some papers. He keeps the papers on the table and glances at his wife, who is conversing with someone over the phone, most probably her mom. Yes, Ruhana and Vineet have purchased a new bungalow and live separately. The latter has requested their parents to live with them but the old couple deny. They visit and stay with them occasionally.

Ruhana smiles at him as she catches him offguard. He's looking at her lovingly, maybe asking her to give him some time, to which she smiles. She walks towards him while talking. He gets up from his place, and hugs her, resting his hands on her protruding belly. She smiles at his action.

Ruhana ends the call and put her hands on his. He kisses her nape and then her head.

"Is there something special today?" she asks her beloved husband.

"Yes! I love you, and that is special," he says pulling her close to himself.

"It will be more special if you agree to what I told you," she says while looking at him.

"I think it's high time, we should tell our story to the world," she says placing her hand on his cheeks.

"Yes, my love. We will tell our story to the world before our baby comes into this world," He says kissing her bulbous belly as if kissing his unborn baby.

She's surprised and looks at him astonishingly while he kisses her forehead softly and cups her face.

"We will tell our story to the world. The story from pain to happiness, hatred to love… " he pauses and gazes at his beautiful wife.

"And the story about **FALLING FOR YOU**, my Love, "she says looking deep into his eyes.

"Yeah and we are ready with our story," He says holding the bunch of papers he's been reading.

Ruhana is surprised while Vineet smiles. He's planned everything. He's publishing the diary that Ruhana used to write. It has all the stories and Vineet's presence is inevitable in it. She's touched.

When you can bring me back to life, give me a beautiful family, then I can tell our story to the world–Isn't it?" he smiles and Ruhana hugs him tightly.

"Thanks, Vineet. It Will be a dream come true. I love you," She says and pecks her cheek.

He reciprocates the feeling and secures her in his arms, keeping one hand on her belly. They are a step ahead towards the beginning to create a new story.

A story of Falling in Love — the story of Falling with Each Other!

About the Author

Roohi, a published author and holder of a Master's degree in Computer Applications (MCA), navigates the literary world with a multifaceted approach. Her journey into storytelling, content creation, and insightful analysis allows her to not only craft captivating narratives but also offer profound insights into the works of her peers.

With a deep-seated passion for creative expression, Roohi actively engages in the production of evocative stories, lyrical poems, and thought-provoking blog content. Her exploration of diverse themes and emotions through writing reflects her commitment to authentic storytelling and connecting with readers on a profound level.

Roohi's dedication to literature extends beyond creation; she is also recognized as an avid book reviewer, sharing her perspectives and critiques to enrich the reading experience for others. Her role as a content creator and reviewer is complemented by her experience in providing remote content writing services to various organizations, where she applies her literary prowess to produce compelling and impactful written materials.

www.ingramcontent.com/pod-product-compliance
Lightning Source LLC
LaVergne TN
LVHW041219080526
838199LV00082B/1013